Are Different

The Rich Are Different

A DAKOTA STEVENS MYSTERY

CHRIS ORCUTT

The Rich Are Different

A Dakota Stevens Mystery Novel

by

Chris Orcutt

First Print Edition: 2014

This is a work of fiction. Names, characters, places, and incidents either are the product of the author's imagination or are used fictiously. Any resemblance to actual persons (living or dead), companies, institutions, events or locales is entirely coincidental and not intended by the author.

ISBN-13: 978-0692208519 (Have Pen, Will Travel)

The cover artist for this book is Elisabeth Pinio, a graphic designer based in the Silicon Valley. The ebook formatter is EBook Converting|High Quality Ebook Conversion: ebookconverting.com

Also by Chris Orcutt:

A Real Piece of Work (Dakota Stevens #1)
The Man, The Myth, The Legend (Short Stories)
One Hundred Miles from Manhattan (A Novel)

www.orcutt.net
www.dakotastevens.com

For Alexas:

My Véra, My Hadley, My Muse

1

FITZGERALD WAS RIGHT

It was a steamy Sunday morning on July 4 weekend and I was being kidnapped.

Okay, not kidnapped exactly. After all, I hadn't been forced at gunpoint and the car I was riding in was a Bentley. Its tangy leather seats and walnut trim made it tough to claim I'd been taken entirely against my will. Besides, people who owned vehicles this nice didn't kidnap, they summoned.

Svetlana sat with her legs crossed, waggling one foot. Her laptop rested on a fold-down table. She was playing chess. Without a game or reading material, all I could do was take in the scenery.

We were on the Long Island Expressway, creeping through a construction zone. A workman sweated on a jackhammer outside, but the Bentley's thick body blocked out the noise so it was barely audible above the A/C washing over my face. Now I knew why the very rich were so aloof: Money insulated them from all things unpleasant. Things like going to a detective's office.

Vivian Vaillancourt, the enigmatic heiress who wanted our help, had refused to come to us. Instead she sent her three-ton luxury tank and her niece: a college-aged girl in Daisy Dukes and a rhinestone "DIOR" T-shirt. Delilah was a decent chauffeur, if a bit lead-footed, and as we reached the end of the construction zone, the big car surged forward, plastering Svetlana and me against the seats.

"Finally!" Delilah said.

Svetlana gave me a look. I leaned into her shoulder and spoke softly.

"So, what is this case about? She must have given you some idea."

"I only spoke to her assistant," Svetlana said. "It is an interview."

"Damn it, Svetlana, you dragged me out here for an *interview?* I'm not even sure I'm ready for this yet."

She touched my arm. "That was a once-in-a-lifetime case. This one won't be like that."

"I don't want to talk about it," I said.

"I know," she said. "But I have to say, it is nice to see you shaved for a change."

"Thanks. I was sick of the Robinson Crusoe look anyway."

We exited the expressway and minutes later glided into a tunnel of stately oaks. Pristine golf courses glistened. This was Sands Point. I rolled down the window and drank in the salt air from the Sound. Driveway gates whooshed by.

"I wonder which place is Daisy's," I said.

"Who?" Delilah's hair flounced on her shoulders. She was a blonde with brunette streaks or vice-versa.

"You know—Daisy Buchanan, from *The Great Gatsby*." I rolled up the window. "Fitzgerald used Sands Point as his model for Daisy's East Egg. Gatsby lived across the water on West Egg. Poor guy spent all his time staring at a light on Daisy's dock."

"Daisy Buchanan, hmm." She glanced over the seat back. The car drifted. "I'm sure I would've met her."

"She must have moved," I said. "My mistake."

I thought every American high schooler had to read that novel. Even Svetlana, a defected Soviet, knew who I was talking about. She smiled faintly and pushed a tuft of hair behind her ear.

At a towering iron gate with a "V" crest, we motored up a gravel drive, curved through a gauntlet of sculpted trees, and ground to a stop in front of a white Italianate mansion with a red tile roof. As I helped Svetlana out of the car, at least two dozen windows glared back at us in the bright sunlight. How many rooms? Twenty? Fifty? The manor's sweeping wings alone made my country retreat look like a tarpaper shack.

When I snapped out of my trance, the Bentley was gone. Still beside me was Svetlana, clutching her Gucci bag. We went to the door and rang. No one answered. As I rang again, the distinctive boom of a shotgun echoed from behind the house.

"What the hell is that?" I said.

Svetlana batted her eyes. "A gun perhaps?"

I sneered waggishly at her and strode across a gleaming lawn in the direction of the gunshots. The thick grass was like walking on memory foam. In the meantime the gun went off again: a blast, a brief silence, then another blast. Sounded like a double-barrel.

I rounded the corner of the mansion. At the bottom of a long gentle slope was a croquet lawn. A man held a remote-control connected to an automatic clay pigeon thrower while a woman stood poised with a shotgun. She wore white jodhpurs tucked into equestrian boots and a shooting vest over a polo shirt.

"Pull!" she shouted.

A pair of clay pigeons sailed toward the beach. The woman followed them with the gun and blew the discs into dust. She was good. While she reloaded, Svetlana and I walked over. The pungent odor of burnt gunpowder hung in the humid air.

"Ms. Vaillancourt?" I said.

She spun around, the breeched shotgun dangling over her forearm. A handmade Fabbri 12-gauge over-under. Elaborately engraved, it cost more than my MIT education. As for the woman, she was sixtyish and trim with pewter hair and imperious features.

"Vivian, not Ms. Vaillancourt," she said loudly. She inspected us through a pair of amber shooting glasses, then snapped the shotgun closed. "You must be the detectives. Bit overdressed, aren't you? *Pull!*"

She blew two more clays to smithereens while Svetlana and I blinked at each other in disbelief. When meeting clients for the first time, we liked to look professional. Svetlana was tastefully attired in a khaki linen sheath and strappy sandals, and I sported a Brooks Brothers poplin suit, pale blue Oxford shirt, and navy and canary striped tie. Maybe I should have worn my safari outfit.

Without another word to us, Vivian Vaillancourt breeched the shotgun over her arm and marched up toward the mansion, where a shady portico beckoned. I flushed beneath my suit, and it wasn't from the heat. I took a deep breath. The man at the skeet trap jogged over in red silk shorts and a T-shirt.

"Louis Zipes," he said.

We shook hands. He was 5'8" of lean muscle, artificial tan, and teeth—the whitest teeth this detective had ever seen. Somehow I got the sense he handled a lot more around here than the skeet trap.

"Dakota," I said. "And this is Svetlana Krüsh."

She shook his hand. "Yes, we spoke on the phone."

"Tell me, Louis." I motioned toward the house. "Is she always this hospitable?"

"You'll have to excuse Vivian. She suffered two horrible blows in two days. First her favorite horse had to be put down, and now her brother's death. She's devastated."

"I'm sorry for her losses," I said. "I assume the case is about her brother."

"She'll have to tell you." He led us up the hill. "I hope you weren't put off by the shooting."

"Are you kidding?" I said. "Gunfire at, let's see"—I checked my watch—"eleven o'clock on a Sunday morning? We love it."

"Delightful," Svetlana said.

Louis shrugged. "Skeet is how she deals with stress I'm afraid."

When we reached the portico, Vivian was stretched out on a steamer chair with her boots crossed, gazing down an interminable lawn at the Sound. Svetlana and

I sat on a bench, but Vivian didn't even blink in our direction. For all I knew, she thought we were a couple of well-dressed houseplants. The shotgun rested on a teak cocktail table in the center.

Louis emerged from the house with a tray bearing a pitcher of lemonade, two glasses and a separate tall drink, which he handed to Vivian. Svetlana poured and handed me a glass. Once Louis left, the silence was heavier than a fallen soufflé.

Ice cubes rattled. A lawnmower droned. Birds batted a song back and forth like a shuttlecock. After a minute, I couldn't take it anymore.

"Nice view." I nodded at the water.

"What?" Vivian plucked earplugs out of her ears and tossed them on the table.

"I said, 'Nice view.'"

"Must be," Vivian said. "I was offered forty million for the place last week."

"Sounds stingy," I said. "I'd hold out."

"Not that I'd ever sell, of course." She gestured with her drink across the bay. "That's Great Neck over there."

I turned to Svetlana. "West Egg."

"Yes, I see Gatsby's place now." She rolled her eyes.

Beyond the peninsula, the blue-gray Manhattan skyline rose out of the haze. A powerboat skittered out of Manhasset Bay and hooked around the point. Vivian swept her free hand at the open Sound.

"And that's Connecticut over there, of course."

"Of course," I said.

I might have been making small talk, but inside I was seething. I wanted to know what I was doing here besides drinking the most exquisite lemonade I'd ever tasted. But if there was one thing I'd learned working for the rich, it was that they loathed being rushed. It could be weeks before she told me what she wanted.

Down at the swimming pool, Delilah emerged from a cabana, lay face-down on a flat chaise and peeled off her bikini top. The panache with which she did it yelled *trouble.*

"I trust you had a pleasant trip out with my niece?" Vivian said.

The shooting glasses gave her eyes an intense yellow glow.

"Sure, if you like NASCAR," I said. "Seems like a nice girl though."

"Ever since she quit Columbia, she's been an aimless little trollop."

Svetlana squinted at the pool. I knew what she was thinking: *That girl went to Columbia?*

"My sister Ursula died when Delilah was ten," Vivian said, "and it fell upon me to raise her. It has not been easy, to say the least."

"What about her father?"

"My sister had Delilah out of wedlock, Mr. Stevens."

I'm an awful therapist. I wished she would get to the case. She drained her cocktail down to naked ice and slammed the glass on the table.

"*Lou-is!* Another Long Island!"

She produced a tin box of Treasurer Golds, jammed one into a cigarette holder and lighted it with a kitchen match. I was mildly disturbed that this woman, who had demonstrated great skill with a gun and was now visibly intoxicated, was walking around with strike-anywhere matches. Louis brought her another drink and retreated into the house. Svetlana crossed her legs.

"How did you hear about us, ma'am?" she asked.

"An acquaintance," Vivian said. "Judith Conover. Said you were helpful in getting evidence on that cad ex-husband of hers."

Svetlana smiled at me. "The sharks."

"Like I'd forget," I said.

The breeze picked up. Down near the water, a wind chime clanged.

"You seem rather young, Mr. Stevens," Vivian said. "Exactly what is your experience?"

"Eleven years with the FBI, including a short stint in the crime lab, and three years with my own agency. For the last couple I've had my highly capable associate, Svetlana Krüsh"—I tossed a hand in her direction—"who also happens to be an international grandmaster in chess."

Vivian swirled her glass. "I recall hearing something about stolen art."

"Our most recent case, a difficult one, and one I don't care to talk about," I said. "Now with all due respect, ma'am, we came out here on a Sunday because we were under the impression your problem was urgent. So if you could—"

I was looking down the portico when a heavyset middle-aged guy rounded the far corner of the mansion. He had a crewcut and wore mirrored sunglasses and an open-collared shirt. As he swaggered toward us, I noticed he wasn't just big, he was tall—my height at least.

"Are you expecting company?" I asked.

Vivian glanced over her shoulder. "Oh, Mr. Roman? Yes, he's my next interviewee."

"What do you mean, *next* interviewee?"

"Well, surely you don't expect me to hire the first detective that comes out of the woodwork."

"Woodwork? You called us." I stood up. "We don't audition for jobs."

Mr. Roman was on top of me. He raised his sunglasses and gave me the hard stare. I'd seen his type a hundred times before—guys who mistake their fat for muscle, size for strength. He stepped into my personal space and rested the toe of his cowboy boot on my Kenneth Cole.

"This the guy, Miss Vaillancourt?" he said. "Forget him—not tough enough."

He shoved me. Not expecting it, I stumbled backwards until I caught myself on the bench. The shotgun was on the table. Roman was smirking as I grabbed it, snapped it closed and cracked him with the stock on the shin.

"Ah, Jesus!"

He crumpled onto the patio. While he clutched his shin and groaned, I buffed the walnut stock with my sleeve.

"Forget him—not smart enough." I put down the gun. "Now if you'll excuse us, your niece can drive us back. We'll send you a bill for our time."

We were halfway to the pool when Svetlana huffed.

"What?" I said.

"That was excessive. He was a strutting peacock. She would have seen it."

"The guy pushed me, Svetlana, and in this business you can't afford to get a reputation as a wimp. Besides, I didn't like her condescension. The next time we—"

"Mr. Stevens, Ms. Krüsh!" Vivian power-walked down to us, flicking the cigarette in its holder. "Please stay. For lunch at least. We're having lobster."

"Wow, did you hear that, Svetlana? *Lobster*."

"You must understand," Vivian said, "I need someone who will stick. I had no intention of hiring Mr. Roman, but—oh, it's all so complicated. There's no one I can trust."

"Listen," I said.

"Please," she said. "Hear what I have to say before you decide."

Shoving my hands in my pockets, I looked around and took in the scene: the sailboat bobbing on the dock, the smug mansion peering out to sea, the personal assistant and possible kept man helping Mr. Roman to his feet, the lazy nymphet waving her tanned legs, and the unstable heiress puffing her cigarette. True, if I took this case I would surely be stepping into chaos, but I needed to be doing something. Although there had been offers of cases, for months the closest I'd come to using my detection skills was watching reruns of *The Rockford Files*. It was time to get back on the horse. I gave Svetlana a questioning look. Subtly, pretending to straighten her hair, she rubbed her thumb and forefinger together. I smiled. Good old Svetlana. She was a ruthless mercenary, and I adored her for it.

"All right, Vivian," I said. "Lose the cigarette and we'll stay."

"Agreed." She plucked the cigarette out of its holder and tossed it on the lawn. "Go, sit." She pointed to a gazebo near the beach. "I'll tell Louis we're three for lunch."

She spun on her heels and quick-stepped up the hill. Somehow her cigarette had found the one patch of dead grass on this showpiece of a lawn, setting it on fire. I stomped out the small flame and ground the butt into the dirt with my shoe.

"You know, Svetlana," I said, "Fitzgerald was right. The rich *are* different."

2

RICOCHET

After lunch—a *long* lunch during which Vivian chose not to say a single word about the case, a long lunch during which she talked endlessly about sailing and her friends across the Sound—a sudden thunderstorm drove us indoors. Vivian showed us into an airy sitting room with four pillowy sofas arranged in a square, and a buttercream carpet deep enough to lose small children in. French doors yawned on opposite ends of the room, and as the breeze stiffened, chiffon curtains swayed indecisively in and out of the house. The room seemed to have been designed for one thing: naps.

It was late in the afternoon and dark outside with the storm, and I was getting sleepy myself. I joined Svetlana on the sofa across from Vivian's and loosened my tie. Svetlana turned on a digital recorder and placed it on the coffee table between us. Pad and pen on her lap, she nodded to Vivian.

"Whenever you're ready, ma'am."

"It's my twin brother, Sidney," she said. "He was killed."

"How?" I asked.

"It was declared a suicide, but that's impossible. Sidney and I were extremely close. I would have known if something was wrong."

"Did he live nearby?"

"No, Montana—on a resort he owned," she said. "He was found hanging from a gallows."

"Excuse me," I said, "did you say *gallows*?"

The lights went out and thunder shook the house.

"Yes," Vivian said. "Just a moment. The generator should come on."

Sure enough, before a minute had passed, the lights came back on. Vivian continued.

"Sidney was obsessed with the Old West," she said.

"Wait," I said. "You said he was found hanging from a gallows. Who found him? When?"

"All I know," Vivian said, "is that he was found by a group of guests out horseback riding. As for details, you will have to find them out yourself. Now, as I was saying, Sidney was obsessed with the Old West. Riding, roping, shooting, all of that. He toured ghost towns, even published a book of photo essays." She nodded at a large book on the coffee table. "With me so far?"

"He loved the Old West," I said. "Got it."

"Mr. Stevens, you have no idea. I don't want to be boorish, but when my parents died, Sidney and I inherited a considerable estate. Not including real estate, we split over a billion dollars."

"You and Sidney were the sole beneficiaries, I take it."

She nodded. "As I mentioned earlier, my sister Ursula died a long time ago."

"So, your brother took his half and bought himself a western resort."

"Well, it wasn't always a resort," Vivian said. "At first it was just an abandoned mining town named Loot. By paying the back taxes, he was able to buy the town and ninety-nine thousand acres. Then he built a resort town near the old one and named it Ricochet. Here."

She handed us a brochure. Svetlana unfolded it. Ricochet was an Old West town with hotels, saloons, a jail, blacksmith, you name it. It even had its own railroad.

"Amazing," I said.

"Everything is one hundred percent authentic to 1885," Vivian said. "Actors play the townspeople, and they live on-site. There's no electricity and only one phone, but believe it or not, it's quite popular. It's incredible, actually."

"Sounds it," I said.

"Unfortunately, the resort comprises a significant portion of his estate," she said. "Sidney made a number of wasteful investments. According to his lawyer, Sidney only has about two hundred million left in cash and equities."

She stated this figure dismissively, like it was change found in suit pockets.

"Ma'am," I said, "let's get back to Sidney's death. When was his body found?"

"Yesterday morning. They're sending his body back today for cremation. The county sheriff, a man named Briggs, is accompanying the body. He was one of the first on the scene."

"We should probably meet with him," Svetlana said to me.

"You're right," I said.

"Perhaps tomorrow morning?" Svetlana said.

"Mention it to Louis," Vivian said. "Briggs will be at the Waldorf, I believe."

I was *persona non grata* at the Waldorf–Astoria, but telling her about it wouldn't enhance my reputation. Svetlana gave me a knowing look.

"No problem," I said.

Svetlana tapped me with her pen. "Perhaps you could also examine the body."

"Louis will make the arrangements," Vivian said. "Just ask him."

The air blowing in was cool and carried the sour scent of ozone. Rain drummed on the awnings outside and lightning flashed over the Sound. Vivian went to a sideboard with liquor decanters on it. The crystal glinted as she poured a glass of whiskey.

"Libation?"

"No, thank you," Svetlana said. "We do not drink during investigations."

"How noble of you."

Vivian closed the French doors and sat down again. The ice clinked in her glass.

"All right," I said, "let's talk suspects. Supposing this was murder—and I'm not saying it was yet—somebody must have had a motive. When you got the news, what did your gut tell you?"

Vivian started to assemble a cigarette and stopped herself. "Right, I promised I wouldn't smoke." She flashed an awkward smile. "Well, the most obvious suspect is a woman named Heather Van Every."

"Who is she?"

"An actress at the resort," Vivian said. "I didn't learn about her until Sidney's lawyer showed me a copy of his will. She stands to inherit a hundred million and control of the resort. A trust of twenty million goes to Delilah, and the rest is earmarked for running Ricochet in perpetuity."

"A hundred million dollars?" I said. "Why did Sidney leave all of that to her?"

"*That* is the question, Mr. Stevens." She sipped her drink. "Apparently, Heather and Sidney have been together for years. This comes as quite a shock to me because Sidney never mentioned her."

"So the girlfriend's a suspect," I said. "Is there anyone else you can think of?"

"I don't know anything about the other actors." She swirled her glass. "But there is the Orlando Fantasy Group, or OFG. You know, the company that owns all of those amusement parks and 'living resorts' for adults. The CEO has made repeated offers to buy Sidney out, but he refused."

Svetlana's pen raced across the legal pad. "Anyone else?"

"You'll need to talk to Sheriff Briggs for the rest," she said.

Vivian drained her glass and deposited it on the end table. Her eyes drooped. A strenuous day of swilling cocktails and shooting clay pigeons will do that to a person. She came to and pounded the sofa cushion.

"I want you to find out who killed my brother," she said. "Man, woman, alien, I don't care—just catch the bastard. Dead or alive, as they say. In addition to your fee and expenses, I will pay a generous bounty."

"Define generous," Svetlana said.

Vivian did, and while I reminded myself how to breathe, Svetlana explained our daily rate. Vivian yawned and tossed us a thick folder.

"Background on the resort, copies of letters from Sidney, and what little information I have on OFG," she said.

Svetlana slipped it into her bag.

"Anything you need, within reason, is yours," Vivian said. "Just get in touch with Louis and he'll arrange it. He'll also arrange with the resort's historical advisor, William McCourt, to send you in undercover as actors."

"Just me," I said. "I'd like Svetlana to have a separate cover."

"She can go in as a guest then. Just speak to Louis about it."

"Thank you," Svetlana said.

"Acting isn't her forte," I said.

Vivian yawned. "Mr. Stevens, you will be playing Sidney's role of marshal. But that's your pretend role." She yawned again. "To ensure that any evidence is legally obtained, I have personally spoken to Sheriff Briggs about having you sworn in as a legal deputy. Now, I'm rather spent, so I think…we…should…"

She slumped over. After she lay there for a moment, I got up and checked her pulse. It was fine. I looked around for a way to summon Louis—an intercom, a bell-pull—but there was nothing. The only sounds were the storm raking against the doors and the distant ticking of a clock someplace. I looked at Svetlana.

"Go find Louis, would you?"

"For this we charge extra."

She went to find him. While I waited, Vivian's posture deteriorated until more of her was off the sofa than on it. Meanwhile, Svetlana showed no signs of returning.

"Okay, Vivian. Upsy-daisy." She couldn't stand, so I picked her up in my arms. In the entry hall, I climbed a *Gone With the Wind* staircase and paused on the landing.

"Which way, Vivian?"

She gestured down the hall.

Vivian's bedchamber wasn't quite large enough for an entire Sudanese village, but it was close, and it took me a moment to cross the room. The covers had been turned down. I put Vivian on the bed, removed her boots and shooting vest, and tucked her in. She let out a girlish sigh and blinked at me.

"Promise me you'll find who killed Sidney."

"I'll do my best."

A glass of ice water sat on the nightstand. I helped her sip some and eased her head back onto the pillow. I closed the bedroom door behind me.

Somewhere in the dark, I made a wrong turn and ended up on a narrow servant's staircase that led down to the kitchen. The room was all black granite and stainless steel, and the halogen lights made everything glare evilly. A familiar voice got my attention.

"So, you taking Aunt Viv's case or what?"

It was very much Delilah. Wearing nothing but the Daisy Dukes and a cherry red bikini top, she leaned against the open Sub-Zero freezer door, eating chocolate chip ice cream straight from the carton. Cold steam swirled around her. A diamond belly ring sparkled at her navel. I looked at her in my periphery so I wouldn't stare. I might have been depressed for several months, but I wasn't dead.

"Yeah," I said. "Listen, have you seen Svetlana?"

"Nope." She held up her spoon, loaded with ice cream. A chunk fell off and landed on her arm. She vacuumed it up with her lips.

"Won sum?"

"No, thanks," I said. "I had a big lunch."

"Big, huh?"

She licked her spoon. The girl was at that enviable age where she could consume nothing but beer and ice cream and still retain her whiplash-inducing figure.

"So," I said. "Any theories about this?"

"About what?"

She looked at me with her plump lips parted, revealing a large pair of incisors. The effect was of a not-too-bright bunny rabbit.

"Your uncle," I said. "His death."

"How should I know?" She dug into the carton again.

A maid stepped into the room, her eyes flashing with alarm when she spotted Delilah. The woman turned around and exited so fast she actually left a breeze in her wake.

"Bitch," Delilah said.

"Listen," I said, "the people in Ricochet. Have you met any of them?"

She snorted. "The actors? Bunch of fakes." She waved the spoon at me. "Look, I hope you're not expecting a ride back now, 'cause it's late and—"

Delilah turned to the doorway. It was Svetlana.

"I have called a car service," she said, and walked away.

Delilah ate a final spoonful and flung the spoon across the room into the sink.

"Well, happy hunting, Mr. Stevens."

She left the ice cream on the counter and the freezer door open and walked straight past me, brushing my arm with her breast on the way by. At the stairs, she gave me a final glance over her shoulder and took her hip-swaying time going up.

I put away the ice cream and met Svetlana outside beneath the porte-cochère. It was dark and the wind was blowing the rain in under the overhang. Somehow Svetlana had an umbrella. I didn't.

"Well," she said, "did you learn anything from the fair Delilah? Besides the fact that she dresses like a slut?"

Through the rain and the shaking trees, a pair of headlights curved up the driveway.

"She likes chocolate chip ice cream," I said. "But never mind that. Where were you?"

"Getting our retainer from Louis."

A Town Car pulled to a stop. I held the umbrella and opened the door for Svetlana.

"It better be good," I said.

She rubbed her fingers together and slid into the car.

3

THE SHERIFF FROM MONTANA

At nine o'clock the next morning, Svetlana and I entered the Waldorf–Astoria Hotel from the more covert Lexington Avenue entrance and boarded an elevator for the 25th floor. I couldn't afford to be recognized, so I wore my sunglasses and kept my head turned away from the elevator camera. Svetlana, meanwhile, freshened her lipstick in a compact mirror.

"How long is this feud between you two going to last?" she asked. "What has it been? A year?"

"Yeah, about," I said. "And it's more than a feud, if you recall. He banned me from the place."

"Surely you are the first P.I. to have this distinction." She snapped the compact shut.

"Yes, my grandparents would be so proud."

At the 25th floor, the elevator beeped and we got off. The sheriff's room was just down the hall. I took off my sunglasses, knocked, and a man answered the door. He was an inch or two taller than me, about my age, and had dark hair and brown eyes. He wore his uniform.

"Sheriff Briggs?" I asked.

"Dakota Stevens?"

"Yes, and my associate, Svetlana Krüsh."

"Pleasure," he said, shaking our hands. "Come in."

The door opened into a sitting room with ornate Art Deco furnishings. The room gleamed with rich wood, sumptuous fabrics and gold trim. Briggs waved at a coffee service.

"Coffee?"

"Thanks," I said.

"Miss Vaillancourt must've ordered it. All this was nice of her, but a bit much for me. I would've been happy in a motel out by the airport."

"I know what you mean," I said.

"Are you staying for the fireworks tonight?" Svetlana asked.

"No, my flight's in three hours," Briggs said. "Have to get back to Montana."

I poured coffee for Svetlana and me, and we all sat down. The couch cushions were stiff. Svetlana pulled out her digital recorder and a notebook.

"Came out with Sid's body yesterday," Briggs said. "Dropped it off at a funeral home in Sands Point."

"I know," I said. "I'm going to see it later with a medical examiner friend."

"Yeah, our M.E. declared it a suicide, so there wasn't any autopsy."

"Vivian mentioned that."

I sipped some coffee. It tasted expensive. Jamaican Blue Mountain was my guess.

"Honestly, though," Briggs said, "I don't know why Vivian went to all this fuss."

"What do you mean?"

"Well, having Sid's body transported back east, having him cremated and put in the family vault, all of that. Sid was a simple guy. He probably would've been happy being buried on Boot Hill in Ricochet."

"That's news," I said. "Do you know if those were his actual wishes?"

"No, just what I know of Sid, that's all."

The phone rang. Briggs answered it.

"Yeah, he's here," he said. "Hold on."

Briggs had a quizzical expression on his face as he handed me the phone. "It's for you."

"Hello?"

"Mr. Stevens," a man said. "Mr. Thompson wants to remind you that you are not welcome at the Waldorf–Astoria. You will leave. Immediately."

"Just tell me one thing," I said. "How did you know? Facial recognition software?"

"Mr. Thompson says if you show up here again, you will be arrested."

"Tell Mr. Thompson no hard feelings, and I wish him a happy July 4."

I hung up.

"Everything okay?" Briggs said.

"It's a long story," I said.

"Please," Svetlana said, "don't get him started on it."

"Can we buy you breakfast?" I said. "There's a good diner nearby."

"I'd like that," Briggs said. "Tell you the truth, this room makes me uncomfortable. Hardly slept last night."

"Just be glad she didn't put you up at the W," I said.

We left and rode the elevator back down to the lobby. A pair of security guards eyed me as we walked downstairs to the street. Briggs held the door open for Svetlana.

"Thank you," she said.

After the cool of the hotel, stepping outside was like slogging through warm oatmeal. Still, even in the oppressive heat Svetlana and I managed to walk at New York City pace, which is about twice that of a country stroll. We had to stop at the corner and wait for Briggs to catch up. We crossed Lexington with the light and headed down 49th toward Third Avenue.

"So," Briggs said to me, "Miss Vaillancourt says you're ex-FBI. Work on anything I might know?"

"Ever hear of the Hagerstown kidnapping?"

"That was you? Read a write-up on that case once. You won a medal or something."

"Service to America," I said. "Finalist, but didn't win."

He grinned. "But it's an honor just to be nominated, right?"

"Right."

The smell of ripe garbage wafted out of an alleyway. An old man walking a Pomeranian passed us going in the other direction.

"And Miss Krüsh," Briggs said, "you're a chess champion I hear."

"Yes."

"She's being modest," I said. "She was number one in the U.S. and number two in the world."

"Boy, that's something," he said.

The diner was a couple of blocks downtown on Third. Inside, we got a booth near the window, and Svetlana and I sat across from Briggs. Once the waitress brought coffee and took our orders, I got down to business.

"So, sheriff, how well did you know Sidney?"

"Fairly well. Only professionally, of course, but I think I had a good sense of what he was made of."

"What's your gut say on this—suicide or murder?"

"Well, again, the M.E. ruled it suicide, so officially I have to tow the line," he said. "But my gut tells me it's suspicious. Sid just didn't strike me as the type. He loved the resort too much."

"Tell me about your department's relationship with Sidney," I said. "What kind of stuff did you do for him?"

He drank some coffee and put the cup down.

"Arrest a few trespassers. Take hunters out of there from time to time. Mainly we just keep an eye on"—he made air quotes—"the *talent*. See, I've got a deal with the Missoula police. When the actors come into town and raise hell, I scoop 'em up and take 'em back to the resort."

"Does this happen a lot?" Svetlana asked.

"Yeah, not that I blame them," Briggs said. "You got to understand, Sid was asking these kids to live cut off from civilization. No electricity, except for the infirmary—they got a generator for that—no Internet, and only one phone. No cell towers anywhere either. It's not easy, especially for people their age. You'll see for yourselves soon enough."

An order bell rang in the kitchen and a moment later our food arrived. Svetlana had poached eggs. I ate my Western omelette and waited until Briggs finished his waffles before continuing.

"You were one of the first on the scene," I said. "Tell me about it."

"There's not a hell of a lot to say." Briggs smiled at the waitress as she refilled our coffees. "Thank you, darlin'. Let's see, day before yesterday, me and a couple of state cops got called out to the resort. We found Sidney strung up on a gallows, and his horse was wandering in the brush nearby. It was pretty clear to the state boys that Sid had committed suicide—you know, by riding up on horseback and having the horse walk away, leaving him hanging there."

"We understand some guests found the body," I said.

"That's right."

"And they all had alibis for the time of death?"

"Sure did."

"And what was the official time of death?" I asked.

"Medical examiner said Sidney died around eleven o'clock the night before," Briggs said.

"And the guests found the body about…"

"Ten hours later," he said.

"Sheriff," Svetlana said, "Vivian fixated on Heather Van Every as a suspect. Perhaps you could tell us about the other actors."

"We only spoke with the principals," Briggs said, "but three of them don't have alibis. Heather Van Every, Kat Styles, and a *really* big guy who plays the villain, named Jack Boone."

"Tell us about Boone and Styles," I said.

"Well, the scuttlebutt is that Sidney was going to fire both of them," he said. "Styles plays the lead prostitute on the resort, and Boone plays the bad guy. Apparently, Boone had been pestering Sidney to be his deputy."

"What are your thoughts about Van Every?" I asked.

"Heather? Believe me, I took my time questioning her," Briggs said. "Pretty upset when she found out. Says she and Boone were together, practicing lines for a new scene."

"Convenient. Any witnesses?"

"Another actor stated he saw them, but that was two hours before Sidney's estimated time of death."

"So all three of them had opportunity," I said. "And Van Every had the strongest motive—a hundred million dollars. Did you know that?"

"Yeah," Briggs said. "Vivian only mentioned it about a dozen times."

The waitress brought the check. Svetlana paid with our Amex and signed the receipt.

"Any hunches?" I asked. "Stuff you know but can't prove, stuff that doesn't make sense?"

"Well…"

I waited.

"I don't think it's any of the actors," he said. "Not even the ones Sid was supposedly going to fire. They're clueless, most of them. I've dated a couple over the years, and long as they've got this sweet gig, they're happier than a grizzly in an RV. But with Sid dead, now they've got plenty of reason to worry 'cause the future of the place is in jeopardy." He lowered his voice. "Ask me, the Indians on the rez are behind this somehow."

"Pardon?" Svetlana said. "Did you say *Indians?*"

"Yeah, if anybody had a motive to kill Sidney, it was them," Briggs said. "A local Indian tribe has been trying to drive him off the land since he bought it. They claim a big chunk of acreage was stolen from them during the gold strike over a hundred years ago. They've made some threats, and there have been a few incidents of them scaring guests away."

"So the case isn't as cut-and-dried as Vivian made it out to be," I said.

"Never is."

I looked at Svetlana to see if she had any more questions. She was packing up.

"That about covers it," I said. "We should go. You've got a flight to catch."

We walked back to the hotel and stood outside the Lexington Avenue entrance.

"I have to tell you," Briggs said, "I had my doubts about this undercover idea, but meeting you I think it'll work. You two investigate from the inside, and I'll help you where I can. You get any solid evidence, let me know about it and vice-versa."

"Sounds good," I said.

"Let's touch base again when you get out to Montana," he said. "We can have lunch and get each other caught up."

We shook hands with him and watched him walk into the hotel. Svetlana hooked her handbag in her elbow. I put my hands in my pockets.

"Thoughts?"

"I think he is trustworthy," she said, "but the plot has thickened. Especially with the addition of this Indian reservation."

"We knew it wouldn't stay so clear-cut," I said. "Besides, I like the challenge."

We headed for the uptown garage where I'd parked the car. The traffic moving down Lexington was light.

"So, I'm going to meet Wendy now," I said. "What are you up to?"

"I am taking the day off," Svetlana said.

"Fair enough. Shall we reconvene in the office tomorrow morning?"

"We shall."

At the corner, she raised her hand and a cab sailed over to the curb beside her. I smiled watching her get in, and trudged across 50th in the stifling heat, alone.

4

RAWHIDE

I was in the prep room of the Sands Point Funeral Home with a gal-pal of mine, Brooklyn Associate Medical Examiner Dr. Wendy Hamilton. We were standing over a hydraulic steel table, examining the body of Sidney Vaillancourt. Sidney had been a medium-sized man in his sixties with graying sandy hair and leathery skin.

With a magnifying glass I studied the rope indentation on Sidney's neck. It looked like it was made by ordinary stranded rope, but there was something strange about the pattern. Above the Adam's apple, within the larger rope mark, was a thin diagonal line. The line broadened out, like writing from a calligraphy pen, until it was flat and rectangular. I pointed at it and handed Wendy the magnifying glass.

"Doesn't look like a rope strand," I said.

Wendy scrutinized the line, then darted around the table and did the same on the other side. After a minute of intense study, she stood up, stared at the wall and smiled.

"Clever. Very clever."

"Somebody killed him first and staged the hanging," I said.

"Exactly. The narrow indentation inside the rope mark. It's thin in some places and flat in others. Like it got twisted. Like a length of heavy—"

"Rawhide?"

She touched her nose with her finger.

"Brilliant, Wendy," I said.

As she stooped to inspect the rope marks again, I couldn't help noticing the svelte body she usually kept hidden under a lab coat. Since this was her day off, she wore a "Girl Power!" T-shirt with Wonder Woman and Batgirl on the front, and a pair of faded jeans that fit her enviably. Girl Power indeed.

"Ahem, Mr. Stevens." Wendy smiled while continuing to focus on the rope marks. "Pray direct your attention to *his* body."

"Yes, Doctor."

Gently, she lifted Sidney's head off the table and peered underneath. "See this impression on the back of the neck? The deep bruising suggests this was the location of the initial trauma, where the rawhide was twisted. A garrote would be my guess."

I snapped several close-up photos with my phone. "Brutal."

"Which the murderer attempted to cover up with a thick rope," she mused aloud. "Probably thought the body hanging overnight would disguise the garrote indentations."

"So, among other things," I said, "I should be looking for a garrote made out of rawhide."

"And a *tall* suspect." Wendy pulled the sheet over Sidney's face. "That would explain the upward angle of the garrote knot. The killer would have to be quite tall or have attacked him from above. I'd look first for a really big, strong man."

I thought of Jack Boone. "There's already a suspect matching that description."

"There you go," she said. "Finally, take notice of these nail scratches around the area. It looks like he was clawing at the garrote to pull it off his neck."

"Why did the original M.E. conclude it was suicide then?" I asked.

"Because it's an instinctive reaction for the hands to go to the throat when something is strangling it." She re-covered the body with the sheet.

We yanked off our latex gloves and tossed them in the wastebasket. Wendy handed back my magnifying glass and picked up her purse. When I reached for the door handle, she put a hand on my arm.

"So, that's it? Get my professional opinion and leave?"

"Well, I—"

"Ask me what I'm doing tonight," she said.

"Okay, what are you doing tonight?"

"I'm glad you asked. Some friends are having a roof deck party in Brooklyn Heights, with a splendid view of the fireworks. It promises to be a fun, cadaver-free evening, an evening ripe with possibility."

I thought about it. I hadn't been out on anything resembling a date since Shay and the art case months ago. I wasn't sure if I was up to it now, and I was concerned about messing up my professional relationship with Wendy. But I also realized that if I had to go on living, I might as well enjoy myself a little.

"Sure," I said. "Sounds like fun."

"I'm nonplussed," she said. "Is the normally tergiversating Dakota Stevens committing to a date with *moi*?"

"He is. Although he has no idea what 'tergiversating' means."

We went upstairs. Vivian was pacing and smoking a cigarette. The funeral director, a wizened old man who looked in worse shape than Sidney, eyed her with a clamped mouth. I introduced Wendy to the heiress. Vivian flicked an ash on the rug.

"So," she said, "what's the verdict?"

"It looks like he was murdered," I said.

"Not by the hanging, I presume."

"It appears something else was the cause," Wendy said. "But it's difficult to say for certain, ma'am. It has to do with post-mortem tissue degeneration."

Vivian made a dismissive gesture. "Should we inform the authorities?"

"Not yet," I said. "If it turns out to be relevant, I'll tell Sheriff Briggs. In the meantime, we don't want the killer knowing we're on to him."

"Fine," Vivian said. "When will you leave for Montana?"

Wendy looked at me askance.

"In a few days," I said.

"Then I'll let you get back to investigating," Vivian said. "But I expect regular reports on your progress."

"I'm sorry, I can't promise that," I said. "I'll be in touch when I have something definitive. Otherwise it's going to be a lot of crying wolf."

"Very well. Just remember, I'm paying you and Ms. Krüsh handsomely, but *only* if you get results."

"Don't worry, we will. And again, my condolences."

The funeral director made a wormlike movement to see us out, but I waved him off. The old-timer didn't have many walks to the door left in him. Wendy and I stepped from a dim 70-degree parlor into glaring 90-degree sunshine. Wendy sneezed.

"Bless you," I said. "Now, about us making fireworks later."

"*Watching* fireworks, Mr. Stevens." She shook her head in mock disgust and pointed to an ice cream truck on the corner. "Come on, let's cool you off."

We got chocolate-vanilla twists and strolled back toward the parking lot.

"What's in Montana?" She licked her ice cream.

"Part of the case. I have to go undercover as the marshal in a mock western town."

She nudged me with her elbow. "You getting to play Clint? Bet she really had to twist your arm."

We reached the parking lot. My one luxury in life, a raven black Cadillac STS, gleamed across the heat-shimmering asphalt. Behind it, a stretch limo with dark windows had blocked it in. I was walking over to ask the driver to move when a pair of blonde sirens got out of the limo. They wore the same outfit—one in pink, the other in powder blue: terrycloth hoodies with matching little boy shorts. Little was left to the imagination.

"Excuse me," I said, eyeing the logos over their considerable breasts, "but I thought OFG was a family company."

Their *glutei maximi* were as hard as walnut shells, and they rested them against the limousine as they talked.

"Mr. Stevens," Pink said. "Mr. Shaw is having a party. We're here to pick you up."

Summoned again. I was getting popular.

"Who's Shaw?" I said.

"He only happens to run OFG," Powder Blue said.

"Never heard of him," I said. "Besides, my grand-mother taught me never to get in cars with strangers."

With a long, tanned and toothsome leg stretched out before her, Powder Blue dipped into her cleavage and produced a nickel-plated .22 auto.

5

OFG

She aimed the gun lazily, as if handing it to me.
"Thanks, but I've already got one." I dropped my ice cream cone. While their eyes followed it, I reached under my untucked safari shirt and pulled out my Smith & Wesson .45 revolver, a gun that snacked on firearms the size she was holding.

"Pretty good, huh?"

Their pupils dilated. Clearly they hadn't counted on such resistance. Between the gun, their breasts and their unbreakable backsides, they'd assumed I would come along quietly. I wasn't.

"Now, ladies," I said, splitting my gaze between them. "Get lost."

Powder Blue put the gun away and opened the rear door. Svetlana leaned out.

"Dakota, what is going on?"

Pink crossed her arms. Suddenly she wasn't a sexy henchwoman anymore, but rather a petulant girl who'd been sent out on an errand and was anxious to get back.

"*Please*," she said. "Mr. Shaw is flying you out."

"Fly?" I said. "Where the hell is this place?"

"Martha's Vineyard," Powder Blue gushed. "We're taking his Lear!"

I turned to Wendy. "Thoughts?"

"Well, aside from the whole abduction thing, it sounds great."

"Come on, Mr. Stevens," Pink said. "It'll be an adventure."

Svetlana spoke up from the open door again. "Yes, Dakota. An *adventure*."

I didn't like people thinking they could force me to go places with them, and in the long run giving in to such demands was bad for business. On the other hand, this would give me a chance to meet one of the suspects face to face.

"Fine." I holstered my gun and helped Wendy into the car.

Svetlana and some guy I didn't know sat close together on the seat across from us. She scowled. As for the guy, I disliked him from the second I saw him, and not just because he had his arm draped over Svetlana's fine shoulders. He had a goatee and smoked a cigarette in that pretentious Continental way, pinched between his thumb and index finger. A haze of smoke hung from the car roof. He appraised me coolly through slitted eyes.

"So, you are great detective Dakota Stevens," he said. "I am concert pianist Alexei Krivtsov."

The car began to move. I reached across the seat and hit the button for the window. The smoke curled out.

"Nice to meet you, Alexei," I said. "Now get rid of the cigarette."

"Dakota," Svetlana said.

Alexei stared at me, but I saw his stare and raised it. Svetlana tipped her head back resignedly and muttered something in Russian. Alexei took a quick puff and tossed the rest of the unfiltered cigarette out the window.

"I should know better than to tangle with FBI man," Alexei said. "Svetlana, she tells me much about your cases. We were going to party this afternoon in Brooklyn."

"So were we," Wendy said. "Where?"

Alexei mentioned it was a roof deck party overlooking the East River, and gave the address.

"Wow, it's the same place," Wendy said.

"And now we go to Martha's Vineyard," Alexei said. "This vineyard, it is owned by Martha Stewart, yes?"

I smirked at Svetlana as if to say, *You sure can pick 'em."* We traded barbed, fleeting looks during the drive, while our dates happily chatted.

Half an hour later, we arrived at Farmingdale airport and pulled up to a Learjet. The plane looked bored. If it had had fingernails, it would have been filing them.

The stair door lowered. We went up.

The interior was cocoa leather, tan carpet and mahogany tables between pairs of cushy seats. Wendy and Alexei sat at a table on the starboard side of the plane; Svetlana and I sat at one on the port side. As the plane began to taxi, our captors buckled in, crossed their legs, and flipped through celebrity magazines. Then there was a tremendous whine and I was sucked backwards into my seat. My scalp buzzed. Nothing makes you feel the magic of flight like a private jet. Meanwhile Svetlana, blasé as always, sat cupping her chin and gazing down at the rapidly retreating coastline.

Once we leveled off, Pink brought us some Pellegrino and two glasses. As Svetlana poured, she nodded across the aisle at Wendy, who was dealing cards.

"*That's* the medical examiner? Girl Power?"

"Yes, and she happens to be a friend," I said. "Look, can we get down to business? We both had other plans, but we probably won't get this close to Shaw and OFG again, so we need to make the most of it."

"You are right," she said.

"Would you like to hear what we deduced from Sidney's body?"

"I can't wait."

I described the mysterious impression inside the noose mark and how Wendy and I believed the killer had used a rawhide garrote to kill Sidney. Svetlana plucked a loose lash from her eyelid and blew it off her fingertip.

"I did some research on OFG," she said.

"I thought you were taking the day off."

"Yes, because Googling 'OFG' is so hard."

"And?"

"Randal Shaw is in deep trouble," she said. "Since he became CEO, the company's stock has dropped from 51 to 13 a share."

"Ouch."

"And there are rumors the company might be in even worse shape, that he has been doing some creative accounting to cover things up."

"A corrupt executive?" I said. "Impossible."

"Market analysts are saying he made a number of foolish investments, like a cable network that went nowhere and an adult resort in Mexico. They have all lost money."

I tilted my drink in her direction. "Which begs the question, why the heck is this guy interested in an Old West resort in Montana?"

Svetlana nodded. "Especially when he might soon be indicted for fraud."

"What else do we know about Shaw?" I asked.

"He spends a lot of company money on private parties," she said. "He loves sports, including tennis, and is quite competitive. People close to him say he has a Napoleon Complex. Oh, and he's a sex addict. Allegedly."

"That's what you get for naming your kid *Randy*," I said. "Anything else?"

"No, but I am curious about his sudden interest in us."

"My guess? Because he heard we were hired on the Sidney case. No matter what, we need to find out why Shaw is so interested in Ricochet."

"You have outlined a strategy," Svetlana said, refilling my glass. "What tactics do you propose?"

"Well…"

Without lingering, I glanced at her aristocratic curves, her enticingly haughty profile, and came to rest on what I considered her best feature: her almond-shaped, predatory eyes. Her brow pinched up as she grasped my meaning.

"Absolutely not."

"Take it easy," I said. "I just need you to keep him distracted while I'm roaming around. Please?"

She glanced over at Wendy and Alexei. The two of them were laughing like high school sweethearts at Reunion. Svetlana sighed. It was the sigh of a woman accustomed to disappointment in romance.

"Fine," she said. "I will do it."

6

LIKE A DOGCATCHER

We were twisting up a narrow lane between sand dunes in a Range Rover. Ahead, a mammoth Neo-Dutch Colonial dominated an oasis of lawn, and beyond it loomed the Atlantic. My ancestors had survived a savage two-month voyage across her, only for my parents to disappear on her during an afternoon sail. If you could resent an ocean, I resented this one.

Wendy shook my arm. "You okay?"

"Yeah, fine."

We parked in a lot below the house and followed Pink and Powder Blue up to a wide porch draped in patriotic bunting. Bartenders stood behind a long bar, and within seconds Alexei ordered a vodka martini. I grinned at Svetlana. She put on her sunglasses. Wendy looked over the drink options, wiggling her lips.

"I will have...a Chardonnay," she said. "Dakota, you?"

"Nothing, thanks."

At the other end of the porch, a covey of trophy wives chatted. One of them turned in my direction. A waifish woman, she wore a canary sundress and had shiny hair and restless eyes. She whispered something to her companions and they laughed, leaving me a tiny bit self-conscious. Maybe it was my safari shirt.

I sucked the salt breeze into my lungs and took in Shaw's property. A few acres of gently sloping lawn encircled the house, with sand dunes on one side and a tennis court and cottages on the other. Far out on a promontory near the water lurked an octagonal building, its dark windows commanding a view in every direction. It had the look of a lair, a place where nefarious plans were hatched.

Powder Blue spoke to the woman in the canary sundress, who walked over clutching a wineglass in both hands.

"Mr. Stevens, Ms. Krüsh," she said. "I'm Madison Shaw. Randal is down at the tennis court. The girls will show you the way."

I looked at Wendy. She sipped her wine and hooked her arm through Alexei's.

"It's fine," she said. "The maestro and I will hang out for a while."

"Dinner is at seven o'clock sharp," Pink said.

Wendy nudged Alexei. "Hey, let's see if they have a piano. You can play something for me." She tugged him into the house.

Svetlana made a sucking sound through her teeth.

"Relax," I said to her. "You know how hard it is to keep a piano tuned by the ocean? I doubt they even have one."

We started across the lawn. Before we got ten steps from the house, Beethoven's "Für Elise" wafted out of a window behind us. Svetlana hitched up her handbag and walked faster.

We hiked down to a hardtop tennis court with a shaded wooden grandstand. The pop of the tennis ball echoed over the swish of the distant surf. When the point finished, our escorts led us into the stands. A dozen pairs of sunglasses whirled in our direction.

"Mr. Shaw," Powder Blue said.

A small-framed man in tennis whites stood up, his thighs failing to add much to his stature.

"Thank you, ladies," he said. "You may leave."

Shaw had wavy blond hair, glittering blue eyes and a slight cleft in his chin. Appraising me with his jaw raised, he clutched my hand by the fingers and shook it like he was trying to open a locked door.

"Mr. Stevens," Shaw said. "Thanks for indulging me with your presence this afternoon. And this, I assume, is your assistant, Svetlana Krüsh."

"Associate," I said.

"I solve the crimes and handle the money," Svetlana said.

"You're divine, whatever you do."

He kissed her hand before she could recoil. We sat down.

"By no means should today be strictly about business," he said. "We're having a clambake later, and I hope you'll stay overnight with us." His eyes vacuumed up Svetlana's legs. "As my guests of course."

"Get to the point, Shaw," I said. "Why did you drag us out here?"

"I understand you've been retained by Vivian Vaillancourt to look into the death of her brother."

Shaw alternated his gaze between Svetlana and me. There was a vulnerable iridescence in his eyes.

"I had nothing to do with Sidney Vaillancourt's death," he said.

I tapped Svetlana. "Well, there it is. We can go home now."

"I would like to hire you and Ms. Krüsh to look into this further," he said.

"We already have a client," I said.

"It's not the same case," he said. "It's related to Vaillancourt's death, or at least I think it's related, but I can't be sure."

"Thanks, but you know, business ethics?" I said. "Or maybe you don't know."

"It's *not* the same case. I don't know how to put it— anyway, we'll get to that later. Do you play tennis, Mr. Stevens?"

"I do."

"And you, Ms. Krüsh?"

"Only when he makes me."

"Fine," Shaw said. "You can partner with me, and Mr. Stevens can pair up with Penny."

Shaw placed a hand on Svetlana's knee. She promptly removed it with her fingertips, as one would dispose of a dead mouse.

"Afraid I can't," I said. "Twisted my ankle recently. Doctor's orders."

"That's too bad," Shaw said.

"I can't either," Svetlana said. "I haven't any sneakers."

"Nonsense," he said. "I keep an assortment of men's and women's gear in the clubhouse. We'll play while Mr. Stevens nurses his injury."

Svetlana's mouth twitched at the corners. Feigning enjoyment was never her specialty.

"And Mr. Stevens," he said, "I'm quite sure my problem wouldn't be a conflict of interest for you. Let's discuss it after dinner."

"Okay."

Once they were on the court and I'd had a chance to proudly observe Svetlana's much improved backhand, I slipped away and jogged up to the house.

I stepped into a dim foyer at the foot of a staircase. Piano music emanated from the next room. Alexei was sitting next to Wendy at a baby grand, teaching her how to play. At least they were occupied.

I wanted to find Shaw's office. The party seemed contained to the ground floor, and the quiet second floor beckoned. I padded upstairs.

On the landing, I strolled down the hall, checking each room. The spartan décor told me these were guest rooms. I kept going.

The master bedroom was decorated in a breezy Caribbean style. A mahogany four-poster bed commanded the center of the room, and a matching armoire, bureau and roll-top desk rested against the sage walls. A stack of magazines lay on an armchair, their pages warped from the sea air.

I went to the desk. The roll-top was stuck and I had to wrench it open. It screeched. I was pulling out papers when the bedroom door opened and clicked shut.

It was Mrs. Shaw.

She leaned back against the door and smiled at me like a dogcatcher.

7

CIGAR AFICIONADO

"Mrs. Shaw, I'm glad you're here," I said. "Do you have a stamp?"

"It's Madison."

"Well, Madison, let me get out of your way."

She turned the lock and studied me for a long moment before pushing away from the door.

"I'd like your opinion about something."

"The decorating?" I said. "Oh, excellent *feng shui.*"

Walking toward me, Madison scooped up her canary sundress and shucked it off. Underneath was a white lace bra and thong. I'd seen my share of craziness on cases, but this was a first.

"You wanted my opinion on something?" I said.

"Do you find me desirable?"

She twirled. Honestly, she was a bit thin for my taste. Slim legs and arms, a fawn's neck—like I said, a bit scant. But one makes do.

"Your husband's a lucky man. Can I go now?"

She narrowed her eyes. "You're a detective, right? What were you looking for?"

Since I'd already been caught, and since Madison probably didn't want her husband knowing about her little strip show, I decided to be direct.

"I need to see your husband's office. Where is it?"

"Why?"

"Let's just say I think he's hiding something," I said.

"I'm sure you're right about that. He's a greedy, skirt-chasing egomaniac. But, he's still my husband." She put her hands behind her back and swayed side-to-side. "I'll tell you...*if* you do something for me."

"Look, Madison, as much as I'd love to—"

"Darling, not to burst your bubble, but right now you could be any mildly attractive man. I don't want sex."

"Then?" I said.

"I want you to slap me," she said. "Hard."

Her eyes were enormous. I sighed like an elementary school teacher.

"I'm not going to slap you."

"All right." She minced across the room, bent over and pulled something out from under the bed. It was a riding crop. She strutted toward me biting her lower lip. At this point, I didn't care if Sidney's killer jumped out of the closet and confessed; I seriously regretted coming in here.

"I'm not whipping you either." I wrenched the riding crop out of her hand and tossed it aside. My eyes landed on the pile of magazines on the armchair. "However, I *will* spank you." I grabbed a copy of *Yachting* and rolled it up.

"Not *Yachting*." She wagged a finger. "*Cigar Aficionado. S'il vous plaît.*"

I shuffled through the pile, found one and folded it in half. Thick and heavy, it was more of a blunt instrument than something you'd spank with, but she had literally asked for it. With a sudden twist of my free arm, I swaddled my hand up to the wrist with her lustrous hair, and wrenched her head back.

"Oh, my," she said. "Somebody wants to play."

I pulled her by the hair and bent her over the chair back.

"Where's your husband's office? What's he hiding?"

"I'll never tell." She wiggled her bottom.

I drew back and smacked her with the magazine.

"His office," I said. "Where is it?"

She didn't answer. I smacked her again: *whap!*

"The octagon," she said. "If he's hiding anything, it'll be out there."

"Where's the key?" I asked.

Whap!

No answer.

"Key!"

Whap!

"Desk." She pointed behind her. "Top drawer."

On my last blow, I had brought down the magazine so hard, the cover tore off. As I got a new grip on the magazine, my stomach knotted up and I realized that I was harboring a profound amount of anger about something. It bothered me, but in a sadistic way I was beginning to enjoy this. Now that Madison had started this little game, I wasn't stopping until I learned everything I needed to know.

"Why is Shaw interested in a resort in Montana?" I asked.

Whap!

"He—Randy—goes out there once a month," she gasped. "To Yellowstone."

"To meet Sidney Vaillancourt?"

Whap!

"No. A woman, I think."

"What's her name?"

Whap!

"I have no idea," she said.

"Why is Randal interested in Ricochet?"

Whap!

"What?"

Her butt cheeks glowed. The pages were shredded.

"Ricochet, why?"

Whap! Whap!

"I don't know," she cried. "Really I don't."

I scaled the magazine across the room and spun her around. Tears rolled down her cheeks, yet she was smiling. She clung to me more than she hugged me. Her body was warm and faintly trembling.

"Thank you," she whispered.

Yeah, the rich are different all right.

"Goodbye, Madison." I shoved her aside, fetched the key and hustled out the door.

I had just stepped outside when Svetlana marched up the hill. She stopped and put her hands on her hips.

"What have *you* been doing?"

"Oh, you know," I said. "The usual."

"You *must* rescue me," she said. "Every time I stoop for a ball, I can feel his eyes on me."

"Svetlana, I know he's a pig, but I need you to keep him occupied. Try to find out why he's so interested in Ricochet. I'm going to check out that building on the point."

"I see you at dinner." She started down the hill and spun around.

"Pimp," she said.

The sun was starting to set and I wanted to search Shaw's office before dinner. Since the octagon was in plain sight from the house, I needed to approach it from the beach. Making sure no one was looking, I jogged into the dunes and was belched out on the shore a hundred yards from the octagon. A long staircase descended from the promontory to the beach. As I jogged along the wet sand to hide my footprints, a sandpiper skittered away from the advancing foam and bobbed its head at me.

"Yeah, I feel you, buddy," I said.

Offshore, at the tip of a sandbar, a powerboat rolled in the light chop. Paparazzi would be my bet. On July 4 weekend, the Vineyard overflowed with celebrities, and while down at the tennis court, I thought I'd recognized a couple of movie stars. Whatever. The paparazzi had pictures to take, I had an office to break into. I started up the stairs.

The octagon was an office in name only. The desk was a bare sheet of glass. No computer, not even a phone. It was a bright, airy space designed more for contemplation than for work, with a Persian rug, several plants and a telescope. I was particularly enamored of the daybed, which must have come in handy when Shaw's brain overheated from creative thought. More likely it was for afternoon delights with Pink and Powder Blue.

On bookcases beneath the windows, besides books sat several thick binders, each one bulging with proposals for new attractions. Flipping through them, I wasn't surprised by the outlandish ideas—not even "Life on Mars," a giant dome enclosing a ten-acre simulated surface of the red planet. What surprised me was what I didn't see: a proposal for an Old West resort like Sidney's. There were no financial records or correspondence of any kind.

The Persian rug struck me as superfluous. I went to it and rolled it back. No safe, no secret hatch—just hardwood flooring. As I replaced the rug, I noticed a fax machine on top of a mini-fridge. I turned on the fax machine and pressed the redial button, but no number came up, as if it had never made an outgoing call. When I opened the fridge, a jar of Vlasic pickles sneered back at me.

They'd be calling everyone for dinner soon, and I wouldn't get another chance like this. Sitting in the swivel chair, I spun around, surveying the room. I saw Columbo do this on TV once, and it worked for him.

If I were a brilliant, creative CEO like Shaw, where would I hide my papers in this office?

I looked at the books on the bookcase: organic gardening, Gettysburg, chaos theory, a Chinese cookbook and a dictionary—there was no pattern to them. They were out of place here. I opened each one and fanned the pages until some folded-up papers fell out of the Chinese cookbook.

I spread out the papers on the desk. They were topographical maps and satellite photos, printed on 8½"x11" sheets of paper. By the blurriness of them, they appeared to have been printed on the fax machine, but there was no sender's phone number on them anywhere. The maps had circles on them, and three of the circles were X'd and dated, with the last date being a week ago. The map names and legends had been cut off, but there were points of longitude and latitude.

The satellite photos showed splotches that looked like woods, two roads in a "T" configuration, and hazy rows of buildings. Circles and dates were scrawled on these, too, just like the maps. I made copies of everything with the fax machine, returned the originals to the Chinese cookbook and put the books back on the shelf. Before I left, I decided to check out the telescope.

It was a simple standing telescope positioned between two windows: one with a view down the beach and the other looking out to sea. I trained the scope on the farthest point on the beach and swept across. Shaw and Svetlana jumped into the frame. They were strolling on the wet sand together, Shaw smiling and gesticulating, Svetlana struggling not to look bored. They were far enough away that they wouldn't make it up here for a while. Down the beach from them, a chest-high orange flag fluttered in the breeze. Some kind of tide marker?

I swung the telescope across the water. The powerboat popped into view. It was beached on the sandbar I'd seen earlier. A person was prone on the sand. At this distance I couldn't tell if it was a man or a woman. I tweaked the focus.

It was a man. A man with a bipod-mounted rifle, aiming at Shaw and Svetlana.

8

Rasping with Panic

I ran outside and thundered down the stairs. At the second landing, I stopped and cupped my hands together.

"Gun! Get down! Get down!"

The two of them were specks far away on the beach. Ten feet off the ground, I vaulted over the railing, landed on the sand, and somersaulted to my feet. Sprinting down the beach, yelling at them to get down, I was still far away when a cloud of blood sprayed out Shaw's back. He took another half-step and collapsed on his face. The sound of the shot exploded over the water and caromed off the sand dunes. Svetlana recoiled from Shaw's body, clutching her face in her hands.

A chill ran down my spine. My throat cinched up.

I ran harder than I'd ever run before, the blood pounding in my ears, my breath rasping with panic. I couldn't let anything happen to her. I couldn't. My legs were leaden and feathery at the same time. I was floating over the sand without getting any closer. I kept my eyes on Svetlana.

And then I was there, slinging my arms around her, tackling her to the sand. I lay on top of her, covering her head with my torso, wondering when the next shot would come. On the open beach we were no better off than driftwood, and the dunes were too far away. I pulled my gun and squeezed off three shots at the sandbar. Hauling Svetlana up, I fired my last three shots, dropped the gun and ran to the water with her. I splashed into the cold surf squeezing her hand.

"Deep breath."

On the crest of the next wave, I plunged us underwater. Clutching her hand, kicking madly, I pulled us away from shore. Her hair swayed in the water like sea kelp. She stared at me in shock.

A muffled hum, like a boat engine, came from the surface. If I was right, the shooter was speeding away in his boat. If I was wrong, I was about to get a bullet through my hand.

I thrust my hand up into the warm air.

Nothing happened.

I surfaced just in time to see the boat skipping over the waves, into the setting sun. Svetlana emerged beside me gasping, her hair slicked against her scalp, her tennis dress clinging to her skin like white latex. Her eyelashes dripped, her chest heaved. We were shaking. I wanted desperately to kiss her, to show how grateful I was that she was alive, but somehow it felt wrong. So I put my hands on her upper arms, she put hers on mine, and we stood there in the chest-deep water staring into each other's eyes as the waves curled around us.

9

GETTING ORIENTED

When we finally returned to Manhattan late the next morning, I felt like a used sponge. Massachusetts State Police had questioned Svetlana and me at the scene, and a detective, last name of Clancy, interrogated me separately until midnight. Then we had drunk celebrity guests and a sobbing Madison to deal with, not to mention an early return flight. The three-story brick townhouse that housed Svetlana's apartment and our headquarters had never looked so good.

While Svetlana went upstairs to freshen up, I went down to the office and started a pot of coffee. Sitting at my desk, I tossed a tennis ball against the wall and pondered the shooting.

Shaw was dead—and then some. The bullet had entered his chest just above the sternum, pierced his heart and blown an exit wound out his back the size of my fist. When Clancy arrived, I showed him the sandbar the shooter had fired from. Approximating the trajectory, they searched for the bullet in the dunes behind Shaw. They didn't find it. However, from the distance, the impact damage and the entry hole, they believed the gun was a .50-caliber long-range rifle, a gun preferred by professional, military snipers. This would explain why he hadn't fired at Svetlana and me after dropping Shaw: he was a one shot, one kill operator. I shivered at the thought.

The only other leads I'd garnered from yesterday's fiasco were the documents I'd found in Shaw's office, and Madison's story about his secret meetings in Montana. It wasn't much, but from a clue standpoint I was better off now than I had been 24 hours ago. I threw the ball against the wall again and caught it.

Shaw could have been murdered by a disgruntled OFG employee or a jealous husband, but given the professional nature of the crime, that theory was unlikely. No, I had to consider the facts, and the facts suggested a connection between the deaths of Sidney and Shaw. One, Shaw had been trying to buy out Sidney. Two, he'd been spending time in Montana. And three, he'd wanted to hire us to investigate a "related" part of Sidney's case.

Then there was the timing of Shaw's murder to consider—July 4, with dozens of potential witnesses around—which meant somebody had an urgent reason to kill him. Maybe Shaw was privy to some vital information about Sidney's case. Then again, maybe I was foaming at the mouth and the two deaths had nothing to do with each other.

I made a bad throw and the tennis ball ricocheted off my desk and rolled into the hall. Svetlana was on her way in, carrying a bag from Murray's Bagels. She picked up the ball and shook her head at me.

The coffee was ready by now. I went out to the break room and poured two cups. Svetlana was already on her laptop when I handed her a mug. She sipped with one hand and typed with the other. I sat on her desk, spreading cream cheese on an Everything bagel.

"What are you working on?" I asked.

"I remembered something Shaw said on the beach last night. You know, before…"

"Yeah, go on."

"He said there was more to Ricochet than the town Sidney built. He wouldn't tell me what it was—he wanted to discuss it with *you* first—but it was clearly why he wanted to hire us. I'll print whatever I find and we can read it later."

"That reminds me."

I fished out the photocopies from Shaw's office. They were still damp. I carefully unfolded them on the desk.

"What are these?" Svetlana asked.

"Clues, I hope."

"They seem to be pages from one large map," she said.

We dried out the pages with a hair dryer, then painstakingly assembled them like a jigsaw puzzle by matching up the contour lines. After we had taped the pages together into one cohesive map, I pointed at the longitudes and latitudes.

"Go to the USGS website and put these in."

I went behind the desk and leaned over her shoulder. She was wearing a subtle floral perfume that brought back memories of a rare, relaxing case together in Scottsdale, Arizona.

"Here," she said.

A topographical map appeared on the screen. It looked very similar to the one we'd just pieced together.

"It's in Montana," she said, "but there's no place name associated with those coordinates."

"They have satellite photos, too," I said. "See if you can find Shaw's."

The moment she found it, Svetlana picked up the laptop and walked across the hall to the conference room. I followed. She flicked on the LCD projector, plugged in her laptop and waited for the image to come up on the white board. The map and the satellite photos appeared side by side.

"*Voilà*," she said.

"*Merci*. Just the map for a sec."

I went to the white board with a dry-erase marker and drew circles on the projected map in roughly the same locations as the ones on Shaw's.

"Okay, three of the circles had X's through them with dates"—I wrote on the board—"here, here and here. We know this is in Montana, and it seems the only place in Montana that Shaw was interested in was Ricochet. We also know he met with somebody in Yellowstone once a month."

"Who?" Svetlana said.

"No idea. Mrs. Shaw told me, but she doesn't know who either."

"How did you get that out of her?"

"Don't ask," I said.

She gave me a pitying look.

"What do the circles mean?" she asked.

"Must be locations of things."

"Assuming the map and photos are of Ricochet," Svetlana said, "perhaps the marks indicate places for future structures or attractions."

"I'd be inclined to agree," I said, "but what about the ones that are crossed out? The dates are all in the past. We'll just have to wait until can see firsthand. When should we leave?"

"Tell me when you want to go and I will book your flight," she said. "I will follow a few days later. My sister Zoya has rented a beach house in Southampton for the month. She wants me to visit."

"Well, we were planning on going out separately anyway," I said. "I should head upstate and pack a few things, close the place up, maybe do a little riding to get back in practice. It'll also give me time to think about the case."

"While you retreat to your Batcave," she said, "I will collect information on the actors in Ricochet."

"Check out Louis and Roman while you're at it," I said.

Svetlana nodded. She held out a hand.

"For saving my life yesterday."

"My pleasure."

For a woman with fine bones, Svetlana had an unusually strong grip.

"Don't do anything stupid up there," she said.

"You know, Svetlana, you really shouldn't be so sentimental."

10

Lined Up

I drove up to the Village of Millbrook, got a sandwich at the deli, and wended my way through the sunny countryside to my modest estate in Clove Valley. I ate lunch on the deck beneath the trees and afterwards decided to practice some shooting.

To get in the Old West mindset, I took out my great-grandfather's Remington 1890, a heavy, single-action pistol, meaning the hammer had to be thumbed back before every shot. The good news was, the weight of the gun, along with how deliberately you had to aim it, made you a lot more accurate, and within three shots I was hitting the paper man targets dead-center. I practiced drawing from the holster and firing, and by the end of the afternoon, while I wasn't exactly the Sundance Kid, I was shooting well enough so I wouldn't embarrass myself out west.

After cleaning the gun and doing some chores around the place, at seven o'clock I changed into riding clothes and walked through the woods separating my place and my neighbor's, Twin Creek Farm. I had called ahead, and Mrs. Gallagher, the owner, was brushing Janie inside the main barn. The prickly smell of hay dust filled the air.

"I would have groomed her," I said.

"I don't mind. Blanket and Western saddle are on the sawhorse over there." She put down the brush. "Finish her up."

I picked up the blanket. Walking back to the horse, I caught a glimpse of a silver SUV parked in the shade on Brush Hill Road. A man stood at the fence with binoculars, sweeping them across the farm. He was too far away to make out clearly.

"Who's the peeper?" I tossed the blanket over Janie's back.

"Handicapper, probably." She glanced out the doorway. "I can't tell you how many times I've had to call the sheriff about them. Ever since Handsome Ransom won at Saratoga last year, they've been hanging around non-stop. Handsome's running in a stakes race at Belmont this weekend and favored to win, so they're trying to see how he looks."

"How *does* he look?" I got the saddle and laid it across Janie.

"Legs in good shape, but he's had a bad cold. Breathing's not a hundred percent. But that's just between us."

"Of course."

I reached underneath and buckled the girth strap, then waited until Janie withdrew her stomach before tightening it. When I finished, I could slip one finger between the strap and her belly.

"Keeping Handsome in the back pasture so they can't see him," she said. "Where you riding? Be dark in a couple hours."

"Just out to the old Brown place and back."

Mrs. Gallagher removed the halter, slid the bit in Janie's mouth and adjusted the bridle straps. I lengthened the stirrups.

"I'll wash her down and feed her when I get back," I said. "I was planning on riding over there first thing tomorrow, too. I'll come early and muck a few stalls."

"Sounds good."

"Thanks. See you later."

Reins in hand, left foot in the stirrup, I grabbed some of Janie's mane and threw my leg over. I nudged Janie into an easy trot and steered her across the road. The man with the silver SUV was gone.

We trotted along the perimeter of a cornfield and onto a path that followed the creek. In a distant field I spied the ghostly gray barn where, only a few months ago, Shay and I had holed up together. I was glad when the barn slipped out of view.

We forded the creek onto an overgrown cow pasture. Deer stood bolt upright, watching us from a distant tree line. Janie bobbed her head and tensed beneath me, and with a gentle slap of the reins she slid into a rolling canter. We walked the last quarter-mile to the Brown place, or what was left of it. Charred timbers lay in a heap where the farmhouse once stood, and on each end of the house's footprint was a stone chimney. I dismounted and led Janie through a crabapple orchard to the aging barn.

I gazed across the open fields and up at Chestnut Ridge. The ridge top glowed orange, silhouetting the abandoned fire tower. It would be dark soon. The barn weathervane, still intact on the edge of the roof, squeaked in the evening breeze. I stroked Janie's neck, and then we rode back in the summer twilight.

———◆◆◆———

When I got home, there was a message from Svetlana. I climbed into bed with the windows open and called her apartment number.

"So," I said, "what's up?"

"I am giving myself a raise."

"You learned something useful, I take it."

"Roman is ex-Marines," she said, "dishonorably discharged after serving two years for assaulting an officer. Also, he is *not* a licensed private investigator."

"Interesting. What else?"

"He worked as a circus strongman once, and he has a pilot's license."

The crickets outside were loud tonight, and I thought I'd misheard her.

"Did you say *circus strongman?*"

"I was testing to see if you were listening," she said.

"I can't believe it, Svetlana Krüsh made a joke. What about Louis? Find out anything?"

"He worked at OFG's main park after college. Eventually he became an assistant in guess whose office."

"Shaw's?" I said.

"Correct."

"Okay. Roman and Louis. We'll have to give them a closer look before we leave. What about the actors in Ricochet?"

"I've assembled dossiers on the leading players," she said. "They all have limited credits. Small theatre companies, slasher films, reality shows and such. For most of them, this is their first steady job. I've included photos of them."

"Well, we can't expect to solve this from a distance," I said. "What they don't know is, there's gonna be a new marshal in town."

"*Please.* I go to bed now."

"Sleep tight, little lady."

I thought I heard her giggle before she hung up, but I was probably just tired. I put the phone in its cradle, shut out the lights and went to sleep.

When the alarm clock rang, I rolled out of bed with re-newed purpose. Today my luck on this case would change for the better—I could feel it. After a quick breakfast, I packed my musette bag. Even on short outdoor jaunts, I always brought some basic survival equipment, including my Leatherman and a first aid kit. An Eagle Scout's hab-its die hard. So do a former FBI agent's: I brought my .45 revolver in its hip holster. I took a bottle of Poland Spring and walked over to Janie's barn.

I mucked a few stalls, and by the time I had Janie ready to go, the horizon glowed pink with the rising sun. I rode up toward Chestnut Ridge Road. The handicapper with the silver SUV was leaning over the fence again. Spotting me, he jumped in his car and drove away. This guy needed a life. I crossed the road, picked up a trail that circled around the surrounding farms, and nudged Janie into a trot.

After several miles of moderate riding, I made it to the once-prosperous and now sadly overgrown Middlemiss Farm. There I turned around and by eleven we were entering the Brown place from the back. Not even noon yet and easily 90 degrees, with humidity so thick you could baste a turkey in it. Mercifully there was a breeze. I stopped at the barn and glanced up at the weathervane. For some reason, it wasn't squeaking today, and a wooden ladder leaned against the peak.

Odd.

When I dismounted, Janie was staring across the open ground between the barn and the fire tower. I squinted to see what she was looking at.

Faintly I made out an orange flag, like the one on Shaw's beach. A jolt of adrenaline surged through me. My mouth tasted metallic.

The weathervane, the flag, the fire tower. They all meant one thing.

I was being lined up.

11

Pinned Down

I dove and landed hard on a rock. Janie screamed. The hairs on the back of my neck sprang up, and an instant later the valley echoed with a high-pitched thunderclap. Janie staggered and collapsed. She moaned, looked imploringly at me as blood gushed from her shoulder. My only chance was to move erratically and find cover. I sprang to my feet and ran full out, zigzagging through the orchard. Something whacked the tree trunk ahead, and a moment later a gunshot ripped through the valley. I kept going, dodging tree limbs, heading for the best cover nearby—the stone chimneys. The shooter would expect me to run for the nearest one. I faked in that direction and sprinted for the second chimney. I leaped over some burnt ceiling beams, skidded across the dirt and collided with the chimney. My head hit a stone. Stunned, I scrabbled backwards into the hearth. A stone on the corner exploded with a loud pop, followed by the rifle crack a second later. I bowed my head and caught my breath. I drew my gun. Unless a second shooter lurked to the west, I was safe—for now.

Sweat poured down my face. My shirt was soaked through. As the adrenaline wore off, my legs twitched and my arm throbbed. Somehow I'd cut my forearm open. Blood oozed out and dripped off my elbow. As things stood, I had the laceration, a goose egg on my forehead and a deep bruise on my leg from landing on that rock. Still, considering the alternative—getting my heart blown out—I was very fortunate.

Janie wasn't as lucky. Every few minutes, the breeze carried her plangent neighs across the orchard. I sat with clenched fists. What could I do? I wanted to put her out of her misery, but the shooter would be counting on that. I bit my lip. Her spotting that flag had saved my life. If I got out of this alive, the bastard who shot her was going to suffer.

Remembering I had my cell phone, I snapped it open and waved it around for a signal. Not one bar. Maybe it was the chimney. Whatever. I was stuck here until nightfall at least.

The cut on my arm needed attention. I took out the first aid kit and applied some disinfectant and a couple of butterfly bandages. Then I drank some water and pondered my situation.

I was pinned down, plain and simple, and I wasn't about to stick my head out to see if the shooter was still around. If this was the same guy who killed Shaw, he was a pro, and lying on his belly for eight hours would be child's play to him. The shooter was probably up in the fire tower. Intuition told me it was the "handicapper" in the silver SUV. How he knew that I would go riding again this morning, and to the same destination, was beyond me. But thinking about it wouldn't help. I needed to focus on the situation and figure out how I was going to escape.

As to the shooter's identity, was it possibly Roman? Svetlana did say he'd been a Marine. Whoever he was, he could circle around to the east, but I doubted he'd waste his energy. He'd wait for me to screw up instead. I sipped from the bottle of Poland Spring and resisted the urge to chug. It was going to be a long, scorching day, and although there was a faint breeze, my shade was limited. All I could do was sit tight.

The sweat continued to pour off me. My head throbbed from the bump and the relentless sun. I pulled a bandanna from my musette bag and put it on my head. It helped a little. I leaned back into the shade as far as I could, but the top of the fireplace was too low for my head, forcing me to bend my neck and tuck my knees into my chest. My only consolation was that the sun would soon be beating down against the chimney instead of me.

A pair of turkey vultures soared in lazy circles overhead. Waiting on Janie. I hoped she was gone and not suffering anymore. The breeze had waned, and an indifferent silence crept over the orchard and surrounding meadow. For half an hour, maybe longer, I sat mesmerized by an ant dragging a dead beetle ten times its size. When it disappeared beneath the charred timbers, I had only the heat to keep me company.

A Piper Cub droned overhead, the sound of the little engine fading until the plane disappeared over the ridge. I wondered what Svetlana was doing. I imagined her in a skirt that showed off her legs, sipping an iced cappuccino, clip-clopping down 10th Street on her way to the Marshall Chess Club. Or maybe she was already at the club, playing speed chess in air-conditioned comfort.

Then for some reason I thought of Shay. I saw her face, her glorious hair, heard her unbridled laugh, smelled her mint shampoo. The heat beating down on me made me think of its opposite—the snow and the cold and riding that toboggan down Brush Hill with her body beneath mine—and I wondered where things between us might have gone, had events followed a different course.

Before I could answer that for myself, a cicada chittered to a high-pitched crescendo, then tapered off to a soft rattle. I sipped some more water. My best chance for escape was in total darkness. But there was something else to consider. Given the careful preparation the sniper had shown so far, I had to assume he was equipped with night vision. With this in mind I devised a getaway route that would give me as much cover as possible: through the orchard, then into the deep drainage ditch that ran through the meadow to the woods. But first I needed a distraction. What foiled night vision?

Light. An intense burst of light.

I dumped out the contents of the musette bag: first aid kit, water, Leatherman, granola bar (which I wolfed down), rope, compass, strike-anywhere matches, mini flashlight and a magnesium fire starter. I always packed the little block in case it rained and I needed a foolproof way of starting a fire. I could scrape magnesium shavings into the bandanna, then set it aflame, creating a blinding flash that would give me enough time to get away.

I got to work.

12

THE HUNTER

When you're waiting for it, darkness takes a painfully long time to fall. The cicadas kept up their shrill song into dusk when the mourning doves took over, their soft cooing like a dirge to Janie. As the sun set, the humidity cooled and settled into a visible haze. Rabbits emerged from their warrens and hopped around warily nibbling clover. Unfortunately the mosquitoes also came out to feed, and they whined in my ears as I scraped away at the metal block. Slowly, a pile of shavings began to accumulate on the bandanna.

When I checked my watch again, it was 11:19 p.m. If I waited any longer, I'd be too cramped to run. I holstered my gun, shouldered my bag and stood up, keeping my back against the chimney. My legs were asleep, and I shook them out until the tingling went away. Finally, with the tied bandanna of shavings in one hand, and a kitchen match in the other, I took a deep breath.

"Here goes."

I lighted the bandanna and tossed it around the corner of the chimney. There was a dazzling burst of light, and I was off, sprinting straight for the orchard. I ran through the orchard, past the barn, past the outline of Janie's carcass, through the meadow, and into the drainage ditch, landing with a mucky splash. There were no shots. Bent double, I jogged down the ditch.

Once the ditch reached the woods, I climbed out, hopped a fence and stole across Mrs. Gallagher's farm. The empty pastures were eerie in the moonlight. I was jogging along the fence that led from the farm to my house when I felt myself slowing down.

Something was wrong here. Getting away had been way too easy, as if the shooter had left hours ago.

What if the shooter was trying to lull me into a false sense of security? Once I escaped, where would he expect me to go? Home. If I were him, I'd have a backup shooting station. A spot with a clear line of sight to my door. And I knew of just such a spot: a rocky ledge in the woods behind my guesthouse. From there, he could take aim on the front and back of the main house and wait for me to show up.

For a moment I thought about ambushing him in his hiding place, but I quickly reconsidered. I was wet, dirty, tired and thirsty, and in no condition to confront anybody. I couldn't go home so I stopped in Mrs. Gallagher's barn and washed up in the office bathroom. I changed into a stable hand's coveralls and drank from the faucet until the parched feeling in my throat went away. To counteract my exhaustion, I found a box of No-Doz in the medicine cabinet and took two. Now, I was ready.

I jogged up Brush Hill with the revolver snug in my hand. The crickets were rowdy tonight, making it hard to hear movement in the trees. Ahead, a silver SUV glinted in the moonlight. It was parked beside the creek that ran along the northern edge of my property, where the look-out spot was. There was a rental agency sticker on the rear bumper, and the license plates had been removed. Clever. I shone the flashlight inside. The doors were locked. I thought about smashing a window to get in there, but the noise would give me away. I'd come back later. For now, I slashed the tires so he couldn't drive off, then headed upstream.

I waded through the shin-deep water, using the current to mask my footsteps. A raccoon skittered up the bank into the underbrush. I kept moving, the gun out and at my side, until a quarter-mile in I found what I was looking for: a hunter's tree stand. The leaves around the tree trunk had been disturbed. I looked closer. Fresh boot prints circled around the tree and faded into the woods. I grinned in the moonlight.

Your ass is mine.

I climbed the ladder and sat on the platform facing the ledge where the shooter was. To get back to his car, he'd have to cross fifty yards of open ground beneath my perch.

Now I had the high ground.

Now I was the hunter.

With the revolver secure in my holster, I settled in for another long wait.

13

FIFTY-YARD FIELD GOAL

The first gray light of dawn trickled through the trees when the shooter came. I couldn't see him, but I heard him, the brush snapping like firecrackers in the still and misty air.

I stood up, rolled my neck and climbed slowly down. Crouching behind the big maple, I flexed my gun hand, drew my gun, and peered around the trunk. The sky rumbled. I sighted down the gun barrel at the mouth of the clearing. And then, apparition-like, he materialized out of the haze.

In the dim light he was only a shape, but as he drew closer I understood why: he wore a gilly suit. He looked like a walking pile of moss and leaves. In one hand he carried a long case—that would be the gun—while his other hand moved stiffly at his side. A military gait.

Twenty yards away, he stopped and put down the case, then removed the gilly suit and shoved it in an empty duffel. He was a muscular, stout man, maybe 5'7".

My ear itched—a mosquito had landed there—but I didn't move, didn't breathe. The shooter reached in his pocket. My hand tightened on the gun. He put a cigarette in his lips, lit a Zippo lighter and raised the flame, revealing a high forehead and bushy eyebrows. The lighter clanked shut.

I let him pick up the case again and take three more steps before I popped out from behind the tree. As I cocked the hammer on the revolver, he stared at me with surprising calmness. I frowned. Usually cocking the hammer had a sphincter-releasing effect on bad guys, and I was annoyed by his composure.

"On the ground," I said. "Face down."

He smiled at me and took another drag from the cigarette. I smiled back, paced casually toward him and booted a fifty-yard field goal into his balls. Falling to his knees, he yelped some gibberish and clutched his groin. Case and cigarette slipped out of his hands. I squashed out the cigarette and kicked him between the shoulder blades, toppling him face-first into last fall's leaves. As I held him down with a knee, he tried to push himself up.

Enough.

I fired into the ground with the gun close to his ear. The shot was deafening to me, so I could only imagine how he felt. He grunted, reached for his ear, swore in what sounded like Russian.

"Simmer down." I tapped him on the head with the gun barrel.

The sky rumbled again. It began to rain. Yanking the rope from my bag, I jerked his hands behind his back and lashed them together. I frisked him and checked the gilly suit. No weapons, no ID, no cell phone. I hauled him up by his bound wrists and aimed him toward my property.

On the ground was a green branch. I stripped its leaves, zipped it through the air a couple times, and whipped him four times across the neck, leaving deep red welts. He cowered and growled something. The rain dripped down his forehead. I whipped him across the cheek and he started to run, tripping on a tree root. When he got up, leaves clung to his face.

"That was for Janie," I said. "All right. Let's go."

Holding my gun on him, I picked up the case and duffel and nudged him forward. We swished downhill through the mulch, the intensifying rain beating the leaves above us.

14

KIDNAPPING

During my eleven-year career with the FBI, I worked on several kidnapping cases, never imagining I'd one day be a kidnapper myself. The scary thing was, I enjoyed it.

I tied him up in the garage. To be precise, I bound him with duct tape to an Adirondack chair and chained the chair to a steel column. I asked him a few questions, including who he was and who'd hired him, but he only smiled and muttered something in a language I couldn't understand. I needed Svetlana.

But first, a little softening up. I taped his mouth and grabbed the switch. He glared at me. I whipped him across the cheek. As a trickle of blood ran down his chin, I held up the slender branch and admired it.

"Ah, the switch," I said. "A great American tradition. There's even one in *Tom Sawyer*, did you know that?"

The shooter stared at a spot on the wall. Clearly there was a language barrier, but I had a hunch he understood more than he was letting on.

"Okay," I said, "since you're not carrying ID, I'm calling you Igor. I think you can understand me, Igor, so here's the deal. You're not going anywhere until I get some information. You killed a man, you killed a horse, and you nearly killed a woman I care about. If I wanted to, I could bury you in the woods and nobody would find you. But it's not going to come to that, because you're going to cooperate."

I went to the slop sink and filled a Styrofoam cup from the tap until it spilled over the lip. I placed the cup on the workbench directly across from him so he couldn't avoid looking at it, and put the switch down next to it.

"You're lucky it's raining today," I said. "Cooler than usual. Tomorrow's looking bad, though. Gets hot in here with no windows open." I grabbed his gun case and left.

Inside the house, I took a shower and cleaned and re-bandaged my arm. My entire body throbbed. Sitting in cramped positions for eighteen hours will do that to a guy. But as much as I wanted to sleep, I had things to do. First, I needed to search Igor's car for ID or some kind of clue about who he was working for, but when I got there the car was gone. The sheriff must have towed it. Next, I had to give Mrs. Gallagher the bad news about Janie. I went over and told her. She was still in shock when one of the farm hands and I took a backhoe over to the Brown place and buried Janie in the orchard.

Igor was asleep in his chair when I returned. Satisfied he wasn't going anywhere, I went into the kitchen, slipped on some latex gloves, and examined his gun.

Without question, this guy was a pro. The gun was a Barrett .50-caliber with a day-night 36-power scope. This was a military-grade weapon often used to take out transformers, generators and engine blocks. A little over four feet long, it had a stubby shoulder stock that made it look more like a spear gun than a sniper rifle. Finally, it was a single-shot, which explained how I hadn't been killed. When Igor's first shot missed, I was able to run for cover while he reloaded.

I leaned on the counter. Despite my exhaustion, I needed to make sense of this. Unless he was acting on his own, somebody hired Igor to kill Shaw and now me. But who? The only person I knew of with a connection to Shaw was Louis, his former assistant. But if he hired Igor, why? And what was the connection to Sidney's death? Assuming there even was one. I closed the gun case.

The key was a stubborn, sweaty man tied up in my garage. I had to make Igor talk, and at the moment, besides his obstinacy, there was a considerable language barrier to surmount.

I called Svetlana. When she answered, I gave her an abridged account of the last 24 hours.

"I am sorry about the horse," she said. "Are you okay?"

"I'm fine, but I need your help. My houseguest—"

"Don't you mean your *prisoner*?"

"Whatever," I said. "I think he's of Russian extraction, so I need your multilingual abilities."

"Doesn't everyone?"

I checked the train schedule hanging on the refrigerator. Muzak played on her end.

"Where the hell are you?" I asked.

"Well, if you must know, in the shoe department at Bloomingdales."

"Listen, I need to question this guy. There's a five-nineteen today, gets in at—"

"That would be a mistake," she said. "I realize you want answers, but you are too tired to be effective right now."

She was right. Truthfully, I could pass out at any moment.

"Okay," I said. "Tomorrow morning take the seven thirty-eight. It gets in at about nine thirty."

"That is quite early, but very well," she said. "Should I pick up any external motivators for the subject? A whip? Some Sodium Pentothal perhaps?"

"Don't kid yourself, I've already got a whip," I said. "But if you wanted, you could wear something low-cut."

"To distract him?"

"To hell with him. For me."

"Good*bye*, Dakota."

"All right, a tight sweater then."

"You're delirious," she said. "Get some sleep."

She hung up.

15

WHEN IT RAINS, IT POURS

The next morning, I picked up Svetlana at the train station. This was only her third visit to my place in Millbrook. Rolling down the driveway and over the creek, we passed under the giant weeping willow, its stringy branches scraping the windshield.

"Isn't this a felony, what you're doing?" she said.

"You mean what *we're* doing," I said. "You're an accessory now."

"The people at FIDE will love that. They especially like having kidnappers among their highest-ranked chess players."

We emerged from the willow tree. All at once the pond, the tennis court and the hill running up to the main house came into view.

"My," Svetlana said, "I forgot how lovely it is, Dakota."

I felt like a dog being petted. "Nice as my place on 77th?"

Svetlana smiled. She'd seen my apartment and was amused by its anachronistic furnishings from the late Eisenhower–early Kennedy period.

"Yes, that is adorable as well."

We parked, went on the deck, and sat at the round slate table in the shade.

"Before we get started with the interrogation, I think we should discuss strategy a little bit," I said.

"Agreed," Svetlana said. "Tell me about the subject. Do you at least know his name?"

"Igor."

"Igor?"

"My pet name for him," I said. "At least until you get his real one."

"Not Ivan?"

"Nah, wait till you meet him. He's an Igor."

A breeze rustled the trees that grew through holes in the deck. It was a beautiful day. Too bad I was about to spend it in a garage interrogating a guy.

"What do you wish to find out?" Svetlana asked.

"Well, first, are there other shooters? Next, who is he affiliated with? The Russians, the Ukrainians?"

"I have already asked my Uncle Viktor," she said. "Such a person does not work for them."

"All right, that narrows it down a bit. We're almost certain he killed Shaw, and somebody's got to pay the piper for his murder. Hold on a sec." I went inside and came back with the cordless. I tossed it to her. "Our detective friend on Martha's Vineyard. Give him a call, find out what he knows." I put Detective Clancy's business card on the table. Svetlana dialed.

"But for God's sake," I said, "don't mention Igor."

"Really?" she said. "You mean I *shouldn't* brag about our little kidnapping? Please."

When Clancy came on the line, she heightened her accent.

"Detective Clancy? This is Svetlana Krüsh, associate of Dakota Stevens. You want we contact you, no?"

I smiled at this not-so-subtle touch. There was a long pause.

"Oh?" She raised an eyebrow. "Yes, I will be sure to mention it. And if you're ever in New York…yes, that would be nice." Svetlana nodded. "Excellent. This fall, then. Goodbye." She hung up.

"They found the bullet."

"Get out of here," I said.

"He and some CSI people combed the sand dune behind Shaw's body and they found it."

"Which means, if they get the gun, they'll have a solid case."

"So," she said, "do we turn Igor over to them?"

"Not until we get some information," I said. "Igor hasn't been cooperative so far, but I'm hoping a long night without food, water or sleep has softened him up."

I considered what I'd just said. If Igor had a military background, there was a good chance he'd undergone torture resistance training, which could make him extremely hard to crack.

"I may have to get rough with him, Svetlana."

"Define rough."

I shrugged. "Depends. All I know is, this guy shot Shaw and Janie and nearly killed the two of us. I have no sympathy for him. At the moment he's nothing but a vessel of information to me." I stood up. "Hey, by the way, what was that about 'This fall then'?"

Her voice assumed a suspiciously KGB tone.

"It is irrelevant," she said. "Come, let us question the prisoner."

When we entered the garage, Igor was slumped over in the chair, and for a split second I feared he was dead. I slammed the door and he came to. His eyes flicked to Svetlana. She sat on a stool and crossed her legs. Igor watched me as I dragged the workbench closer to him.

Without a word, I produced several items from a paper bag: a pair of cowhide work gloves I wore when splitting wood, a big bottle of Pellegrino with the condensation rolling off the cold glass, a container of Morton salt, and a 500,000 volt stun gun. I placed the items in a neat row on the workbench and gestured at them like a *Price is Right* model. Then I picked up the switch and tore the duct tape off his face.

"Wakey, wakey," I said.

His head swayed. He grunted. He opened and closed his jaw a few times—hopefully getting the muscles warmed up to talk. Svetlana sat up straight and twirled a foot.

"Russian? Ukrainian? *En español? Auf Deutsch? Ou devrais-je essayer le français? O forse chiedergli in italiano?*"

"Showoff," I said. "Russian first. Find out his name."

Svetlana spoke in Russian, her voice sharp and authoritative. Igor didn't answer.

"Again," I said.

She put the same question to him, barking it this time. Igor rolled his eyes.

"Can you believe this guy?" I knocked on the workbench. "Tell him I didn't bring this stuff for fun. I want his name."

Svetlana translated. A second later, his mouth opened and a name croaked out: "Igor."

He grinned. I grinned back and whipped him three times across the face until one of the cuts reopened. Then I grabbed the salt container.

"When it rains, it pours," I said.

Holding up the container, I poured the salt in a long, dramatic arc into my open palm.

"Last chance," I said. "Tell him."

Svetlana translated. He pretended not to care, but I noticed his forehead was perspiring. We were getting to him, if ever so slightly. I waited for an answer. When none came, I held my salt-filled hand over his cheek. He huffed through his nose. The second the salt dropped into the cut, he yelled and thrashed in the chair. I let him have a good dose of pain before throwing the cup of water in his face.

"Forget it," I said. "His name isn't important right now. Who hired him and is there a second shooter?"

Svetlana rattled off the questions from her perch. When Igor refused to answer, she raised her voice and asked again. He was silent.

"Ask him if he wants another boot in the nutskies," I said.

"*Nutskies?*"

"My Russian is limited."

"So is your imagination."

She translated. While we waited for an answer, Igor licked his lips and ogled her. He whispered something. Svetlana gave a start and put a hand to her chest.

"What did he say?" I asked.

"I cannot. It is too vulgar."

My rage must have shown because the smug expression on Igor's face vanished and for the first time since I'd captured him there was fear in his eyes. I opened the Pellegrino and waited for it to stop fizzing before taking a drink. Then I calmly put down the bottle, pulled on the work gloves, and punched Igor square in the jaw with the hardest straight right I'd ever thrown. Svetlana winced. I followed up with a left hook that rocked him in the chair and banged his head against the steel column behind. His eyes glazed over and his head went limp.

"Let's give him a second," I said.

I drank some more Pellegrino. When he began to stir, I walked over and dumped another handful of salt on his face. *That* woke him up. And this time, I didn't wash it off.

"Ask him again," I said.

She did. In reply, he spouted a stream of obscenities.

I took off the gloves and grabbed the stun gun. He spat at me, bloodying my shirt. A tooth bounced off my chest and clicked across the floor. He tightened his cheeks to spit again, and I rammed the stun gun into his neck, letting the crackling voltage pump into him for a count of five, staring into his eyes as he soaked in the juice. He thrashed in the chair, his wrists straining at the tape. When I released the button, the garage reeked of ozone. Igor's face glistened with sweat.

"Ask again," I said.

She did, but I'm not sure he even heard her. He was slumped over, panting. I put down the stun gun.

"This isn't working."

"You *think*?" she said. "You almost electrocuted him."

"It only affects voluntary muscle, Svetlana." I leaned against the workbench. "We need an expert, somebody skilled at getting information out of people."

Svetlana blinked at me several times until her eyes widened. She knew who I meant, and she didn't like it.

"No," she said. "No."

"You have a better idea?"

She shook her head and went outside. The moment the door closed, I grabbed a coil of rope from the shelf. It was time to get Igor ready for a little trip.

In my trunk.

16

FALCONE

After I got him well-hydrated, I hog-tied Igor and dumped him in the Cadillac. Slamming the trunk, I shuddered at how much my behavior resembled that of the kidnapper-murderers I'd once investigated. But even so, I had no pity for the guy. Like I'd said to Svetlana, he was just a vessel of information to me, and I wanted answers. Once I changed my shirt, I put a jacket, tie and Igor's gun case in the back seat, and we headed south to see Falcone.

Francis Falcone provided services equivalent to mine as a "finder" for New York's five families. You name it, and for a fee he'd find it: cars, cash, jurors, jewels, bodies, boats, drugs, snitches, hookers, pimps, thieves and killers. As the Mob's private detective, he resorted to methods I wouldn't even consider. But he got results. Which was why I was bringing Igor to see him.

We reached Belmont Raceway at two thirty. I parked in the shade and opened the trunk to give laughing boy some fresh air. Standing over him, I put on my jacket and tie.

"The clubhouse is semi-formal," I said to Svetlana.

"Is what I'm wearing okay?"

She wore a knee-length navy blue dress with white polka-dots, and her hair was tied with a bow of the same polka-dot pattern. White pumps completed the outfit.

"Gorgeous." I nodded at our friend in the trunk. "Right, Igor?"

He tried to say something under the muzzle of tape, but darned if I could understand him. I checked his ropes, patted my brow with a handkerchief and closed the trunk.

Inside the gate, we got lemonades and a *Daily Racing Form*.

"Let's have a look at the ponies," I said.

We went to the paddock and leaned over the fence drinking our lemonades. Svetlana tapped me on the arm with the rolled-up *Racing Form*.

"I let you pick," she said. "The horse I know best is the one on the chessboard."

One by one the strappers led them in, but the horses were either too skinny or frothing at the mouth from the heat. I was about to give up when Number 3, a good-sized filly, clip-clopped out of the shade. With her chestnut coat, rippling shoulders and eager muzzle, she was a heart-stopping reincarnation of Janie.

"Number three," I said. "What's her name?"

"Princess Jessica."

The electronic board put her odds at 4 to 1. Other horses were better favored, but I had a feeling about her.

"It's the Princess," I said. "Come on, let's place our bet and get upstairs."

After a brief argument, Svetlana coughed up $500 of Vivian's retainer, which we put on Princess Jessica to win. Upstairs in the clubhouse dining room, men looked up from their lunches to examine the pretty filly that had just walked in—Svetlana.

Falcone and Dominick were sitting with two surprisingly waspy-looking women at a large table overlooking the track. Falcone waved and the maitre d' escorted us over. I pulled out a chair for Svetlana and sat down next to her.

"Hello, Triple-X," Falcone said.

Svetlana stared at him with endgame eyes.

"Hello, *Francis*."

The girl beside Falcone leaned into his shoulder. "Triple-X?"

"The secret agent from *The Spy Who Loved Me*," Falcone said. "Ladies, allow me to introduce Svetlana Krüsh, one of the top chess players in the world."

The women cooed.

"Oh yeah," Falcone said, "and this is Dakota Stevens, an ex-FBI pain in my ass."

Falcone and I smiled at each other like a couple of duelers. The table was well stocked for an afternoon at the races: a tray of shrimp, two bottles of champagne on ice, and six small binoculars. Falcone poured champagne for us.

"Put in your bets?"

"Princess Jessica," I said. "Five hundred to win."

"A friggen dog," Falcone said. "Jackinthebox, that's the one to beat."

"Did you visit the paddock?"

"You kidding?" he said. "Hot out there. Besides, you can look now till Sunday and it won't matter. The handicappers have it all figured ahead of time."

"Maybe."

"Dakota," Svetlana said, "remember the package we have in the trunk. It *is* perishable."

"Right."

The two women excused themselves to the bathroom. I waited until they left before mentioning them to Falcone.

"They don't seem like your usual girls," I said.

"Kim and Daria?" Falcone said. "Yeah, coupla grad students at Princeton. Met 'em over there when we were looking for a kid screwing around with Mr. Ianucci's daughter. Turns out the *kid* was a psych professor."

"Gotta watch out for them," I said. "All that Freud."

Dominick cleaned the glass on a pair of binoculars. "He's not the first academic we've had to pay a visit."

"I was starting to think you were mute, Dominick," I said.

"Never mind that," Falcone said. "Tell me about this package."

I told him how I came to possess said package, then described the interrogation methods we had tried and our limited results. Falcone snorted.

"So, basically you got dick." He glanced at Svetlana. "I mean—"

"We have been unsuccessful," Svetlana said.

"And what makes you think Dom and I can do better?"

"Because we all know Machiavelli's your personal hero," I said. "Hell, you've probably got 'The ends justify the means' framed in your office."

The waiter brought a tray heaping with sandwiches. Falcone, Dominick and I each took a corned beef. Svetlana had one of the club sandwiches.

"I know exactly who to use," Falcone said, glancing at Dominick.

"Who?" I asked.

"Sick Vinny."

"Absa-friggen-lutely," Dominick said.

Svetlana nudged me. "Who is this 'Sick Vinny'?"

"I have no idea."

Falcone slathered Grey Poupon on his sandwich. "Let's put it this way. He's an unmitigated expert in his field."

"When should we come?" I asked.

"Make it ten tonight," Falcone said. "Only comes out after sundown, that guy. Now, what incentive are you offering?"

Out on the track, the horses trotted by the grandstand. The race would be starting in a few minutes.

"I have some information that might interest you," I said.

"Like?"

"Help us extract what we need from the package, and I'll share what I know about a certain horse scheduled to race here this weekend."

Falcone stopped in mid-chew, considered the offer and nodded. Just as Kim and Daria returned from the ladies' room, the bugler sounded the first call. Falcone refilled our champagne flutes, and we all turned to the window. Svetlana crossed her fingers between our chairs. We picked up our binoculars and trained them on the starting gate.

The bell rang. They were off.

17

THE MISSING SAILBOAT
AND THE WHEELBARROW

At the cashier's window, Svetlana's phone rang. She took the call; I got our money. It had some heft. When she hung up, I knew immediately something was wrong.

"That was Vivian's niece," she said.

"Delilah? What, trouble in paradise?"

"Louis has disappeared, along with Vivian's sailboat and the cash from her safe. Apparently, Vivian is quite distraught."

"The fun never ends over there," I said. "Okay, let's go check it out."

On our way to the car, I took Svetlana's hand and slapped the cash into it.

"What is this?" she said.

"A bonus. For your vacation with Zoya."

She looked at me with level eyes.

"You are a good man, Dakota Stevens."

"Yeah?" I put on my sunglasses. "Tell me that when I don't have a guy locked in my trunk."

At Vivian's, I parked in the shade of the porte-cochère and checked on Igor. He wasn't looking particularly peppy. I gave him some water and fresh air, tightened his ropes and slammed the trunk shut.

"What if he dies?" Svetlana said.

"That would be bad."

We went to the door and rang three times. After waiting a minute with no answer, we strolled around back and bumped into an idle lawn crew. They leaned on their mowers, staring at the scene before them.

Stretched down the lawn, all the way to the pool, was a long yellow Slip 'n Slide. A queue of bikini-clad girls waited at the start. Delilah, in the same Daisy Dukes and red bikini top as the other day, climbed out of the pool. Her arms, like the rest of her body, were tan and toned. She joined a bevy of 20-year-old girls lounging on the cement. Two of her friends I recognized from a vacuous reality TV show.

I scanned the portico for Vivian. Her steamer chair was empty. Delilah noticed us and ran up the lawn. She was dripping wet and her blonde-brunette hair was tightly braided with beads on the ends, like Bo Derek's in *10*.

"Dakota Stevens." She leaned over to catch her breath. "What's up?"

I removed my sunglasses. "What's up? You called us. Where's your aunt?"

"Chill. She's inside, resting."

She waved to her friends. I grabbed her by the chin and swiveled her head to face me.

"Where inside?"

"I don't know. *Inside*."

"Go make sure she's okay, will you?" I said to Svetlana. "This one is taking me to Louis's room."

"Bungalow, actually," Delilah said.

Svetlana looked at me. "Remember the package."

Delilah tugged me down to her friends and introduced me as a P.I. The blonde hotel heiress lolled on a chaise lounge.

"Do you, like, have a gun?"

I opened my jacket, revealing my shoulder holster.

"That's hot," she said.

"Yeah, hot," her friend added.

"I'm taking the P.I. over to Louis's," Delilah said. "I might be a while."

Barefoot, like some kind of hillbilly chick, Delilah skipped down to the croquet lawn and onto a path through the trees. She spun around and walked backwards so she faced me. Her tan was admirable, the spaghetti straps on her bikini top deliciously fragile.

"What package was she talking about?" she asked.

"Nothing," I said. "Forget it."

The Daisy Dukes barely clung to her hips. Her belly ring glinted. Every inch of this girl was fearfully and wonderfully made. Even the scratch on her thigh was sexy. She stopped short, and I bumped into her. Staring into my eyes, she ran her fingers along her braids.

"Wanna feel my cornrows?"

I seized her by the throat and pulled her into me. Her skin was cool and wet. Her pulse throbbed fast against my thumb.

"Look, sugar britches," I said. "I'm here to do a job, so stop with the *Lolita* routine, all right?"

I doubted that she knew who Lolita was, but her eyes said she got the message.

"Good," I said. "Now, show me his place." I spun her around and nudged her down the path.

Emerging from the trees, we passed a small stable and crossed another sumptuous lawn to Louis's bungalow. It had the same Italianate design as the mansion. Delilah bypassed the front entrance and led us to a small patio on the side with a sliding glass door. She put her hands in her back pockets and rested her head against the glass.

"Should be open," she said. "Was last time I came over."

"When was that?"

"Yesterday afternoon."

"Yesterday afternoon?" I said. "When was the last time anybody saw him?"

She played with the beads on her braids.

"I don't know. Yesterday morning, I think. Or maybe the day before."

"So you guys noticed he was missing yesterday, and you didn't call me until today?"

She shrugged. "Auntie Viv didn't think anything of it. Sometimes Louis takes the boat out and stays overnight on it. But she got worried when he didn't show up at the house this morning. That's when she noticed the boat was still gone and the stuff was missing from the safe."

"Okay, let's go in." I grabbed the door handle. "Now, don't touch anything."

We went inside. Draped over a chair was a terrycloth bathrobe. I tossed it to Delilah.

"Please," I said.

"Thought you said not to touch anything." She stuck out her tongue and slipped into the robe.

I surveyed the room. It was one large open space—kitchen, dining and living areas—with a hallway that I assumed led to the bedroom and bathroom. Piles of clothes, CDs and some dumbbells covered the floor. The bookshelves had empty spaces where books or pictures had been. Somebody had packed in a hurry. But the kitchen island told a different story: three empty wine bottles, with only one glass, and no food or plates.

"Was he a big drinker?" I asked.

"Not that I know of." Delilah paced in the robe. "Can you hurry this up? My friends are waiting."

"Was Louis depressed about something?"

"Like?"

"Like did he get any bad news recently?" I asked.

She looked at the floor.

"I need your help, Delilah."

"I shouldn't."

"He might be in serious trouble," I said. "Believe me, Louis will understand."

She let out a petulant moan and flopped onto the sofa.

"Some guy he knew was killed," she said. "He was upset. I think they were, you know…" She made a so-so motion with her hand.

"Lovers?" I said.

"Maybe."

"What about your aunt and Louis? Are they—"

"Screwing?" Her eyes shot open. "Are you kidding? Like clockwork. Monday and Friday mornings, 'ole

Louis has to drop everything and satisfy Auntie. And let me tell you, the old gal is a *goer*."

"That's enough." I walked down the hall.

Sand coated the floor on the way to Louis's bedroom. The bed was made. On the bureau stood pictures of him with Vivian, him with other women, and one of him and Shaw on a yacht. A pair of muddy, sand-caked sneakers were kicked off in the corner. I had brilliantly deduced that Louis had small feet when Delilah walked up behind me.

"You almost finished or what?"

I noted the tread pattern and put down the sneaker.

"The guy that was killed," I said. "Do you know where?"

"I don't know." Then she snapped her fingers. "Wait a sec. A couple days ago, I overheard him on Auntie's phone, saying something like, 'I'm not taking the ferry.' Does that help?"

Martha's Vineyard? Did he leave to attend Shaw's funeral?

"That's very helpful." I took out my phone and called Madison Shaw. A servant answered. A moment later Madison's breathy voice came on the line.

"Mr. Stevens, this better be important."

"I'll be brief," I said. "Do you recall a Louis Zipes at your husband's service?"

"Doesn't ring a bell. My assistant made the arrangements, though, so don't hold me to it."

I described Louis to her.

"Half of the OFG executives look like that," she said. "What about my husband's murder? Are you working on it?"

"Among other things."

"Well, if you need additional information, give me a ring," she said. "And if you happen to be on the island sometime…"

Ah, the grieving widow.

"Yeah, I'll bring my best paddle. Goodbye, Madison."

I hung up and gave Louis's closet and drawers a cursory search. Not finding anything, I went back out to the main room. Delilah was at the refrigerator. She snapped open a can of Heineken and slurped the foam.

"Want one?" she said.

I shook my head and squinted at the scene one more time. Something wasn't right here. Delilah sidled up to me and fondled my tie.

"You know, you're kinda cute…for an older guy." She sipped some beer.

"Thanks."

"Wanna fool around?"

Her lips were parted and shiny with lip gloss. She gave me that not-too-bright bunny rabbit look, clutched my tie, and stroked it suggestively. I grabbed her wrist.

"We older guys prefer a more subtle approach," I said.

Then I remembered a detail Vivian had mentioned when we took the case.

"Something just occurred to me," I said. "*You* had motive for killing Sidney."

"Kill my uncle?" She stared up at me in disgust. "Are you high?"

"You're only getting twenty million from him. But had she lived, your mother's share of the estate would have been over three *hundred* million."

Delilah went to the counter and shimmied out of the robe, then boosted herself up and wriggled her tush until she was comfortable. She guzzled some beer and wiped her mouth with the back of her hand.

"Look," she said, "you might not believe this, but I'm not worried about money. When you live in your aunt's mansion, use her cars and she pays for everything, twenty mil goes a long way. I was doing fine before, and that was with zero mil." She took a drink and flapped her legs. "Besides, when Auntie goes, I'll be the sole heir. I'll get everything then."

"You've got it all figured out, don't you?" I said.

She shrugged, held up her beer can and jiggled it. I went to the refrigerator and got her another one. She rolled the cold can on her face and neck before snapping it open.

"I don't have time to kill anybody anyway," she said. "I've got a very busy social life, you know."

"I'm sure you do."

"Yeah? Well, I was busy enough the night my uncle was killed."

She stretched across the counter and rummaged through a stack of mail.

"Ah, here." She pulled out a recent issue of *New York* magazine, flipped to a photo spread and slapped the page. "My famous friend out by the pool? Her movie premiere was the same night Uncle Sidney died. Sorry to disappoint you."

There Delilah was, standing on a red carpet in a slinky cocktail dress with a bottle of champagne in her hand, right next to the famous blonde heiress.

"I was at after-parties all night," she said. "Not friggen *Montana*."

She put down her beer and studied me for a moment before slithering off the counter.

"Dakota, you look stressed." She walked over touching her belly ring. "And I know the perfect stress-reliever." Her eyes flicked toward Louis's bedroom, then back to me.

"Still not subtle, but better." I opened the sliding glass door.

"You're no fun."

She grabbed her beer and stomped out to the patio. I closed the sliding door behind her, put the robe on the chair, and went out the front.

Embedded in the mud at the foot of the doorstep were Louis's sneaker prints and a fresh tire impression. I kneeled down for a closer look. The tire tread was straight, not knobbed like a bicycle tire, and there were two small impressions, each about eighteen inches from the tire mark, so the three formed a triangle. A fully loaded wheelbarrow had been here recently. Delilah came over.

"What's the holdup?"

"Has the gardener been working over here?" I asked.

"Like I'd know." She crushed her beer can and threw it in the flower bed. "You're boring me. Goodbye."

I was vaguely aware of her storming away as I stooped to follow the tire track. It crossed the front yard and continued through a small meadow and down to the shore. The tide had washed away a section of the tire track and Louis's footprints, but I picked them up again farther down the beach. Twice the wheelbarrow got stuck. Whatever Louis had been carrying, it was heavy.

The trail veered off to the lawn and terminated at Vivian's dock. I walked out to the end and stared across the Sound, basking in the late afternoon sun with my hands in my pockets. Sailboats drifted across the horizon. Beneath me, waves lapped hypnotically against the piers.

Where are you, Louis?

Did you borrow Vivian's sailboat to go over to the Vineyard to pay your respects, and get caught in a storm? Did this have something to do with Shaw's interest in the resort? Or maybe you simply got tired of being a kept man, so you took a wad of Vivian's money and sailed away into the night. But then why the three bottles of wine? And what were you carrying in the wheelbarrow that was so heavy?

I headed up to the mansion shaking my head. The pool was quiet now that the girls were gone, and the hillside hissed with lawn sprinklers. Svetlana met me by the pool. Light glinted off the water.

"How's Vivian?" I asked.

"Depressed. Sidney's funeral service is tomorrow."

I nodded grimly. "You didn't say anything about Louis once working for Shaw, did you?"

"No."

"Good. There might be a connection between Louis's disappearance and Sidney's death, but I don't think this is the best time to tell her. Agreed?"

"Yes," she said. "Oh, I had Vivian show me the safe. It has an electronic keypad, and only she and Louis know the combination."

"Any signs of forced entry?"

"None."

Up on the portico, Vivian emerged from the mansion in white linen pants and a white polo shirt, like she was going to play some 1920s tennis. She stretched out on her usual steamer chair and crossed her legs.

"Okay," I said, "let's go talk to our client."

We sat on the portico with Vivian and had iced tea. Vivian wore sunglasses, but her nose was red so I knew she'd been crying. After a while, I felt comfortable asking her a few things.

"Vivian," I said gently, "your sailboat, could one person pilot her?"

"Louis could," she said with a sniffle. "He often did."

Svetlana put down her glass. "I contacted the Coast Guard. They and all the harbormasters along the coast are searching for it."

"Was there rough weather out there last night?" I asked.

"No, a dead calm," Svetlana said.

"If he was in some kind of trouble," Vivian said absently, "why didn't he tell me? He didn't need to steal. There's nothing I wouldn't have given him."

"Did you two have an argument?" I asked.

Vivian stood. "Please excuse me. I'm not feeling well."

She disappeared into the house, leaving Svetlana and me looking at each other. The tinkle of wind chimes floated by on the breeze.

"Are we having fun yet?" I said.

Svetlana blinked slowly, twirled a leg. I chugged the rest of my iced tea and put the glass down with spirit.

"Let's go air out the package."

18

SICK VINNY

At ten o'clock Svetlana and I showed up at Falcone's converted warehouse apartment in the Williamsburg neighborhood of Brooklyn. With 15-foot ceilings, the place was cavernous. The far end held Falcone's office and living quarters, but the other two-thirds was a giant clubhouse for his crew, with every amenity a bunch of goodfellas could hope for: jukebox, pool table, raised stage with a pole for strippers, batting cage and illegal casino. Everything looked like dollhouse furniture in the yawning space.

We reached Falcone's office and were about to go in when Dominick came out pushing a flatbed cart. Falcone followed behind him.

"Where's the package?" he asked.

"My trunk," I said. "Need any help?"

"Nah, let Dom handle it. He's got a system."

I tossed Dominick my keys. Falcone escorted us over to the conversation pit and stepped behind a bar. Across the East River, the Manhattan skyline glowed.

"How about that view, huh?" Falcone put ice in a glass. "Drink, Triple-X?"

"No, thank you," Svetlana said.

"How about you, numb nuts?"

"Look," I said, "whatever happens, don't let this Sick Vinny kill him. I don't feel like being an accessory to murder. I'd also like to maintain a shred of humanity here."

"Yes, no killing," Svetlana said.

Falcone waved a hand as he poured some designer vodka.

"Relax. Vinny's like this karate master I read about once. Scared opponents away before he ever had to throw a punch. Vinny's an artist, I'm telling you."

Dominick returned with Igor on a cart and handed me my keys. He laid out a plastic tarp, placed a chair on top of it and tied Igor to the chair. Then he stood three portable floodlights around the chair and switched them on so they blinded Igor. Our captive was looking rather listless until Dominick forced him to swallow a couple Dexedrine. Now he sat pricked up in the chair, his eyes darting around the place.

The elevator started down. Dominick went over to the closed-circuit monitor.

"It's him," he said.

Falcone pointed at a leather recliner. "Triple-X, you take that chair." He strolled over to Igor sipping his vodka and gave him a friendly slap in the face. "Get ready to do more talking than you've done in your whole life."

Svetlana sat down. I stood beside her. When the elevator came up, Dominick hauled the grate open and a wiry man in his fifties stepped off, pushing a metal tool cabinet on wheels. A cigarette dangled from his lips as he wheeled the cabinet precisely to the tarp edge.

"My friend," Falcone said to Igor, "I'd like you to meet Sick Vinny."

Perspiration beaded up on Igor's face. Vinny paced around him, puffing his cigarette, flicking the ashes on the floor, sizing up Igor like Michelangelo appraising a chunk of marble. Falcone watched with his arms folded across his chest, grinning in admiration.

"So, Vin, whaddaya think?"

Vinny squinted one eye, studied Igor with his head tilted, and nodded, as if he had just made a momentous decision. Without a word, without the faintest expression on his face, he opened the cabinet doors. Hanging inside were a five-pound hammer, several knives, and a variety of curved, pointy tools that looked suspiciously like medieval disembowelment instruments.

Reaching deep into the cabinet, Vinny pulled out a loaf of rye bread, a jar of deli mustard, a spreading knife, paper plates, and—bending his knees to drag it onto the tarp—a deli slicer. My shoulders stiffened. Removing an industrial extension cord from a drawer, Vinny plugged in the slicer and handed the other end to Dominick, who walked it over to an outlet.

"Ah, sandwiches," Falcone said. "Hey, not too much mustard on mine, Vin."

"Me neither," Dominick said.

My throat went dry. It had taken me a moment, but now I knew why he was called Sick Vinny. Svetlana sat silently in her chair, clutching the armrests. I smiled at her to ease the tension. Not that it helped. Maybe because I harbored doubts myself. Igor was scum, but I wasn't sure this level of torture was justified. Would the information even be worth it? He might say *anything* to avoid pain. Besides, what did it say about my abilities as a detective if I had to rely on the Sick Vinnies of the world to get answers?

Vinny retrieved a long dowel from the cabinet and poked Igor in the rump. Then, with a magician's flourish, he spun around and tapped the deli slicer. Igor's jaw quivered.

Falcone turned to me. "He's all yours."

"All right, Svetlana," I said, "same stuff as before. Who is he and who hired him?"

Svetlana translated. Igor was silent. She asked again. Nothing.

"Triple-X," Falcone said, "tell him that Vinny *will* slice his ass if he doesn't talk."

Svetlana gulped and translated that, too. Still no response.

Vinny snapped his fingers and Dominick untied him from the chair. Igor thrashed, tried to bite him. Dominick punched him in the gut so hard it lifted him off the ground. While Igor was doubled over, Vinny unbuckled his pants and stripped off his shorts. They dragged him to the deli slicer. Igor flailed, whimpered something in Russian.

"What's he saying?" I asked.

"I can't understand him," Svetlana said.

They shoved him down on the slicer so his behind lay in the path of the slicer arm. Vinny turned it on and grabbed the handle. In the stillness of Falcone's airplane hangar, the slicer whirred with gruesome meaning.

"Hey, Vin," Falcone said.

With a reptilian jerk of the head, Vinny turned to him. "Make mine *extra* thin."

19

BASH BISH FALLS

Words spilled out of his mouth in blubbering, rapid Russian. It was as if a dam had broken. Dominick and I heaved him up, buckled his pants and shoved him back in the chair. Vinny lurked in the shadows smoking a cigarette as we listened to Svetlana's translation. Considering the shape Igor was in, I was amazed by his clarity and detail.

His name was Vladimir Pratasevich, and decades earlier he had been a Soviet sniper in the Afghanistan campaign. As soon as Communism collapsed, he made his way to the United States and hired himself out as a mercenary and hit man. And his latest client, the person who had hired him to kill Shaw and me? Mr. Roman.

I tapped Svetlana on the arm. "Does he know why Roman wanted us killed?"

Svetlana asked, listened to the response, shook her head.

Dominick nudged Falcone. "Wonder if this guy's whacked anybody we know."

Falcone leaned back in his chair with his hands behind his head. After a moment of deliberation, he turned to Svetlana.

"Ask if he did a guy down in Atlantic City, ran a restaurant called Sharkey's."

She asked. Vladimir nodded.

"I knew it," Falcone said. "Mr. Ianucci would *love* to meet this guy. Tell him, Svetlana."

She did, and the remaining color drained out of Vlad's face. He began to jabber, his eyes darting between me and Svetlana.

"He says—"

"Doesn't matter," I said, standing up. "He's coming with us."

"Look, Stevens," Falcone said, "if I'm right, there's still a nice chunk of change on this guy's head. You give him to me, I'll cut you in for a piece."

"No," I said. "Vlad here might be a scumbag, but I'm not handing him off to you so some *gavonne* can bury him down in the Pine Barrens. Somebody has to answer for Shaw."

"Who the hell is Shaw?" Falcone said.

"Another guy he killed. I've got Vlad's gun, and a cop on Martha's Vineyard has the bullet. He's coming with me."

Falcone contemplated me for a long thirty seconds with one finger against his cheek. Finally, just when I remembered I was carrying a gun, he nodded.

"Stevens, you're the only guy that can talk to me like that and continue to walk erect," he said. "Okay, we'll stay on the sidelines—for now. But before you go, I want that horse tip you promised."

"You know Handsome Ransom? Running in the stakes race this weekend?"

"Yeah, sure. Tomorrow. Big favorite."

I shook my head. "Bad chest cold. Definitely won't win. Probably won't even place or show."

"And you know this how?"

"My next-door neighbor boards him."

"In the city?"

"Yeah, the Upper West Side," I said sarcastically. "Of course not. Upstate."

"Not bad," Falcone said. "Does this mean—"

"No, it doesn't. It's a one-time thing. Now, if you'll excuse us, it's past Vlad's bedtime." Sick Vinny was packing up his tools. I gave him a nod. "Thanks for your expertise, sir."

Sick Vinny acknowledged me with a jut of the chin. Svetlana didn't even look at him as she grabbed her handbag and went to the elevator. I took Vladimir and we left.

Out at the Cadillac, I handcuffed Vlad to the door handle in the back seat. It was a luxury suite compared to his previous accommodations, and he thanked me profusely for it.

"That's sweet," I said, "but he's still going to jail."

"Now what will you do with him?" Svetlana asked.

"I'm driving him up to Bash Bish Falls State Park in Massachusetts, chaining him to a tree and calling Detective Clancy to have him picked up—that's what I'm doing with him. Now, where does Roman live?" I put the car in drive and headed for the Williamsburg Bridge.

"Ronkonkoma," she said. "But you're not going out there tonight, are you?"

"No, I'll swing by the office in the morning and we can pay him a visit together."

I turned onto the ramp for the bridge. Across the river, Manhattan glittered with its usual false promise. I was tired, and my mind was wandering. I mused aloud.

"What I can't decide is, tomorrow morning, when Roman opens the door, should I kick him in the balls or punch him in the solar plexus?"

"Well," Svetlana said, "since you recently used the kick-in-the-groin gambit on Vlad, I recommend the solar plexus."

"I agree. A classic."

On the way uptown I caught only green lights. Svetlana hopped out at her building and spoke sharply in Russian to Vlad.

"What'd you tell him?" I asked.

"Who my father is, and that he had better cooperate."

I shook my head admiringly and zoomed away, into the Manhattan night.

20

A PUNCH IN THE SOLAR PLEXUS

At eleven the next morning, Svetlana and I parked in front of Roman's split-level ranch at the end of a cul-de-sac. We walked to the door. The second he opened it, I was going to punch him square in the chest.

"Step aside, my dear."

I cracked my knuckles, pressed the doorbell and bounced on the balls of my feet. We waited. I rang again, waited, and put my ear to the door. Nothing. An SUV was in the driveway, so I was pretty sure someone was home. I rang several more times, but no Roman.

"Call him," I said. "If he answers, just say you got the wrong number."

Svetlana pulled out her iPhone, dialed and waited. I heard the phone ringing inside. Then she hung up.

"Answering machine," she said. "Absolute *dumbest* message I've ever heard."

"My, a bit testy this morning, aren't we?"

"I'm hungry. All I've had is coffee."

"Don't worry, soon as we finish here, I'll take you to lunch." I jumped off the stoop. "Hooters is right up the road."

She called me a name in German that I'd never heard before.

"That's a new one," I said. "Be right back."

I ducked around the corner and came upon a high wooden fence. The gate was unlocked. I went in.

The fence encircled the backyard, and thick foliage grew over the top of it from the other side. Across the yard, Roman lay on a chaise lounge, badly sunburned. I slammed the gate shut, expecting to startle him, but he didn't move.

Why didn't the slamming gate startle him?

As if in response to my question, the wind shifted and I was treated to the enchanting aroma of rotting flesh. I walked up to the body pinching my nose.

An orgy of flies buzzed around Roman's head. Maggots covered his nostrils and eye sockets. From what I knew about forensic entomology, the presence of maggots indicated that he had been dead 1–2 days. I leaned closer. There was a small hole at the top of his forehead, but no exit wound in the head that I could see. From his face to his toes, Roman's skin was deep red and shriveled, but the half of him against the chair was pasty with dark blotches where the blood had settled. The *livor mortis*. A longneck Budweiser sat between his legs. Around him were several empty chaises, a barbecue grill and a patio set.

Stepping back, I got a sense of what had happened here. In the chaise fabric near Roman's ear was another bullet hole, behind which the sliding glass door was shattered. Conceivably, whoever had shot Roman wasn't skilled with a gun and had missed with the first shot. The second shot caught Roman in the throat and exited with a good-sized hole, and just as Roman sprang up in the chair, the third bullet entered at the hairline. From the tiny entry hole and lack of exit wound on the head, I decided it was a small-caliber gun. As for witnesses, the high fence and the thick foliage would have prevented anyone from seeing the murder, and even if someone *heard* what happened, the person would have written off the gunshots as firecrackers. I went back to the gate. Svetlana was on her way in.

"Trust me, you don't want it," I said. "One of those things you didn't sign on for."

"Ah."

"Get us some gloves and meet me at the front door."

I wiped down the gate handle with my shirttail, closed it and searched on my hands and knees in front of the body for shell casings. I didn't find any. Either the murderer collected them all or he used a revolver. I dusted off and went inside the house. It was a '70s-style recreation room, complete with bar, Foosball table and artificial turf carpet. Classy. I went upstairs to the front door and pulled Svetlana inside.

"What's going on?" she asked.

"Let's just say Mr. Roman is indisposed at the moment."

She looked at me as though I'd tried to move a knight like a bishop.

"Dead?"

"Or getting one hell of a Coppertone tan," I said.

We slipped on the gloves, continued upstairs and stopped cold. In one sweep we managed to take in everything bad about '70s interior design: dark brown paneling, plaid living room set, orange countertops and spring green wallpaper with giant white daisies.

"I hope we're not here for decorating ideas," Svetlana said.

"Let's stick to finding clues—and fast," I said. "I'm surprised Roman's neighbors haven't smelled the stench yet. You take the kitchen and living room, I'll take the rooms down the hall."

I was concerned about the amount of time we spent, but I was also thinking about the first principle of forensic science: Locard's Principle. *Every contact leaves a trace.* With a dead body out back, we needed to limit our contact with things in the house. This and the lack of time meant that I couldn't do a thorough search. I would have to stick to general impressions and any clues that were obvious. I opened the first door.

It was a bathroom, with a dirty sink, an overflowing hamper, and a pile of pornography on the toilet tank. A typical bachelor's bathroom—I got the picture.

Next, a small bedroom. Crates of comic books covered the floor and a twin bed. There was no other furniture in the room. In the closet, more comic books. I moved on.

The master bedroom. Here I found an unmade bed, a messy closet, a .45 ACP in a bureau drawer, and one interesting item—an escort guide next to the telephone on the nightstand. I flipped through it. None of the escort services were circled or dog-eared, which made it a dead end for me. I left it for the cops and went to the next room.

A cluttered den. The walls were filled with antlers. In between were dozens of photos of Roman and other hunters posing around their kills. Stacks of magazines, including *Field & Stream* and *Soldier of Fortune*, sat on the floor. I walked around them to a cabinet full of hunting rifles. It was locked. Beside it was a desk. No computer on the desk, but a sea of papers instead. There were bills and overdue notices, but no credit card statements, and the utilities had been paid in cash. The desk drawers contained nothing but junk and a checkbook—a checkbook with a blank register and only a few checks torn off.

But then, underneath the phone, I found a clue.

It was the most recent phone bill, and among the twenty or so long-distance calls, half were to numbers in Montana: West Yellowstone, Gardiner and Ricochet. *Yes.* I wrote the phone numbers in my notebook and went out to the kitchen. Svetlana was stooped over a large cooler on the floor. It brimmed with bottles of Budweiser, the labels peeling off from soaking in the water.

"It appears he was expecting company," she said.

"Which explains the setup out back. Anything else?"

"No."

I picked up Roman's phone, dialed 911, told them I found a body at this address and hung up. We left through the front door and zipped out of the development. Back on the expressway, I threw our latex gloves out the window and gave Svetlana the Montana phone numbers.

"I'll look into them," she said.

"And call your Coast Guard contact again. Maybe Louis turned up."

She gave me a look that said, "I doubt it."

"Yeah," I said.

Sidney was dead, Shaw was dead, Louis was missing, and now Roman was dead. I had about as much idea of what was going on as an Alzheimer's patient in a hedge maze. I pounded the steering wheel.

"Damn."

"And you were *so* looking forward to punching him," Svetlana said.

I sighed wistfully.

"Well, the trail leads elsewhere." She patted my shoulder. "Go west, young man."

21

PEACEMAKER

Missoula International felt more like a hunting lodge than an airport. Great vaulted ceilings towered overhead, elk heads adorned knotty pine walls, and a stuffed grizzly reared up near the baggage claim. There was even a massive stone fireplace. It was the first airport I'd ever regretted leaving. I went out to the curb.

My ride—Sheriff Keith Briggs—wasn't here yet, so I plopped down on a bench and unfolded Shaw's map. I'd met some interesting people in first class over the years, and today's flight from New York was no exception. On the New York–Denver leg, the man sitting next to me was a builder, and when he'd noticed me studying Shaw's map, he remarked that the circled locations could be places earmarked for soil tests or perc tests. Before building in a spot, he explained, engineers had to know whether the ground could withstand the weight or whether it drained properly. When I got to Ricochet, I'd check out each location for evidence of surveying or testing.

Briggs still wasn't here. I put the map away and passed the time perusing dossiers on the four leading actors.

First was Jack Boone's. According to his stats, Boone was a freakish 6'8" and 270 pounds, but his headshot only showed thinning brown hair, squinty eyes and a razor-sharp jaw line. He was scowling, not smiling, in the picture, as if he knew casting directors would only consider him for bad-guy roles and he was already angry about it.

Next, Kat Styles. Mid-twenties. Biracial with Medusa hair and smoky eyes. A clipping from a review of one of her off-Broadway shows read, "Kat Styles is a mesmerizing figure, all slinking and scheming." It seemed fitting that she played Ricochet's most expensive prostitute.

The mayor of Ricochet was played by Prentice Keller, a Gary Cooperish man in his mid-fifties. His character owned the mercantile. All I could say about him was that I hoped to look that good twenty years from now.

And on the bottom of the pile—Sidney's girlfriend, Heather Van Every. The woman with the strongest motive for killing Sidney—$100 million. She played the cafe owner's widow, but from the way Vivian described her—as a conniving gold-digger—I'd imagined a casting couch ingénue. Instead I saw a woman in her early thirties with an honest beauty made of laugh lines and tiny crow's feet. Finished, I put the dossiers away.

It felt good to be out of the East, away from where I'd had nothing but failure since I started this case. Maybe it was the clean air, but something made me believe I'd have better luck here in the West. At the same time, the idea that I was starting from scratch, with no substantial leads whatsoever, was depressing. The only links I had between the East and the West were some phone calls from Roman's to Montana, a map, and some satellite photos. I was literally starting my investigation all over again.

When I looked up next, Sheriff Briggs was at the curb in a department SUV. I tossed my bag in the back seat, and a moment later we were cruising on I-90 toward Missoula. Briggs drove with his head tipped back slightly. The top of his cowboy hat scraped the ceiling fabric.

"Hungry?"

"I could eat," I said.

"Good, got just the place. Nice-'n-quiet, so we can talk."

He took us into Old Downtown Missoula, a grid of broad streets and four-story brick buildings from the early 1900s, and parked in front of a place that looked suspiciously like a bar.

"I know what you're thinking," he said. "Guy drinks on the job. But it's not like that." He cut the engine. "Best damn burgers anywhere. C'mon."

The Missoula Club was vintage through and through: smoke-stained wood, brass boot rail, grimy mirror behind the bar, and framed photos of loggers, miners and movie stars. We took stools facing the street and placed our orders with the bartender. Behind us, college kids played pool badly.

"So, how's it going?" Briggs asked.

I told him about examining Sidney's body, and our conclusion that he had been killed with a garrote.

"Boy, I don't know how our guy missed that one," he said.

"It wasn't obvious by any means."

I then told him about the connection between Shaw, Roman and the sniper, as well as Louis's disappearance.

"You've been busy," Briggs said. "Not a heck of lot has happened on this end."

The bartender arrived with a tray of food: two half-pound burgers with steak fries, and chocolate shakes.

American cuisine at its finest. We didn't talk again until the bartender took the plates away.

"That was the best beef I've ever had," I said.

"Whole different animal out here. Slaughtered yesterday, probably."

"Please don't ruin it." I tossed my napkin on the bar. "You were telling me about what's been going on out here."

"Yeah," Briggs said. "I went over to the rez and talked with some of the Indians. Couple days ago, somebody threw a Molotov cocktail at Sidney's train."

"Wow, anybody hurt?"

"No, turns out the guy missed. Scared the hell out of the guests though. I don't know if the rez is behind the train incident or Sidney's death, but they're hiding something, that's for sure. Guy you'll want to see goes by the name of Carries Bison."

I raised an eyebrow. "So does he prefer 'Carries' or 'Mr. Bison'?"

Briggs pointed at me.

"Don't screw around with them," he said. "You go in there and get your ass kicked, there's nothing I can do. No jurisdiction. And believe me, they don't take kindly to smart-ass remarks from white Easterners. End up with a damn spear through your chest."

"I'll tread lightly." I put two twenties on the bar.

"C'mon," Briggs said. "Take you to the station, get you sworn in. And I got a present for you—Colt Peacemaker, a real one. Single-action of course, but better'n nothing."

"Shoot real bullets?" I said.

"Yep."

"Then it sounds fine by me."

22

WYATT EARP, EAT YOUR HEART OUT

After a harrowing ride up and down a series of switchbacks, Briggs pulled onto the shoulder at the intersection of two dirt roads. The sun was low in an endless azure sky. A narrow lane faded into evergreens with a modest wooden sign pointing the way to Ricochet Depot.

"Check-in center's up there," Briggs said. "Drive you in, but they catch us together and we're screwed."

I grabbed my bag and hopped out. The window rolled down.

"Hey, Stevens. Watch your back."

I squinted. "What happened to, 'Where seldom is heard a discouraging word'?"

"Not discouraging," he said. "Realistic."

We shook hands through the open window, and then he turned around and roared away, kicking up dust. I hadn't felt this alone since my first day of kindergarten. I started walking.

About a mile in, I reached the train depot. It was a long wooden building with a sloping overhang that covered the train platform. Watering troughs and hitching posts adorned the front, along with a sign overhead: "Ricochet Depot, est. 1870." I went inside. The room was hot and smelled like dry cardboard. I walked past a row of benches to a barred ticket window, where a portly man gave me a reserved nod. He wore a hat that read, "Stationmaster."

"Dakota Stevens," I said. "New town marshal."

"Walt," he said. "Nice to meet you. Got your credentials?"

I handed him the materials Vivian had arranged: an Actor's Equity card and a letter of employment from the resort historical advisor, William McCourt.

"New York, huh?" Walt said.

"Yup."

"Broadway?" he asked.

"Off-off-off Broadway actually."

"Gotta start somewhere, right?"

He handed me my Equity card along with a map of the resort. Then he waddled over to an old-fashioned box phone and turned the crank.

"Train just left. I'll check with Mr. McCourt, see if we can get him out here on the next one."

"He's pretty important, I take it."

"Yeah, with Sidney gone he pretty much runs the show around here."

I sat down on one of the benches. Walt raised his voice into the phone.

"'Course I'll wait. What else'm I gonna do?" He covered the mouthpiece and looked at me. "McCourt's place is down the street a ways, so it might take a few."

"No problem," I said.

We waited ten minutes, during which time I got well acquainted with the map. It included Ricochet, Loot, all of the trails and roads, and a grayed-out section indicating the nearby Indian reservation. I put it away as Walt hung up the phone.

"Train's just getting in over there now," he said. "Mc-Court's gonna ride back on it, meet you here. I was you, I'd take a shower. Last one you'll get for a while. Actors' locker rooms are on the right. Then go see the quartermaster, pick up your costume. Oh, one more thing. You can't go into Ricochet with anything from later than 1885. Don't bother with a cell phone either, 'cause there's no towers around, so it won't work anyway." He checked his pocket watch, pointed down the hall. "Better move. Got less than an hour."

"Thanks." I paused at his Dutch door. "Say, Walt, is it true what my agent told me? The guy who owned this place was murdered?"

"Died. Suicide, they say. Why you askin'?"

"Just curious what I was getting into. I've come a long way for this gig, so tell me—with the owner dead, this thing isn't going to fold, is it?"

"Not a chance."

Walt looked around the empty room. He lowered his voice to a whisper.

"See, here's the thing. Sid—he was the owner—Sid loved this place, so I'm sure he left plenty of dough to keep it going. Besides, his gal, Heather Van Every, she's one of the stars here. She went out to his funeral yesterday, and I'd be mighty surprised if 'ole Sid didn't leave her a little something. If a man was smart, he'd cozy up to that little lady right quick."

"You've put me at ease, Walt. Thank you." I walked down the hallway to the locker room.

After my shower, a sign directed me to "COS-TUMES," where a middle-aged woman with old-fashioned spectacles sat reading a book. A heavy velvet curtain hung behind her. Still damp beneath my bathrobe, I bellied up to the counter and smiled.

"Dakota Stevens, new marshal, reporting for duty."

She dog-eared the page in her book and sized me up, then disappeared behind the curtain. A minute later she handed me an armload of clothes, a gun belt, and a ratty carpetbag, which she patted.

"Three pairs of socks, extra shirt, one change of underclothes, kit with personals—tooth powder, talc, razor, soap, et cetera—and an envelope with fifty Ricochet dollars in it. Your real paycheck comes here, first of the month."

"Yes, ma'am." I held up the clothes she'd given me. "What if these don't fit?"

"They'll fit. Hats and boots in the next room." She sat down and picked up her book again. "Break a leg, marshal."

I tried on half a dozen hats before settling on a black wool Dakota with a moderate crown and slightly curved brim. For boots, I chose a pair of square-toed ones with spurs already attached.

Back at my locker, it took me twenty awkward minutes to get into all of the clothes: cotton long-johns, pinstriped wool trousers with suspenders, a white shirt with a high band collar, a silk string tie, a vest and a charcoal wool Western frock coat. The heavy clothing was hot and itchy already, and I'd been wearing it for all of thirty seconds.

I pinned my tin star to the vest, put the chained pocket watch in my vest pocket, and slipped on the gun belt. The belt had two holsters, but only one gun, so I kept the fake Smith & Wesson Schofield (Jesse James's weapon) in its holster and put the real Peacemaker in the other. This way I would have ready access to a real gun if I needed it, and the fake one for playing the marshal.

Finally, I stepped back and eyed myself in the mirror.

Wyatt Earp, eat your heart out.

23

THE NICKEL TOUR

I grabbed the carpetbag and walked outside. Between the gentle swish of my frock coat and the soft clink of my spurs, in moments I found myself transported back to 1885, so by the time I stood on the train platform with a dozen other men and women, I felt far away from the 21st century. It would be easy to fall under the spell of this Old West charade if I wasn't careful. I needed to focus on why I was here—to find Sidney's killer—and avoid buying wholeheartedly into the illusion like the others around me.

The men puffed cigars and laughed; the women twirled parasols and chatted. One of the men I recognized as the founder of a computer company. His companions had that self-absorbed, CEO look, like Shaw had had before he got shot. At the far end of the platform stood a tall, silver-haired man in a gunslinger's outfit.

Somewhere in the distance, a train whistle shrieked. I squinted down the tracks. Black smoke billowed over the trees.

Out of nowhere, a blonde woman in a form-fitting calico dress ran onto the platform. It was Heather Van Every. She was out of breath.

"Okay, miss?" I asked.

"I can't believe I made it."

She had a pair of chatoyant ice blue eyes that seemed stuck in a perpetual sense of wonder. Whereas most beautiful women relied on the promise of sex to get men to do what they wanted, this one had only to flash those eyes, and instantly she appealed to every man's deepest desire—to be the hero.

"I know what you mean," I said. "Came in from New York today myself."

She gave me a questioning look. "New York? Wow, I was just there. Are you here on vacation?"

The train emerged from a hole in the trees and blew a long whistle.

"Actually, I'm one of the actors. Dakota Stevens, Miss…"

"Van Every. Call me Heather."

We shook hands.

"And what role are you playing, Mr. Stevens?"

"Town Marshal."

She swallowed and was about to say something when the train rolled in, blasting steam. She forced a smile.

"Well, break a leg, Mr. Stevens."

"I hope we can talk again," I said. "And please, call me Dakota."

She nodded. "I'm sure our paths will cross. Ricochet's a very small place."

The train stopped. It was a narrow gauge locomotive with a coal tender, passenger car, open platform car and caboose. A conductor stepped off, followed by another man—late twenties, about 5'10" and slender. Everything about him said he hadn't done a hard day's work in his life. He clattered down the stairs and stood in front of Heather and me. He wore a suit with a bowler hat and had long sideburns.

"Mr. Stevens," he said. "William McCourt."

Like a lot of academics, he exuded an air of distraction, a sense that he'd be working on an important problem if he didn't have to deal with *you*. I shook his hand. It was surprisingly rough and callused, like a mason's. Once the other passengers detrained, the computer mogul and his entourage boarded.

"Heather," McCourt said. "You didn't have to rush back."

"I know, but the show must go on, right? Besides, Vivian Vaillancourt made it pretty obvious she didn't want me around."

"I'm sorry to hear that," he said.

She gave me a grim smile, and as I tipped my hat she scooped up her skirt and climbed aboard. Walt ran out of the station office and traded a canvas sack for one the conductor held. That would be the mail. Sometimes my skills of deduction amaze even me.

"Ready?" McCourt said.

"Lead the way."

I picked up my carpetbag and boarded the passenger car with him. Horsehair seats faced each other on each side of the aisle. The walls were carved mahogany and ornamented with brass oil lamps. Clearly, Sidney hadn't skimped on the details. The passengers jabbered with each other, except Heather, who sat alone in the last seat, staring out the window. I put my bag on the overhead baggage rack.

"All aboard!" the conductor bellowed. The whistle gave a short blast and the train lurched forward.

"Let's go outside," McCourt said.

It was a flatbed car that had been converted to provide outdoor seating. Steel rails encircled the deck, and bench seats ran down the center.

"So," he said, sitting down, "what do you think so far?"

"This place must employ a heck of a lot of people."

"A small army," he said. "Besides the actors, we have a large support staff doing the day-to-day work like cooking, caring for the horses, repairs, all of that."

"Is there reason to suspect any of them in Sidney's death?" I asked.

As the train picked up speed, he took off his bowler hat and held onto it.

"I hadn't considered that. No, I can't imagine it. Sidney worked everyone hard, but he compensated us well, so I don't see the motive." McCourt stood up and waved me over to the railing. "Care for the nickel tour?"

"Okay," I said.

A shallow river ran parallel to the railroad bed. Stretched out beyond the river were rolling hills followed by a stand of trees with the Bitterroot Mountains looming in the distance. The train traveled at about 25 mph, and except for a couple of times when the wind shifted and we got a whiff of coal smoke, the air rushing by was green and fragrant. McCourt gestured at the passing vista.

"Ninety-nine *thousand* acres. That's a little over a hundred and fifty square miles."

"How is it that it's never been built up?" I asked.

"Too remote." He pointed at the wooded hills around us, the hills Briggs and I had switch-backed over to get in here. "We're wedged in. Too difficult to build a major road. No good for mining anymore because it's dried up. Although, there's a legend that the miners hid a sizable cache of gold in one of the mines." He shook his head. "A fool's errand, I'm afraid."

Spanning the river ahead was a wooden trestle bridge, and the train curved in its direction. As our long shadows moved across the flatbed platform, I realized how late it was. I'd been traveling since dawn, and my limbs were leaden with exhaustion. A bed tonight was something to look forward to.

"We'll be passing Loot in a few minutes," McCourt said.

A high-walled ravine swallowed up the train, and when we came out the other end the waning sun flickered through the trees. We chugged up a mild grade, passing several mounds of rocks worn smooth from the elements.

"What are those?" I asked.

McCourt gestured like he was sending back food.

"Tailings piles. Leftover rock from the mining. Hideous, aren't they? All over the resort. Guess they didn't feel obligated to leave it pretty."

"Guess not."

We rounded a bend, the trees disappeared, and we were looking across a broad meadow at the ruins of two dozen buildings, their wood bleached gray by the sun. Several roofs had collapsed.

"Loot," McCourt said. "Ironic, isn't it?"

"Must have been prosperous at one time."

"Loaded. Until they cleaned the gold out anyway."

While we talked, I glanced at the one brick building among them and thought I saw something move in an upstairs window. Before I had a chance to take a second look, the train plunged into the trees.

"About five minutes now," McCourt said, putting his hat back on. "Let's go."

We went inside the passenger car. I took down my bag and sat quietly while McCourt chatted with Heather. The whistle blasted twice and the train began to slow. By the time McCourt and I got off the train, the stagecoaches had pulled away.

"There goes our ride," I said.

"Not at all. We're around front."

The station was little more than a shed with a ticket window. No brass band to welcome the new town marshal. No photo-op with the mayor for the *Ricochet Gazette*. The place was cricket-empty and the sun was going down. Two horses waited at a hitching post, swishing their tails.

"Yours is the chestnut gelding," McCourt said.

Once aboard, I held the carpetbag in one hand, the reins in the other. We moved out at a trot.

"Vivian mentioned you're a historian," I said. "This must be the ultimate gig for you. How'd you get it?"

"My doctoral thesis was on the sociological mores of boom-bust towns in the late 19th century American

West," McCourt said. "Sidney heard about it and asked me to be his historical advisor. So here I am."

"Where'd you get it?"

"Get what?"

"Your doctorate," I said.

"Oh, out your way, actually. NYU."

"Really? That's right near my office."

"Small world, I suppose," he said.

The horses clomped along side by side. I filled my lungs with the cool piney air. We climbed a short hillside and then the ground leveled and across a barren plain stood Ricochet, forty to fifty buildings glowing in the sunset. I stopped my horse. McCourt pulled alongside.

"Listen," I said, "this might be our last chance to talk openly for a while. Any ideas on who did this?"

"I'm a historian, Mr. Stevens, not a detective, and I'd rather not speculate. I'll do what I can for you in terms of information, but the last thing I want to do is prejudice you against someone. The fact is, it could have been anybody."

Spoken like a true academic: turgid and noncommittal at the same time.

"Understood," I said. "But I need a list of where everybody was the night of Sidney's death."

"I'll give you what I can."

As if sensing our conversation was over, the horses started moving again. McCourt pointed to a tiny house on this end of town.

"Well, I hope you don't mind, but I have some paperwork to catch up on. I assume you can manage on your own tonight."

"Sure. Where do I go?" I asked.

He made a chopping motion with his hand.

"Keep heading into town. Go through the intersection and the marshal's office will be on your right. Your apartment is above the office. Put your horse in the livery down the street, and one of us will drop by in the morning to take you to the meeting."

"What meeting?"

"The story meeting," he said. "A few times a week we convene to discuss the skits we'll be putting on for guests. Don't forget, Mr. Stevens, you're supposed to be an actor. You won't be memorizing dialogue *per se*, but there are a few stories you'll need to stick to. Have some breakfast and somebody will find you, at the cafe or your office."

We shook hands from our saddles.

"Goodnight, Mr. Stevens."

He veered off, and once again I was alone, a stranger in a strange land.

24

A Warm Welcome

As my horse shuffled into town, figures appeared in the windows. Sadly, no women ran into the street half-clothed and crazed with desire to greet me. Inside the 24 Karat Saloon, piano music twanged and men roared. Farther down the street the noise faded, and before I knew it I had reached the marshal's office. I rode ahead to the livery and left my horse with the stableman there.

"Do I pay you now?" I asked.

"You're the new marshal, right?"

"Yup."

"Town pays for it," he said. "Welcome to Ricochet."

I went over to the office. It was as if Sidney had used the one in *High Noon* as a model: desk, potbelly stove, rack of rifles on the wall, and a ring of keys near the entry to the jail. Behind the thick oak door lay barred lodgings for four bandits. The layer of dust on everything told me the place hadn't seen much action. Hopefully that was about to change.

I went upstairs to the apartment. Despite his wealth, Sidney's quarters were monastic: double bed, bureau, washstand, nightstand and oil lamps. A pair of framed sepia photos—Sidney with Heather, Sidney with Vivian—sat on the bureau. The room was uncomfortably still, and in the waning light the red paisley wallpaper looked like blood. Sleeping up here, at least on my first night, was out of the question. I took the maps and satellite photos, and left.

The sunset behind the Bitterroot Mountains was spectacular, and as I plunked myself down on a bench to watch it, I wondered what Svetlana was doing tonight. Whatever it was, I was certain that she and her sister had a dozen men doing their bidding. Together those two were a dangerous force of beauty. Meanwhile, 2000 miles away, the raucous swells from the saloon only reminded me how alone I was.

I watched the last wedges of sun dip behind the mountains, then went in my office and lit a lamp. Unless I went to a hotel, there weren't many options for sleeping tonight. I stared at the door to the jail. I went in, shook out a blanket on a lower bunk and got undressed. A faint breeze washed through the tiny barred window near the ceiling, and as I drifted off with the air brushing my cheek, it morphed into the back of Heather's hand.

We were at our wedding reception, greeting guests, but each time I looked over at my bride, she had changed—from Heather to Shay to Svetlana. The best man proposed a toast, and as the glasses clinked, they all shattered.

I sprang awake in the inky cell. I could have sworn the breaking glass was real.

My throat was parched from the dust. Wearing only my long underwear, I staggered outside and looked for a well pump. There was the outline of one across the street, in the alley next to the cafe. I wasn't keen on going over there barefoot, so I turned around to get my boots.

And that's when I saw the fire.

25

MARSHAL DAKOTA STEVENS

Flames boiled out of the apartment window over the jail. I sprinted across the street, filled a bucket from the pump and ran back shouting, "Fire! Fire!" I felt like an idiot, but there *was* a fire—a damn *big* fire.

I ran up the stairs, paused at the door and touched the knob. It was cool. I turned it and pushed the door open. Flames curled up the wall from behind the headboard. The bed coverings were burning and my carpetbag had caught fire as well. I pitched the water at the wall, but it might as well have been gasoline for all the good it did. On my way to get another bucketful, I kept yelling for help, and in no time a bucket brigade had formed. Thick smoke plumed out of the door. We aimed the buckets at the area around the bed.

When the fire was out, people began to ask questions, but I couldn't see their faces. "What the hell happened?" a man shouted. "What'd you do?" said another. They stood around awhile to make sure there were no flare-ups, and then, one by one, they walked away grumbling until I was alone again.

I went back in the jail. Water dripped all over from cracks in the ceiling. Lovely. I went outside, grabbed a few buckets, and placed them around the office. Then I went in the cell. I stripped out of my soaked underclothes, hung them to dry, and collapsed on the bunk. Every cell in my body was spent. As I fell asleep this time, I thought of what the man in the livery had said: *"Welcome to Ricochet."*

When I awoke, I was determined not to let the previous night's attempt on my life intimidate me. Someone didn't want me here, but whoever had set the fire needed to see that I didn't scare easily. I rolled out of bed while the dawn was still gray, got dressed and went to fetch my horse. The livery man—Kurt, I learned—was already mucking stalls, and after some small talk about the fire, he saddled me up and sent me on my way.

Riding down the main drag, swaying in the saddle as the sun rose, I found myself looking around in awe. I'd been too tired to appreciate Ricochet when I arrived last evening, but now, in the soft morning light, I could see that this place *was* the Old West.

A treeless dirt street divided two long rows of buildings. Wooden sidewalks ran the entire length of town while hitching posts and watering troughs waited at regular intervals. False fronts trumpeted every business and amenity that might have existed in an 1880s Montana town, and then some: laundry, newspaper, barber, bank, cafe, claims office, post office, blacksmith, mercantile, livery, three hotels with restaurants, two saloons, a church and more. Every detail was pitch-perfect, right down to the **WANTED** bills posted in front of my office. The quiet of the street, the lilac-tinted mountaintops, the bright golden haze in the air—if this were a musical, and if I could sing, I would have broken into "Oh, What a Beautiful Mornin'."

As the horse clomped along, I consulted Shaw's map and devised a plan. This morning I'd explore the south side of town; this afternoon, the north side. I folded up the map and snapped the reins.

I started by heading east out of town, toward the gallows where Sidney had been found, and passed some smaller tailings piles along the way. Even though I was certain any evidence there would be long-gone, I wanted to see the gallows just the same. The resort map showed it southeast of town, and at a fork in the road a sign pointed one way to Prospect Creek, the other to Boot Hill. It made sense that they'd put the gallows near the graveyard. I nudged the horse in that direction.

The path soon disappeared and we clomped across a barren and stony expanse. At the top of a bare knoll stood a dozen or so wooden grave markers, surrounded by a battered picket fence. Alone at the base of the hill was the gallows.

I studied the ground around the gallows, and just as I thought, there were way too many foot and hoof prints to make sense of them. There was nothing resembling evidence here. I rode south. It was time to look for the spots on Shaw's map. It was the best lead I had and I needed to follow it.

The vastness of the Montana countryside had me disoriented at first, and it took some time for me to get my bearings. Meanwhile, the horse must have thought I was nuts because I took us in meandering loops across long stretches of pasture, into the woods and back into open fields. Each time I reached a spot that seemed to correspond with one on the map, there was nothing noteworthy there. A boulder maybe, a fallen tree, or just barren ground. I couldn't imagine anyone wanting to build in these locations, and there seemed to be no pattern to them whatsoever.

Two hours later, I cantered back into town hungry and annoyed, and pulled up at Heather's cafe. I was charged a dollar of play money for overcooked scrambled eggs and burnt toast. I paid and stepped into the sunlight, glad that at least nobody had stolen my horse.

Down the other side of the street, Prentice Keller was sweeping the porch in front of his mercantile. Our eyes met, and he waved one-handed with his thumb still connected to the broom. I waved back. Taking in the other side of town, I noticed the silver-haired gunslinger from the depot, standing at the corner of the "T" intersection, watching me. Something about his stare was unnerving, as though it wasn't a coincidence that he was watching me, but I concluded I was just being paranoid. Besides, it was too early for confronting anyone, and I had work to do. I crossed the street to my burned-out apartment, hoping to find a clue from the fire.

Bad as it was, most of the damage was isolated to the side of the room nearest the windows. The bed and bureau were now wet cinders. My carpetbag, along with all my personals, had burned up too.

Although not an expert on arson, I knew that a fire's point of origin is usually the lowest point where you observe the results of the most intense burning. I was also pretty sure the fire had been started by something thrown through the window. My hypothesis was that it had landed on the floor at the corner of the headboard. I went over and squatted.

Without a doubt, this area had borne the most intense heat. I fingered the ashes. Mixed in among the cinders were shards of brown glass. Groping under the bed, I found what I was looking for: the neck of a bottle. I pulled it out by my fingertips, blew off the ashes and smiled. Embossed on the glass was a brand I knew well: Bass Ale. At least the arsonist had good taste in beer.

There was a charred piece of wick still in the bottleneck, and although I couldn't see any prints on the glass, that didn't mean there weren't any. I took the bottle to the post office, boxed it up and mailed it to Briggs, omitting his title to foil any snoopers. I included a note about it and asked for a complete fingerprint check.

When I got back to the office, Heather was there, studying a map of Ricochet on the wall. I closed the door and she whisked across the room to me.

"What happened last night?" she asked.

"Just a little fire. No problem. Although I can't believe the best you guys have for firefighting is a bucket brigade."

"I think there's equipment, but they keep it hidden," she said. "The only fires we have around here are small anyway, like yours. Are you okay?"

"Never better."

"How did it start?"

"Clumsy," I said. "Not used to those oil lamps. I feel awful about it. You know, it being Sidney's room and all."

"Objects can be replaced, Mr. Stevens. You can't." She took my arm. "Anyway, it's time for the story meeting."

"You're here to take me?"

"I try to look out for the new folks."

She opened her blue eyes wide. Instantly I could feel myself being sucked in, ready to do just about anything for her.

"Ready?" she said.

"Yeah."

Outside, the town was awake now. Proprietors chatted in front of their storefronts, and a group of male guests stood outside the Bonanza Hotel, gathering for their morning constitutional. At the "T" intersection, Heather turned us left and let go of my arm when we reached the church.

"Well, Mr. Stevens, here we are. Break a leg."

Once she was inside, I waited a moment, then slipped in quietly. With giant clear-glass windows that drenched the room in sunlight, the church was bright but hot. Leaning over their pews, the talent gestured grandly and gossiped. Someone sang. A Native American woman made eye contact with me, elbowed the girl next to her, and she the next girl, until half a dozen actresses had eyeballed every inch of me, like bidders at a steer auction. Just as unnerving were the male actors, who ignored me altogether. Heather, I noticed, sat alone in the front row.

Onstage, McCourt clapped his hands.

"Okay, people, let's settle down. We have quite a lot to cover, so if you please." He scanned the room. "Where's Kat?"

"Here, unfortunately," said a woman from the doorway.

Kat Styles strutted in wagging a giant fan of peacock feathers. Her dress was plum silk with a high collar, tight bodice and prominent bustle. Despite the layers of clothing, she somehow managed to walk like she was stark naked—and proud of it. She joined a clique of girls and flapped her fan.

"You may begin now."

McCourt glared at her, then cleared his throat.

"People, you know what I'm here to talk about. There have been too many instances of anachronistic items being found in the resort."

"Translation, please!" Kat said.

The other actors laughed.

"You all know very well what I mean," he said. "Wrappers from smuggled-in food, battery-operated DVD players—"

"And *other* battery-operated items," Kat said, smirking at the girls.

More laughter. McCourt continued.

"Cosmetics, beer cans, flashlights. Need I go on?" The room hushed. "People, our guests pay a lot of money to experience the nineteenth century. Yesterday I found a condom wrapper in front of the mercantile. This cannot continue."

"You're right, McCourt," Kat declared. "If *I* can't get laid in the middle of Main Street, nobody should be able to."

The room howled. Kat stood up and gave little bows all around.

"Thank you, thank you! I'll be here all summer."

McCourt had just opened his mouth to speak when a shadow appeared in the doorway. It stretched all the way down the aisle. Everyone turned.

"You're late, Mr. Boone," McCourt said.

The guy was a walking monolith. So tall, others would strain their necks talking to him for any length of time. So broad, he had to walk with his torso pivoted—a habit no doubt developed from having to enter rooms at an angle. If I weren't playing the hero, I would have gulped.

"Maybe if you didn't have me living in the sticks," Boone replied, "I wouldn't be."

McCourt turned to a man with unruly hair, maybe 30, seated behind him.

"Irving, talk to him, would you?"

The man walked to the edge of the stage. His shirt sleeves were rolled up and he clutched a sheaf of papers. Maybe it was the exasperation on his face, but he looked overworked and underappreciated. He had to be the writer.

"Mr. Boone, we've been through this," the pale writer said. "You're the stranger."

"Save it, I've heard it all before."

Boone sauntered to a chair in the corner and lowered himself into it. The chair actually groaned.

"Let's get this bullshit over with," he said.

McCourt sighed. "Mr. Irving will now discuss story lines."

"Guys, gals," Irving said, "remember who we're here for."

The entire room droned, "The guests."

"That's right," he said. "And it's the little moments that make it real. Remember, verisimilitude." He let the word hang in the hot air for a moment. "Next. Improv, improv, improv. Make it your mantra. Ladies, if you're in the mercantile and a guest walks in, strike up a conversation about the weather, complain about your husband's drinking, gossip—heck, you're all good at that—but do it in character. Guys, same goes for you. Talk about your businesses, politics, the pretty girls. Rib each other at the saloons. This goes for everyone. If a guest is around, you've got to be *on*."

He shuffled papers.

"Now, we're sticking with our tried-and-true story lines: the cheating gamblers—Eric, Maggie, keep up the good work there—the shooting contest, and tonight we'll do the fight at the 24 Karat, featuring Kat, Mr. Boone, and our new marshal—"

Kat sprang to her feet. "Damn it, when are we going to talk about it?"

"Talk about what?"

"What do you think? The gigantic elephant in the room—Sidney's death. What are we going to do, pretend it never happened? The guy was our benefactor, for God's sake. We need to do something to remember him."

McCourt stepped to the edge of the stage. "And what would you suggest, Kat?"

"I don't know. A monument, something. Write him into the story maybe. Heather, you want to help me here?"

I was leaning against the back wall when I got an idea.

"What if the new marshal was looking into the old marshal's death?" I said.

The entire room went silent and turned to face me.

"Who the hell are you?" Kat said.

I strode up the aisle, my spurs clinking with each step. When I was standing over the exotic terror, I opened my frock coat to reveal the tin star.

"Name's Dakota, miss."

"Kat Styles. Charmed, I'm sure."

She held out a gloved hand, but her eyes drifted to my groin. I raised her chin with two fingers.

"I'm up here, darlin'," I said.

She grinned and leaned back in the pew.

"Everyone," Irving said, "I'd like to introduce Marshal Dakota Stevens."

I touched my hat brim. From his chair, Boone spoke up.

"So, we're supposed to revolve our stories around the new guy, is that it?"

"Yeah, Boone's right!" shouted an actor in the back.

"That's for Mr. Irving to decide," I said.

"Actually, Mr. Stevens," McCourt said, "it's for me to decide."

Boone was about to say something when Keller stood up. The room hushed. He had an upstanding posture that, with his height and lean build, gave him an air of integrity.

"Well, I think it's a great idea," he said. "About time we got some new blood in this place. Seems to me, a story about Sidney's death is just what the doctor ordered."

I nodded, turned to Irving. "Any ideas, you know where to find me."

I walked out.

26

MISERY LOVES COMPANY

With a canteen of water, a saddlebag of sandwiches and my Colt Peacemaker, I set out to explore the area north of town. For three hours I wound through a small canyon looking for landmarks that corresponded with Shaw's markings. I found nothing, nada, zip—not even a boulder shaped like a President. Discouraged, I plopped myself down in the shadow of a cliff and gnashed into my so-called lunch.

Thinking about the fire, I couldn't be sure the arsonist had meant to kill me. For all I knew, it had nothing to do with Sidney's death and was instead the desperate act of a jealous actor. However, as Sherlock Holmes said, it is a cardinal mistake to form theories before you have the facts. I needed to talk with all of the main suspects first, and Carries Bison was one of them. According to the resort map, the reservation was just a few miles away, with Boone's place along the route. I ignored the uneasiness in my gut and climbed back in the saddle.

Once out of the canyon, I picked up a trail that ran along the railroad tracks. Boone's cabin was on the edge of a stream. He was outside, chopping firewood. Despite his size, he was terrible at it, the axe glancing off the log each time. I rode into the clearing. He stopped in mid-swing.

"What do you want? You got *some* balls coming over here."

"Let me guess," I said. "You don't get many visitors, do you?"

Boone swung the axe, burying it in the chopping block. My horse shied away as Boone walked over.

"If this is part of that storyline you got for yourself, you can quit acting, asshole. Nobody's around."

I steadied the horse. "I was in the neighborhood and wanted to ask you a question. Where were you on the night Sidney was killed?"

"Screw you. I already talked to the cops about it. *Real* cops."

"And you don't care to add anything?"

"No, I don't," he said. "But I'm glad you stopped by. I'm looking forward to tonight."

"Why?"

"You'll see."

He walked back to his axe and resumed chopping. I rode away without saying anything. Take that.

It was time to check out the Indian reservation. Consulting the map, I rode over hill after hill of tall prairie grass with the sun beating down on my neck. Since I was approaching the reservation via the backcountry, there were no signs to tell me when I'd reached it. The grass simply ended and I was on beat-up asphalt. Half a mile down the road, a group of double-wides huddled around the Stars and Stripes and what looked like a tribal flag.

When I got there I was greeted by something you don't see in the East anymore—a phone booth. Since I couldn't use the phone in Ricochet for fear of blowing our cover, this was perfect. I jumped down, wrapped the horse's reins around a fencepost, and called Svetlana collect.

"Let me guess," she said. "You solve case, we get big check, and you send Zoya and me on vacation to Hawaii."

I could always tell when Svetlana had been around her Ukrainian relatives because her English went to hell.

"Not quite."

I told her about the fire, my failure to locate the spots on Shaw's map, and my current foray into the reservation.

"Misery loves company," she said. "I will be there Thursday, late afternoon. That is three days from now. I assume you can survive without me until then."

"I'll try. By the way, the food here is terrible."

"Noted."

Something brushed against my leg. A scruffy brown mutt stared up at me, wagging its tail fast. I scratched behind its ears.

"Any word on Louis?" I asked.

"The Coast Guard searched the entire Sound, including the ports. They even sent a search plane all the way to Martha's Vineyard. Nothing."

"What about those Montana phone numbers from Roman's?"

"Well, one is the Ricochet number," she said. "Another is a park administration office in West Yellowstone, and the third belongs to a Patrick Hollis in Gardiner, Montana, just north of the park."

"We'll have to follow up on them. You and Zoya having a good time?"

Out in the yard, my canine pal smiled at me and chased its tail.

"Wonderful, thank you," Svetlana said. "We went to a few celebrity parties the other night."

"Whose?"

"No idea. We just walked down the beach from one to the next."

"Something only you two could get away with," I said.

"Yes. Oh, I saw Delilah's friends, but not Delilah. I thought she was a socialite of some kind."

"Maybe the bouncers wouldn't let her in," I said. "Not famous enough."

"Or not clothed enough," she said.

"Or that."

There were footsteps behind me.

Four brawny Native Americans were headed my way.

27

THE WELCOMING COMMITTEE

"Look, the welcoming committee's here," I said. They were fifty yards away. I measured my words in footsteps.

"Listen carefully. Pick up a GPS, a couple of Mini Maglites and two small walkie-talkies with the longest range you can get. Download topographical maps for this area onto the GPS and smuggle it all into Ricochet."

The men formed a semicircle around the phone booth.

"Gotta go," I said. "Kiss Zoya for me."

"*Zadnitza*," she said disgustedly. "Goodbye."

I hung up and turned to face the men. Hulking and impassive, they looked like four Easter Island statues. I thumbed over my shoulder.

"American Express—lost my traveler's checks. They're sending a guy out."

The tallest one glanced at my horse. The dog sat down next to me, panting.

"Your dog likes me." I scratched its ears again.

"Who are you?" the tallest one asked.

I considered telling them I was from the Bureau of Indian Affairs, but they didn't seem the type to appreciate bureaucratic humor.

"Dakota Stevens. I've come from Ricochet—you know, the resort? I need to speak with Carries Bison."

"About?"

Loquacious, this one.

"That's between us," I said. "Consider me an emissary."

They looked at each other. The tall one waved for me to follow.

They piled into a king cab pickup truck and fishtailed out of the parking lot. I trailed behind on the horse. Ahead, a dirt road descended into cut forest. They turned in. I followed.

The narrow lane ended at a vast clearing with a sprawling building under construction in the middle of it. One end of the four-story building had a domed roof and was nearly completed, while the other was exposed metalwork and wood framing. Men moved around on each floor. Saws whined and nail guns popped. Nearby, a pair of bulldozers ripped out tree stumps and graded. The air reeked of diesel fumes.

The Indians' pickup was parked in front of a trailer with a sign on the door that read, "BISON CONSTRUCTION — OFFICE." Three of the Indians stood expressionless beside pallets of lumber and cement, while the tallest one talked to a man in crisp linen shorts tapping a two-way radio against his leg. I tied off the horse and walked over.

Imagining the stereotype, I had expected Carries Bison to have long hair pulled back in a ponytail. Instead, it was black and spiky. A pair of Bruce Lee sunglasses reflected the afternoon sun as he gazed at the building. Unlike his brawny colleagues, he was built like a surfer.

"I got this," he said.

He waited for the tall Indian to shuffle away, then turned to me. It was somewhat unnerving not to be able to see his eyes.

"All right, Ricochet, what's this about?"

"What are you building?" I asked.

"Nothing that would interest you."

"Looks like a hotel and casino."

"You must be some kind of idiot," he said. "White man, coming in here asking questions."

"Actually, I'm part Native American myself," I said. "One-sixteenth."

"Yeah, what nation?"

"Passamaquoddy. They're from Maine."

"Passamaquoddy," he snorted. "Sounds like something my old lady says during sex."

"Your wife says Passamaquoddy during sex?"

"You better get to the point. *Right now.*"

He jabbed me in the chest with a finger. I could have broken it, but it seemed like a bad idea.

"Okay," I said. "Did you kill Sidney Vaillancourt?"

"Vallen *who*?"

"Nice try. The man who owned the resort next door. Died over a week ago. Found hanging on his own gallows. Maybe you heard?"

"Ironic," he said, "but no, I didn't. Now, who are you?"

"Dakota Stevens. Actor hired to play the new marshal. Heard the two of you had some words a while back. I just wanted to find out what I'm getting into here."

"Nothing that concerns you."

Behind him, perched on a stack of plywood, was a single Bass Ale bottle, half-full in the bright sunlight.

"You let your workers drink on the job?" I raised an eyebrow. "Does OSHA know about this?"

He looked at the bottle, crossed his arms over his chest.

"Keeps them motivated," he said.

"Bass Ale, huh?"

"So?"

"So," I said, "somebody tossed one full of gasoline through my window last night."

"Foolish. Waste of five cents. Ten in Michigan."

I glanced at my horse, about fifty feet away. Something told me a Jesse James getaway was in my future.

"Let's stop jerking each other around, shall we?" I said. "Just tell me about your relationship with Sidney Vaillancourt and I'll go away."

"I've got a better idea." He gestured at the four men leaning against the trailer. "How about I have them beat you to a pulp and bury you someplace?"

"Ah, but you're forgetting one thing," I said. "If I fail to report, double-oh-eight replaces me."

Carries Bison waved for the men. They marched in unison across the lot. Quickly calculating the odds, I determined that despite my training, these guys would be a handful. Besides, their boss looked like he knew how to handle himself, too, and he had another forty or fifty workers in reserve. Under the circumstances, there was nothing undignified about a hasty retreat.

"For the record," I said, backing up toward the horse, "I didn't come over here to start trouble."

I turned and went for the horse, but Bison's men caught me. One of them grabbed my arm and whipped me around, while a second one threw a punch at my head. I slipped it and it landed on my shoulder, like a friendly punch from a buddy except a hundred times harder. Still locked in the first one's grip, I was whirling backwards from the punch when a third guy kicked me in the leg. I started to fall, but before I hit the ground a fourth one kneed me in the ribs. I landed hard on the dirt. They stepped away and reared back to gang-kick me when I snapped out the Peacemaker. They froze.

"Relax," Bison said, "it's one of those cap guns."

I focused on the beer bottle behind him. Thumbing the hammer back, I took careful aim and shot it, sending a spray of beer and glass at the trailer. The blast was deafening. My assailants backed away. Holding the gun on them, I stumbled to the horse, grabbed the reins and slung myself aboard, feeling the pain jolt through my shoulder, my leg, my ribs. The entire construction site was silent. I wheeled the horse around and pointed the gun at Carries Bison.

"A pleasure meeting you," I said. "Goodbye."

I holstered the gun and cantered into the trees, wondering if I'd made a mistake coming over here. There were already plenty of people in Ricochet who didn't like me. I didn't need more.

28

LATE FOR AN EIGHT O'CLOCK CALL

It was late afternoon when I made it back to Ricochet. Walking from the livery, I heard banging coming from my apartment. I went upstairs.

Keller and two other men were assembling a new bed. Everything burned had been removed, the broken windowpanes replaced, and the floors swept clean. Even the sooty walls were scrubbed. Except for the smell of smoke, it was as if the fire had never happened.

"What's going on?" I asked.

Keller stood up. "Just fixing up your place, marshal."

"Who told you to do this?"

"Well, I *am* the mayor, Mr. Stevens, but it was Heather's idea. Said it wasn't fitting for the marshal to be sleeping in his own jail. Thought it'd be a nice surprise for you."

"What'd you do with all the burned-up stuff?"

Keller tipped his hat back. "Why, threw it out, of course. I saw that your bag burned up, too, so I had the bureau stocked with new personals for you. Hope that's all right."

I nodded. The men stood up beside the new bed. "All set, Mr. Mayor."

"Hear, marshal? You're back in business."

We shook hands.

"Appreciate it," I said.

"Pleasure."

They walked out. At the last second, Keller stuck his head back in.

"Oh, Kat wanted me to give you a message. There's an eight o'clock call for your scene at the 24 Karat."

"Which is?"

He grinned. "You arresting Boone."

"A cinch," I said. "Tell her I'm looking forward to it."

As soon as he shut the door, I collapsed onto the new bed. For a second my bruises from today's fight flared up, but the pain dissipated and I began to relax. The mattress was excellent. I yanked off my boots and stared at the ceiling.

Well, well, Heather. Fixing up my place was mighty neighborly of you. Then again, it was also a smart way to get rid of evidence. For all I knew, you might have searched the place beforehand as well.

The window was open and a soothing breeze washed over the bed. Promising myself only a catnap, I fell asleep atop the quilt with all my clothes on.

I was jolted back to life by pounding on the door. I staggered out of bed and answered it. Kat stared back at me.

"You're late, marshal."

Dark curls dripped down her cheeks. Her nostrils flared as she brushed past me.

"Your call was an hour ago," she said.

"And a good evening to you."

While I poured some water in the basin and splashed my face, she examined my room.

"See they got you fixed up."

I checked myself out in the mirror. Besides needing a shave, I was short about twenty hours' sleep. Behind me, the bed squeaked. Kat was bouncing on it.

"Mmm, nice and firm," she said. "I'll say one thing for Heather—girl doesn't waste time."

She kept bouncing, her breasts squeezed together, her hands pressed down between her thighs. Ten more seconds of this, and neither of us would be showing up at the 24 Karat.

"Please stop that." I slipped on my boots. "What were you saying about Heather?"

"That's right, you're new." With a final bounce, she sprang off the bed and strolled around the room, gliding her fingertips over everything. "Well, it's no secret she was having a thing with Sidney."

"For how long?"

"Before I showed up. Couple years at least. Anyway, it's *so* obvious the little slut wants to get in bed with the new marshal." She ran her fingers across the nape of my neck. "That's you, sweetie. Little warning, though—she's got another one on the side."

"Another actor?" I asked.

"Nope. Some bloke down in Yellowstone. Never met him, but she's been going down there to meet *somebody* for months. Every weekend."

I thought about the phone calls from Roman's in the East to Yellowstone and Gardiner. Was Heather's other boyfriend the Patrick Hollis that Svetlana had mentioned? As the room glowed with the last light of sunset, Kat paused in front of the mirror to tweak her hair.

"Come on, we've got a scene to do," she said. "I'll explain on the way."

29

STAGE COMBAT

I was sitting in a rocking chair across the street from the 24 Karat, waiting for my cue. The saloon blazed with light, and the laughter and piano music told me it was crowded in there. I didn't want to be doing this—acting, that is. I wanted to be investigating. But this was the price I had to pay to be undercover. I decided to suck it up and deal with it.

It was that magical time of night between sunset and moonrise, and the sky was dark and starry to the east and still glowing to the west. A full moon hung coyly behind the mountain peaks. People behaved strangely on a full moon, and I wondered how this one would manifest itself tonight.

Brisk footsteps approached from down the wooden sidewalk. A shape emerged out of the dark and stopped in the light of the hotel window. It was McCourt. He frowned.

"Where were you today?"

"Simmer down, McCourt." I lowered my voice and rocked in the chair. "I'm not here for my acting skills, remember."

"I realize that, but you're putting me in an untenable position. I can't be seen as playing favorites. And what was that nonsense about pretending to look into Sidney's death? Now you won't get anything out of them."

"Look, McCourt, I don't work for you, and the last thing I need is a history Ph.D. lecturing me on detective work. You don't see me telling you how to write a thesis statement."

With a huff, he reached in his jacket pocket and shoved a folded sheet of paper at me.

"The information you requested. Don't open it here, but maybe it will give you a lead." He adjusted his hat. "By the way, I couldn't help noticing you and Kat at the meeting this morning. Be careful with her. She—"

A palpable shriek rose up from the saloon.

"Excuse me, McCourt," I said. "My cue."

I strode across the street and parted the saloon doors. The room was well-lit with period gas lamps and it took a second for my eyes to adjust. Twenty or so men stared up from their cards at the balcony. A petite ingénue with long brown hair leaned over the railing with blood dripping from her mouth. I knew it was one of those packets of fake blood, but it was nauseating just the same. Behind her, Kat flew out of a room and ran to her side.

"My God, Lizzie, what happened?"

The girl wailed.

"Let's get you a drink," Kat said.

She led the girl downstairs. I followed them over to the bar.

"It's okay, Lizzie," Kat said. "The marshal's here now. Tell us what happened."

She dabbed the girl's mouth with a handkerchief. The male guests leaned closer.

"It's…"

"Come on, Lizzie, out with it," I said.

Kat glared at me. Lizzie sniffed.

"Mr. Boone, he…"

A voice bellowed from the upstairs landing: "He *what?*"

All of the guests whipped around, their eyes dilating the instant they took in Boone's mass. I'm not ashamed to admit that mine dilated a bit as well.

"I told him to stop and he hit me!" Lizzie said.

"That's a lie!" Boone shouted.

He clomped down the stairs one at a time, like Frankenstein. Every step groaned.

"You aren't welcome here, Mr. Boone," Kat said. "Please leave."

Boone reached the foot of the stairs and stood there strangling the banister scroll. I sauntered over to him.

"We'll be having words, you and me."

At this point, Boone was supposed to fake-punch me repeatedly until I pulled my fake gun and fake-shot him. Boone would fall against the banister, exploding the fake blood packet concealed in his shirt. That's what was supposed to happen.

Instead, Boone said, "Get the hell outa my way," heaved all 200 pounds of me up by the gun belt, and tossed me like a sack of walnuts at a very real poker table. The table didn't break, so my back took the brunt of it, and my head slammed against the high keys on the piano.

Through the daze in my head I heard a collective gasp, and as I stumbled to my feet, a flush of embarrassment swept over me. Boone wasn't acting. The freak was at the bar now, clutching Kat by the arm and shaking her. She cried out, looked to me for help. What was happening? Unlike these actors, I'd never been trained in fake fighting, or stage combat. Beyond shooting him in the back, there was only one thing I could think of to take this maniac down.

I snatched up an empty chair and swung with everything I had at the side of Boone's knee. He yelled and hit the floor with a thud that made the poker chips jump.

Kat and Lizzie were flattened against the bar, covering their mouths. A hand grabbed my ankle and squeezed. It was Boone, staring up at me, panting through his teeth.

"You sonovabitch!" he said.

I wrenched my leg out of his grip and stepped away, rubbing my head. I had lost my hat. I picked it up. A guest scurried outside covering his mouth like he was about to vomit. The room echoed with lackluster applause, as though the onlookers couldn't tell if the scene had been real or not. Through all of this, the bartender had been grinning. I grabbed him by the collar and dragged him halfway over the counter.

"Fetch the doctor," I said. "A *real* doctor."

I marched out the doors.

30

A Levitating Kiss

I needed to relax and think, and since I tended to do both pretty well in a tub of hot water, I went back across the street to the Ricochet Manor Hotel and ordered a bath. The staff placed oil lamps around the room and gave me perfumed soap, a back brush, a shaving set-up and a swivel mirror mounted on the side of the tub. They gave me everything a person needed for a pleasant bath except hot water. The water was tepid at best.

I soaped up the brush and scrubbed my back, trying to wash away some of the guilt I felt for reacting the way I did. As an FBI agent, I'd defused situations far more difficult than the one with Boone. Plain and simple, my ego had gotten in the way.

I reached for the paper McCourt had given me. It was a list of the principal actors and their whereabouts on the night of Sidney's murder. Most of them had had the night off and were seen in Missoula. The only ones unaccounted for were Boone, Kat and Heather. Big surprise. I shoved the list in my boot and slumped down in the water.

The answer to the question I'd been hired for—"Who killed Sidney Vaillancourt?"—seemed further away than ever. Heather Van Every, the suspect with the strongest motive, had ordered the "cleanup" of my burned apartment. She was unaccounted for on the night of Sidney's death and, according to Kat, she had another boyfriend down in Yellowstone. The woman was hiding something. For the time being, though, I would continue to investigate all lines of inquiry.

The water was cold now, and I wasn't feeling brave enough to try and shave with a straight razor, so I left my beard alone, got dressed in my dirty clothes again, and went back to my apartment.

Lamps were lit. I smelled perfume. Kat came into focus on the wingback chair, her hair askew, her chest rising and falling pleasantly in the tight plum dress. I put my hat on the bureau.

"Honey, I'm home."

"What the hell was that scene?" she said. "Have you had *any* training?"

"Look, Kat, I'm hungry, I'm exhausted and I've been beaten up twice today. Can't this wait?"

"Answer me. Have you had any training?"

"Of course."

"Where?"

"Emerson College," I lied.

"Yeah? They teach you anything about blocking, what it means to upstage somebody? And Boone, what was that all about?"

"Nothing. When I saw him hurting you, I decided to take him down."

"Oh," she said, "you just *decided* to take down a three hundred pound psychopath?"

I shrugged. "Pretty much."

"Well, they took Boone to Missoula in an ambulance," she said. "You really did a number on him, sweetie." She leapt out of the chair and stood a foot away from me, studying my eyes. "Why do I think you're lying about who you are? You're not an actor."

"Yes I am."

"All right, what's your audition piece?"

This I hadn't expected. Maybe I should have memorized something ahead of time, but presumably I was a detective, not Laurence Olivier. I thought of movies I'd seen more than once.

"Fine," I said. "Ready?"

"Just go."

I rasped up my throat to get into character.

"'I know what you're thinkin',' " I said. "'Did he fire six shots or only five? Well, to tell you the truth, I've forgotten myself in all this excitement.'"

"Stop! What the hell is that?"

"*Dirty Harry*. A classic."

She started to slap me and I grabbed her wrist. I was going to let her go when she gritted her teeth and tried to yank free. She kicked at me. Still clutching her wrist, I grabbed her upper arm with my other hand, pivoted and pushed. Having no choice but to go where I aimed her, she scurried backwards across the room until the chair caught her at the knees. She collapsed into it at cartoon speed.

For a minute, she just sat there, eyes closed, chin down, utterly deflated. I was admiring her cocoa skin in the lamplight when she began to cry. This could be another actor trick. I would proceed with caution.

"What's really bothering you?" I said. "It's not my lack of acting ability."

"You wouldn't understand," she sobbed.

"I might."

"It's this place. The job, the people, everything. Twenty-five and look at me. In the middle of nowhere, playing a prostitute in a glorified theme park."

"Go on," I said.

"Outside of here, all I can get is bit stuff because casting directors don't want half-breeds. Not Asian enough to play the exotic stuff, they say, and not black enough to do urban."

"You're unique, that's all," I said. "Maybe a little harder to place, but it'll happen. Someone with your charisma? It's just a matter of time before you get noticed."

"You really think so?" She dried her eyes with her sleeves, leapt out of the chair and touched my chest. "Sidney was going to do a showcase for me. You know, fly in a bunch of producers and casting agents. Such a nice man, and now he's dead."

"Were you here when it happened?" I asked.

"When what happened?"

"When Sidney died."

She looked away. "No, I had the night off. Why?"

"Nothing," I said. "The whole thing's creepy, that's all."

"It is."

A breeze came in and made the lamps flicker. I rubbed her shoulder.

"Well, next time I'll rehearse with you and I'll nail that scene, I promise."

"Not with me you won't," she said.

"What do you mean?"

"McCourt took it away from me. When they get somebody else to play the big bad guy, I won't be playing that scene."

"But what happened wasn't your fault," I said. "Do you want me to talk to him?"

"Thanks, but it wouldn't do any good." She stepped closer to me, stood on her tiptoes and sniffed my neck. "You smell nice."

"Just took a bath. Perfumed soap."

She touched my cheek. "You could have shaved."

"All they gave me was a straight razor and—"

"Enough about your bath," she said. "Look, if I tell you something, you have to promise—no, *swear*—not to tell anyone. It has to do with McCourt."

"I swear."

Even though the room was empty, she looked around and licked her teeth, the gossiping thespian engaging in her favorite pastime. She tugged me over to the bed and sat us down on the edge.

"Okay, check it out. McCourt, he's supposed to be this big deal Ph.D., right? Well, last Christmas, I'm doing a show in New York and I go to this dinner party and there's a couple of history profs there. Anyway, I get talking with them about Ricochet and I ask them about McCourt, and they tell me that the guy never *got* his Ph.D., that he started having an affair with somebody."

"Who?" I asked.

"I don't know, but I got the sense it was another professor's wife, and the Dean got wise and kicked him out." She let out a long, satisfied sigh. "I can't tell you how long I've been holding that one in. But please don't say anything. I could get fired, okay?"

"I won't."

"Thank you for listening," she said, and without warning she wrapped her arms around me and kissed me.

I wondered if they taught actors how to kiss in acting school. It was that good. She put her entire being into the kiss. It was a levitating kiss, a kiss for the ages.

But when I closed my eyes to enjoy it, I thought of Shay and my enthusiasm waned. All I could think about was the minty smell of her hair and our plan to live together. Kat toppled backwards onto the bed with me. Just then, my stomach growled. I pulled away.

"Wow," she said. "Sounds like someone's hungry."

"Starved. Hey, let me ask you something. The food— has it always been bad? I haven't had a decent meal since I got here."

"Hell, no. When I first got here, back when Sidney ran everything, it was amazing—like eating at Spago every day. But McCourt kept nagging him about it, the little prick. Kept saying it wasn't realistic. All that crap about *anachronistic*. Over time, McCourt took over the food and ruined it."

"I'm getting the idea you don't like the guy," I said.

"Let's put it this way." She stared at a spot on the wall. "I'd ram a pair of scissors through his temple if I knew I could get away with it."

"Remind me not to get any haircuts from you."

She ran a hand down the length of my arm. "How about we go get some dinner, then come back and resume this?"

I thought about it. I could always eat and then say I wasn't feeling well, which, given the awful food, wasn't much of a stretch.

"Sure," I said.

She kissed me again, pressing her body against mine, and then she melted off me and was standing in front of the mirror, straightening her hair.

"I'll go over to the Bonanza and get us a table." She turned and stared at me. "A private table." She opened the door. "See you in ten minutes?"

"Okay."

She left. I lay on my back on the mattress for a moment, waiting for Kat's kiss to dissipate, and when I finally got up, I went to the washstand and splashed cold water on my face. For settling the nerves after an encounter with a beautiful woman, I had yet to find anything as effective as cold water.

My feet were sweaty in the boots, and I wanted to douse them in talcum powder and put on a fresh pair of socks. I opened the top drawer of the bureau and reached inside.

Out of the silence came a hissing sound, but by the time I heard it, it was too late. Whatever it was lashed out of the dark drawer and struck my forearm. I jerked my arm away.

I couldn't see it in the dim room, but I heard its telltale sound.

I'd just been bitten by a rattlesnake.

31

Turning Point

I stepped back and kicked the drawer shut. The sudden quiet underscored the seriousness of what had just happened. I'd never been bitten by a snake before, but I knew from my survival reading that it was crucial I not panic. Panic would elevate my heart rate, which would spread the venom through my body that much faster. I needed to keep the venom isolated to my arm and get to the doctor immediately.

I tore off my string tie, made a small lasso from it, cinched it snug around my upper arm, and tied it off. I left, walked calmly down the stairs and asked some passersby where the resort infirmary was. It was around the corner, across the street from the church, they said. I started walking.

Under my coat sleeve, I felt a burning sensation. I ignored it and kept walking. Across the street was the Bonanza, where Kat was waiting, and it occurred to me that she was alone in my room before I got there. Maybe she planted the snake.

I kept my breathing steady and walked at a moderate pace. Turning left at the intersection, I passed the silver-haired gunslinger going the other way. Something about him didn't add up. Could he have planted the snake? No time to find out now. I kept walking.

The infirmary windows glared with light as I climbed the stairs and went inside. I wondered how they had all this light, and then I remembered the infirmary had a generator. Must have been in a soundproof room because I couldn't hear anything. It seemed a foolish thing to think about at a time like this. A woman in a period nurse's uniform sat at a desk at the entrance.

"Please tell me you're a real nurse," I said.

"I am. Why?"

"Get the doctor. I've just been bitten by a rattlesnake."

"What?"

She jumped out of her chair and hurried into a back office. A moment later, a graying man in a lab coat hustled out.

"What's this, young man? Something about a snake?"

"Doc, please tell me you have antivenin here."

"We should," he said. "Go in back with Charlene and I'll be right there."

Nurse Charlene took me behind a curtain and sat me on an examination table. She helped me remove the cinch, my coat, vest and shirt, and it was then that I got my first look at the snakebite. My forearm around the bite was already swollen. The nurse cleaned the wound, administered an IV, and took my vitals. My temperature was 99.6, my pulse was elevated, my mouth and throat were parched, and my forearm burned.

The doctor scooted inside the curtain wearing latex gloves and carrying a small red box. He winced as soon as he saw me.

"Ouch." He pointed at the fresh bruises on my shoulder and ribs. "Play rugby?"

"No," I said. "Slipped on some soap."

"Well, the bruises can wait. Let's see that bite." He examined the wound and glanced at my frock coat. "You were wearing that?"

"He was, doctor," Nurse Charlene said.

"You're lucky. Only one of the fangs punctured the skin, and it appears to have gone in just a couple of millimeters. How long ago was this?"

"Maybe fifteen minutes," I said.

"Well, we caught it fast, and I have more than enough CroFab here, so you're not going to die."

"That's good news."

"But," he said, filling the syringe, "you're probably going to feel a lot worse before the night is through. The effects of antivenin can include itchiness, hives and something called 'serum sickness.' I'm afraid you're going to be out of commission for a while, marshal. At least a day."

"How did you know—"

He pointed at my vest on the chair. My tin star shone in the strong light.

"Busy night for me," the doctor said. "You put Mr. Boone in the hospital."

"Believe me, I'm not proud of it," I said.

"Now, you're sure it was a rattlesnake?"

"I've seen the Discovery Channel, Doc. I know what they sound like."

"Not that it matters." He injected the syringe contents into the intravenous tubing. "CroFab is a polyvalent crotalid antivenin, which means it's for all pit vipers—rattlesnakes, copperheads and cottonmouths."

"It was a rattlesnake, I'm sure of it," I said.

"Where was this, by the way?"

"The snake is in my room above the jail. Bureau, top drawer."

"Your drawer?" the doctor said. "That's odd. But I suppose they can crawl into just about anything."

"Yeah," I said.

"I'll tell Kurt from the livery," the doctor said. "Once in a while he has to catch snakes and other critters around here. He'll take care of it."

"Tell him not to kill the snake," I said. "It wasn't being malicious. Just have him take it way out in the woods someplace and leave it."

"That's what he does."

"One other thing, Doc—and you, too, Charlene. Please don't tell anyone about this. I just got this gig and I don't want to lose it."

I also wanted to be able to surprise the person who planted the snake, when he or she saw me walking around alive.

"Your medical condition is private, Mr. Stevens," he said. "Neither of us will say anything. Right now it's essential that you rest so the antivenin can do its work. We'll stay here through the night to monitor your vitals."

"Thanks, Doc."

Once the doctor left, Charlene took me to a bed in a screened-off area and gave me a hospital gown to put on. By now my forearm around the bite was yellowish and swollen—so swollen, it looked like an egg was trapped under the skin. As I changed and lay down, I thought of Kat waiting over at the Bonanza and considered asking Charlene to get a message to her, but by then the serum had started to take hold, making my entire body woozy and weak. I felt seasick, and no matter how hard I tried, I couldn't shake the vertigo sensation. The room spun. I vomited and collapsed. My throat was parched and several times I had to ask Charlene to bring me water.

I lay there through the night, unable to sleep, the nurse checking my temperature and blood pressure every half-hour it seemed, and when morning came the nausea had abated but I was still weak and at a new low mentally.

Once again my work had almost gotten me killed. First a sniper, then a band of angry Indians, then a 300-pound psychopath, and now a rattlesnake. It was enough to make me question why I did this work in the first place. To make matters worse, I had no sense that I was getting close to solving this case. Lying in bed, watching the sun come up outside, hearing the town come to life outside, lying there alone and with no one to talk to, I felt further from the solution than I had when I agreed to take this case.

Out of nowhere, I missed Svetlana. When I'd landed in the hospital during the last case, she had miraculously shown up. But not this time.

At noon the doctor came by and said the immediate danger from the snakebite had passed, but I would continue to feel weak from the serum sickness for another couple of days. A new nurse checked on me a couple of times, but otherwise for hours upon hours I lay there alone, lightheaded, staring at the ceiling in the empty infirmary. A cook came in at dinnertime with a cut finger, but the rest of the time the place was dead silent. They gave me some chicken broth and toast, but I ate very little of it. I was haunted by questions, chief among them being, "Who planted the rattlesnake?"

It was a useless question to ask because it could have been anybody: Heather, Boone, Kat, Keller, Carries Bison—hell, even Kurt from the livery, since he handled all of the snakes and critters around the resort. Asking the question of who did it only reminded me of how much I didn't know, and it made me angry. Angry that up to now I'd been an utter failure on this case.

The anger I felt was so intense that I caught myself sitting up in bed and strangling the blankets. Whoever was behind all of this was out there right now, laughing, feeling smug and superior to me, thinking there was no way I'd catch him or her. For some reason this bothered me more than all of the injuries I'd sustained. Maybe my pride was hurt.

No, the real problem was, ever since I arrived in Ricochet I'd been distracted by the Old West facade and had temporarily forgotten what I was here to do, which was investigate. Find Sidney's killer and bring him or her to justice. From now on, I wouldn't forget that.

This, I decided, was the turning point. Still sick or not, still weak or not, in the morning I was yanking the IV out of my arm, buckling my gun belt and going out and solving this case.

Tomorrow I would start fresh.

32

DETECTIVE WORK IS ANYTHING BUT SEXY

I awoke before sunup planning to make a clean break from the infirmary, but when you're as sick and injured as I was, getting dressed is an ordeal. Thankfully the nurse had left me clean underclothes. Twenty minutes later, I slipped out and returned to my apartment to fetch my hat. The bureau drawer was open and the snake was gone.

"Don't worry," Kurt said when I got to the livery, "I took that snake miles out of town. We won't be seeing him again." As he saddled up my horse, he added, "And I didn't tell anybody about it either. Your secret's safe with me, marshal." I thanked him and made my way out of town.

My plan was simple: to search Boone's place now that he was away in the hospital, and to return to the reservation construction site before work started and see what clues I could pick up there.

It was dawn by the time I got on the trail. Everything was cloaked in a cool fog, and July or not I was thankful for the heavy frock coat. I turned up my collar and nudged the horse along. I was less steady in the saddle today, and every bounce and jostle on the horse made me queasy and painfully aware of the cuts and bruises on my body. Still, it felt good to be investigating again. I was looking forward to searching Boone's cabin.

There was only one problem.

The place was burned to the ground. Smoke rose from the ashes. I circled around the footprint, hoping to see a clue, but it was no use. The one thing untouched was Boone's axe, which rested in the chopping block.

I rode on, arriving at the reservation construction site a few minutes after seven. The lot was empty, the machines silent. I tied up the horse in the woods and walked over to the trailer. The door was locked and solid metal so I couldn't peek in. I had my lock-picking set, but the door would take half an hour to open. Besides, something told me Bison's men would begin work early, while it was still cool, and I was in no condition to fight anyone right now.

The windows were shut tight. I circled the trailer, searching for fake rocks and magnetic "Hide-a-Key" containers, but came up empty.

Over in the trees, the horse snorted. Birds sang. It promised to be a picture-perfect Montana day. Now if I could just find a clue. My eyes wandered across the lot until they fell upon a Dumpster.

Had it really come to this? Unfortunately, yes.

The reality of detective work is anything but sexy.

I walked over to the container and flipped the lid. White bags of household trash were mixed in with heavy black contractor's bags. I couldn't avoid it: I'd have to get dirty. I removed my frock coat and climbed in. Some of the household trash was covered in maggots. I grabbed the bags that weren't infested, pulled them out with me and sifted through coffee cups, half-eaten sandwiches, empty water bottles and paper. The paper was what I wanted to see.

Tsk, tsk, Mr. Bison. Should've bought a shredder.

I had just started reading when two pickups barreled into the lot and parked in front of the trailer. I crouched behind the Dumpster. Workers piled out and shambled into the construction site. I collected the papers, shook off any clinging maggots and quietly lowered the remaining garbage back into the Dumpster.

I slipped into my frock coat. The horse was across the clearing, ten feet into the woods. I paced across the gravel, just another guy in 1800s garb out for a stroll. The lot echoed with hammering and sawing. Head down, I kept walking.

The second I stepped into the trees, someone shouted, "Hey, it's that guy again! Get back here!"

I rammed the papers in the saddlebag, climbed aboard the horse, and went into a trot, zigzagging through the slender trees. The voices faded as I moved deeper into the woods, but something told me I hadn't seen the last of those guys.

33

THE DAMSEL AND GARY COOPER

Back at the jail, water was still dripping from the ceiling after the fire a few nights ago, so I hid the papers under the one dry mattress in the place and went over to the cafe for so-called breakfast. I was there to talk to Heather, though, not to eat.

Across the dining room, the silver-haired gunslinger eyed me as I walked in and sat near the front window. He didn't seem like a guest. For starters, of the three or four times I'd seen him, he'd always been alone. Never trust a guy with no friends. I thought about going over and confronting him, but before I could decide, the waitress brought my food. Once again my eggs were overcooked.

Heather chatted with diners and refilled coffee. When she saw me, I studied her face for any sign of surprise that I was alive, but she only smiled. This didn't necessarily mean she was innocent, though; she could be a good actress. She walked over and refilled my cup.

"Thank you," I said. "And thanks for the new bed."

"Don't be silly. You're the town marshal. We can't have you sleeping on cinders."

I kicked out a chair. "Take a seat."

The coffeepot was speckled graniteware. She put it on the table and sat down. Her ice blue eyes were operating at full power again this morning.

"What happened between you and Boone?" she asked. "I heard they took him to the hospital."

"I think he's been hanging around Ricochet too long," I said. "He was starting to believe he *was* his character."

I decided not to say anything about Boone's house burning down. I wanted to see if anyone else mentioned it first. Heather looked around the crowded cafe and lowered her voice.

"I probably shouldn't be saying this, but he won't be missed."

"You didn't like him?" I said.

She shrugged. "Boone caused a lot of trouble for Sidney. I'm pretty sure Sidney was going to fire him."

"I heard Sidney died suspiciously," I said. "Could Boone have had something to do with it?"

"Maybe, but the police already did their investigation. What's it to you, anyway?"

"Just doing my job, ma'am. Being the new marshal and all."

"Can I give you some friendly advice?" she said.

"Shoot," I said.

"You're not going to last around here unless you start keeping a lower profile. You may be the town marshal, but to the other actors you're just the new guy. Take it from me, if you're not super popular, this can be a very lonely place."

"I'll take it under advisement," I said. "In the meantime, I'm curious about something."

"What's that?"

"Who decided to fix up my room? You or Mr. Keller?"

"It was a mutual decision—me, Mr. Keller and Mr. McCourt. Your room burned up, you had no place to sleep. We agreed it made sense."

"And you had no other motivation," I said. "Just helping out the new guy, is that it?"

"What other motivation could I possibly have?" She stood up and grabbed the coffeepot, holding it at a precarious angle over my lap. "Now if you'll excuse me, I have guests to attend to."

She whirled around, her skirt whipping across my legs, and stormed off toward the kitchen. The guests stared, but when I looked around, the silver-haired gunslinger was gone. Since I was sitting near the front door, he must have slipped out the back.

As interviews with suspects go, the one with Heather was an abject failure. All I'd done was make her angry and more wary of me. The problem was, since I was supposed to be an actor, I couldn't be my usual self and ask direct questions. For my next interview, I resolved to use more finesse to get the information I needed. I put on my hat, dropped a dollar of play money, and left.

Outside, I stood in the warm sun for a moment watching the actors go through their routines. As I strolled down the sidewalk, a guest couple said hello. I tipped my hat and glanced at the mercantile across the street. Keller was the only major player I hadn't spoken with yet. I went over.

Once again, Sidney had spared no expense on the details. From the restored cigar store Indian outside to the wood and glass cases of period merchandise inside, the mercantile was every inch 1885. Keller, wearing a crisp white apron over his clothes, chatted with two women at the counter. He saw me coming and gestured in my direction.

"Ladies, I'd like you to meet the new town marshal, Dakota Stevens."

They were two of the women I'd seen on the train platform the first day. My smile had a 50/50 effect: the tall one sneered, but the petite one looked at me as though I'd just untied her from a set of railroad tracks. I removed my hat.

"Ladies," I said.

"Mr. Stevens is looking into the death of his predecessor," Keller said. "How's it going, marshal?"

I was distracted by movement in the corner. McCourt was in a phone booth, jabbing a finger as he talked. He stopped moving when he noticed me watching him.

"Marshal?" Keller said.

"Sorry. Not much progress yet. Actually, Mr. Keller, I wanted to talk with you about it."

"Me?"

"Yes," I said. "As owner of the main store in town, you hear most of the scuttlebutt. Do you have a moment?"

"Sure." He nodded at the women. "Ladies, I'll bring your purchases by the hotel." He waited until they left, then turned to me. "How can I help?"

I glanced at the phone booth and thought about the calls from Roman's to Ricochet.

"By the way, is this the only phone in town?" I asked.
"Afraid so."

"Is there some kind of log of who uses it?"

Keller chuckled. "No way. As you can see"—he waved a hand—"it's being used all the time. Hell, sometimes I get a dozen actresses in here waiting to use it."

"There you are!" McCourt charged out of the phone booth. "We need to talk. *Now*."

"I'm busy at the moment," I said.

"Your behavior has been unacceptable."

I put my hat back on. "We've already had this conversation, McCourt."

"Now you listen—"

"I'll be in my office in a little while," I said. "If you have a grievance, we can discuss it there. In the meantime, Mr. Keller and I were speaking—alone. Good day, sir."

McCourt's face turned as red as Madison Shaw's backside. I couldn't tell if it was due to embarrassment or apoplexy, and didn't care. Wisely he backed away and walked out the door.

"He always this uptight?" I asked.

Keller came around the counter and leaned against a case of pistols.

"Pretty much. But lately he's gotten worse."

"Worse how?"

"Like you said—uptight. Used to do his job, but never got carried away. Then Sidney died and he became a real stickler. Started docking the actors' pay if he caught 'em with contraband."

"Contraband?" I said.

"Yeah, any modern stuff. Conveniences. Heck, we all want to make this real for the guests, but the actors are only human, and the girls, well, they want to look pretty, and you can't do that with 1885 stuff. Couple of 'em quit the other day."

"Was he like this when Sidney was around?"

"Beginning of the season, 'bout the middle of May, he and Sidney had some words," Keller said. "McCourt was searching guests' bags. Still is, I think. Anyway, it got around and attendance dropped off. But stuff like that was the exception. Mostly Sidney gave him a free hand. Ask me, William's trouble is of the romantic variety, if you know what I mean."

"One of the actresses?" I nodded at a couple of them passing on Main Street.

"Don't think so. Hear him on the phone a lot with somebody. Don't know if the person is male or female, but I do know that he talks low, like he's embarrassed or something. Want my opinion, the man's just pent up."

"It would explain a lot."

I went over to the glass case and leaned on it like Keller. During a course at the FBI Academy on questioning witnesses, the instructor had emphasized the importance of mirroring their body language. If you weren't overt about it, the witness often relaxed and opened up to you.

"Listen," I said. "For real for a second—not acting—I need to know what I'm getting into here. Given what happened to my predecessor, should I be concerned for my own life?"

"The police said it was suicide."

"Let's pretend they got it wrong."

"All right." Keller stroked his cheek. "What are you asking? Do I think any of the actors killed Sid?"

"Yes."

"Can't imagine it." Keller walked over to a row of candy jars, got a couple licorice twists and handed me one. "Sidney was good to us. Take me, for instance. Not a lick of acting experience."

"What did you do before this?" I asked.

"Owned a lumber company in Missoula, supplied a lot of the stuff used to build this place. Once she was built, Sidney comes up to me, asks me to do this. I figure, what the hell, why not?

"We were a little family here," he continued. "I mean, sure we bickered, but when it came right down to it, we all liked the work, and everybody felt pretty fortunate to be making a living doing this stuff."

"Is it a decent living?"

"Sure, Sid paid us well," Keller said. "Health insurance, the whole nine yards. I just can't see any of the actors biting the hand that fed them."

"What about an outsider?"

Keller tore off a piece of licorice with his teeth. He wagged the remainder in his hand.

"Only time I seen Sidney lose his temper was when this sawed-off corporate type showed up one weekend and kept pestering him to sell the place. Sid got fed up and had him tossed him out."

This sounded like Shaw.

"When did this happen?" I asked.

"Oh, let's see…end of last season. Would've been early September sometime."

"Anybody get the guy's name?"

Keller pointed his licorice stick at me. "You know, for a guy that just about broke Boone in half, you're one nervous Nellie."

As I bit into my licorice, the taste for some reason made me visualize black ink, which led in strange, rapid succession to signatures and hotel registers. I'd check for Shaw's name later.

"I suppose you're right," I said. "Seems foolish to worry about it." I pointed at the phone booth where McCourt had been a moment before. "What about him? Could he be involved in Sidney's death?"

"Not a chance," Keller said. "Ricochet is McCourt's life. He'd have nothing if it weren't for this place, and with Sid gone the future of the place is uncertain. No, the only thing McCourt is guilty of is being a historically accurate pain in the neck."

"One more thing," I said. "What do you think of Kat Styles?"

"As an actress?"

"In any way."

"A handful." He lowered his voice. "Always thought she was a bit uneven myself. Fella that takes up with her oughta sleep with one eye open."

"Thanks," I said.

"Drop by anytime."

We shook hands. I glanced around the store.

"Say, you wouldn't have a back door, would you?"

Keller grinned. "Now you're learning. Most of the time, you see McCourt around, best to just duck out. Follow me."

34

CURIOUSER AND CURIOUSER

All three hotels in town—the Mountain View, the Ricochet Manor and the Bonanza—had rear entrances, so I was able to examine their guest registers without being hassled by McCourt. I was looking for two things: evidence of Shaw's presence in September, and the names of people who checked in or out around Sidney's death.

Eighty-six people checked in or out, but none of the names meant anything to me. They were probably useless anyway. If the killer was a guest, he would have used an alias. However, on the question of Shaw, the Bonanza's register showed an "R. Shaw" checking in September 7 and leaving the next day. I didn't know what Shaw's signature looked like, so it was impossible to verify, but the timing of the entry corroborated Keller's statement.

In the Bonanza hotel restaurant, I had "lunch"—a charred baked potato and a steak that ate like the prototype for a new bulletproof material. Somehow I forced myself to eat it and began counting the hours until Svetlana got here. Only one day left.

In the meantime, I needed to press on with the case, and for starters I wanted to see the gallows again. My gut told me I had missed something there. I retrieved my horse and headed out of town. From the sidewalk in the front of the laundry, Kat waved a handkerchief.

"Marshal! *Yoo-hoo, mar-shal!*"

I touched my hat brim and kept riding. The woman might have kissed like Aphrodite, but my detecting mojo was coming back, and I didn't want to do anything—or talk with anyone—that would interfere with that.

The gallows site appeared the same. As for the gallows itself, it was simply constructed of two heavy square posts joined at a right angle with a diagonal cross-brace. In short, it was built for show, not actual hangings. I dismounted, circled the gallows and tried to picture Sidney's murder.

Either the killer had lured Sidney here or he had killed him elsewhere and brought the body out on horseback. The gallows was far enough from town that it was unlikely Sidney or the killer had walked. This meant that unless they came on one horse—highly doubtful—at least two horses were here. The crossbeam was ten feet off the ground, and there were no pulleys or other mechanical aids. Just a cleat for tying off the rope. Even if the killer had used one of the horses to hoist up the dead body, there were other problems, such as securing the rope, controlling the other horse and keeping lookout. And that's when it hit me:

This murder was a two-person job.

For a moment I just stood there, shaking my head, pleased with my conclusion yet annoyed with myself for not coming to it sooner. From the beginning I had assumed Sidney's murder was the work of one person. This new theory fit certain facts, like the simultaneous absence of Heather and Boone on the night Sidney was killed. Heck, for all I knew, Heather might be behind Boone's attack on me at the 24 Karat. She might also be behind the rattlesnake. Heather and Boone could be working together, with Heather the brains, Boone the brawn.

I fetched the canteen from the saddlebag and drank some water. Hypothesizing that Heather and Boone were working together might have answered some questions, but it raised others. Like, was there a connection between Heather and Boone in the West and Roman in the East? And, was it true that Heather had another boyfriend in Yellowstone? Still, despite these loose ends, at the moment the Heather-Boone hypothesis was the most straightforward one, and as Occam's Razor tells us, the simplest explanation is often the right one.

I took off my hat and poured some water over my scalp. To the west, bruised and towering clouds lumbered over the mountains. Not having rain gear, I needed to get back soon. I was starting to remount when a flash of light stabbed me in the eyes. The reflection came from a flinty ridge half a mile away.

Another sniper.

There was no cover and the trees were too far away. I wheeled the horse in front of me, ducked and waited for the shot.

Nothing happened.

After a minute, I felt myself being watched. Thankfully Sidney knew there would be times when he needed at least one gun that fired real bullets. I reached over the saddle and yanked the Winchester .45 lever-action rifle from its holster. The chances of hitting this person were laughable, and while I didn't want to kill anybody, I did want to put a scare into him. I jacked a round into the chamber and took aim to the side of him. Just before I fired, he ran out of sight over the ridge line. I fired two more shots to make sure he got the message, then mounted the horse and went after him.

After switch-backing through the pines and yanking the horse along on foot when it became too steep to ride, half an hour later I finally reached the top. The summit was bare rock with some gnarly sagebrush eking out an existence in the cracks. On the backside of the ridge, a path snaked down the slope, and when it reached a meadow at the bottom, there were tracks in the grass.

Tire tracks. From a four-wheeler.

Far off, the faint buzz of an engine puckered the air. The horse clomped a hoof, as if eager to continue. I snapped the reins.

The tracks were easy to follow across the meadow, but once we forded a creek, the terrain turned to dry scrubland, and the treads barely showed in the hard-packed dirt. Then, as though to point out the futility of this chase, the clouds opened up. I turned around.

Approaching the creek bank again, I noticed something shiny in the thick grass. I jumped down. It was a rock hammer. Brand new, not a speck of rust on it.

Rain sluiced off my hat brim. I tucked the hammer into the saddlebag and remounted.

"Curiouser and curiouser," I said.

The horse snorted and began to move.

35

BLANK LETTERHEAD

On the way back I took a wrong turn and ended up in the ghost town of Loot. By now it was a steady downpour, and without any rain gear I was drenched. The horse and I plodded down what had once been the main drag. Half-dead trees lined the street in front of once-proud buildings that were now bleached shanties. Shards of glass clung in the window frames, and the spaces behind them were dark and silent. Only one building looked remotely habitable, and that was the brick Hotel Meade.

Tomorrow Svetlana would join me, and with any luck, she'd spot all the clues I had failed to recognize. Then, the following night, we'd be back in New York, counting our money.

Sadly it never happened that way.

If this were any other case, at this point I'd be able to focus my energies on a single suspect. This time, however, I wasn't so lucky. Over the years, most of my cases had followed a linear pattern—A event points to B suspect points to C event and so on—but this time I had a lot of pieces, with no idea how they connected, if they connected at all. The best I could do was run down each line of inquiry and see where it led. Hopefully I'd discover a connection soon.

Back in Ricochet, I left the horse at the livery with Kurt, asking him to add extra oats to the feed, and headed to the Mountain View in the cold and driving rain. The menu described my meal as "Roast pork loin *au jus*, creamed carrots, mashed potatoes and gravy," but in no way did it resemble food. I returned to the office still hungry, closed the curtains and locked the door behind me.

The room was dank. I built a fire in the potbelly stove and, as the place warmed up, fetched the papers from under the mattress. Half of them were soiled and impossible to read. I threw those in the fire, as well as the tribal council correspondence and office supply packing lists.

However, there were a couple of interesting items, like brochures for Indian casinos, and a letter from the Montana State Gaming Board wishing the reservation well with their project. One thing was clear: Carries Bison was building a casino. I wished there were bank statements or even deposit slips, but the only financial documents were invoices for building materials. Scrawled on each one was "PAID, R.C." and a date. I assumed "R.C." were the bookkeeper's initials until I found several balled-up sheets of letterhead for an R.C. Development Corp. Aside from the address, the pages were blank. Why would Carries Bison have another company's blank letterhead? I thought about this as the rain drummed on the wooden sidewalk outside.

I pitched everything into the fire except the Gaming Board letter and one sheet of the letterhead. These I rolled up and slid down the barrel of a shotgun on the gun rack.

There were footsteps outside. The front doorknob rattled. Someone knocked on the door. Instinct told me it was either Kat or McCourt. Tired and sore from the lingering effects of the serum sickness, not to mention from riding all day, I didn't have the energy or patience for either one of them right now. I stepped into the shadow of the jail vestibule and waited until I heard the footsteps walk away. Then I shut off the lamps, put on my coat and hat, and went out, locking the door behind me.

I was about to go upstairs when, through the rain, I saw the silver-haired gunslinger standing on the covered porch across the street. He smoked a pipe, and light from the cafe silhouetted him. He appeared to be watching the jail. I threw open my frock coat to have ready access to the Peacemaker, and crossed the street. Silver-hair didn't move. Just stood there smoking. Rain ran off the roof and splashed into a watering trough between us. I had to speak up to be heard above the rain noises.

"Did you just come looking for me at the jail?"

He puffed on the pipe. "Nope."

"Who are you? Why are you here?"

"I'm going to let you figure that out yourself." He turned and paused at the cafe door. "Marshal Stevens."

36

The Cavalry

Despite my encounter with the mysterious silver-haired gunslinger, I awoke the next morning feeling hopeful, and not just because I had several new clues to follow. Svetlana arrived this afternoon. Picturing her face, I took a deep breath of cool, tangy air from the window, got up, got dressed and left.

The rain had stopped overnight, leaving a soupy mess on Main Street. Perfect conditions for following new tire tracks. This morning I would follow up on that four-wheeler.

I rode straight to the ridge top and down the other side, forded the now-swollen creek and headed in the direction the four-wheeler had gone yesterday. Today the hard-packed dirt was sour mud, and the horse's hooves made sucking noises as we crossed the open ground.

By mid-morning I found the four-wheeler tracks. They were fresh. I followed them into the resort, but when the tracks cut into the woods on the loamy ground, they became fainter until I lost them entirely. I turned around and followed in the other direction. This time the tracks led to the construction site on the reservation. I watched the clearing on horseback from the tree line.

There was movement inside the trailer. A few pickups sat parked in front, but no four-wheeler. My stomach growled. Men drank coffee, moved lumber. Wheelbarrows of bricks went by, reminding me of the wheelbarrow Louis had used back on Long Island and making me wonder what he'd been carrying in his that was so heavy. My stomach growled again. Cement trucks pulled in. Carries Bison supervised the pouring.

An exciting morning to be sure.

Not interested in watching cement dry, I headed back to Ricochet, pondering one question over and over as I rolled in the saddle: Why was some guy gallivanting around the resort on a four-wheeler with a rock hammer?

Tying up the horse at the jail, I noticed two papers tacked to the office door. The first was a handbill advertising a "Grand Tour" of the north side of the resort. The tour was tomorrow and all guests were invited. This was a problem because I had planned to check out the marked sites in that area using the GPS Svetlana was bringing. I'd need a distraction.

The second paper was a notice about a special meeting with Irving down at the church. I checked my pocket watch. It was going on right now. This was a perfect opportunity to search the actors' quarters.

Keller's apartment was above the mercantile. The door was locked, but it was an old-fashioned lock and I'd brought a skeleton key. It was a suite. I started in the living area, and when I finished the only thing I could say he was guilty of was anal-retentiveness. Moving on to the bedroom, I found Keller's diary. No one kept a diary anymore, and I felt like a degenerate for reading it.

He loathed Kat and McCourt, and he thought Heather was an angel, but there was nothing incriminating in the diary. I also learned that Keller was a widower, and the entries about his late wife were deeply personal. I put the diary back and left the apartment.

In Kat's room above the saloon, I didn't find any garrotes or other damning evidence, but I did find a drawer full of Victoria's Secret lingerie and other anachronistic contraband, including an iPod. I left all of it alone and moved on.

Heather's place, above the cafe, was next. Like Keller, she too had a suite. Around the apartment were several photos of her and Sidney, as well as her and a tall young man. Could this be the Yellowstone boyfriend Kat mentioned? According to a daily planner on her desk that showed her schedules and story lines, she had this weekend off.

Footsteps echoed on the stairs outside. I looked for an escape route. The front windows opened onto Main Street, but the one in her bedroom faced the alley. I ran to it, heaved it open and climbed out on the overhang. The door inside opened just as I closed the window. I lowered myself down, brushed myself off and walked across the street to my apartment.

I had a few hours to kill until Svetlana got here, and I was exhausted, so I lay down for a nap. I fell asleep in record time.

I was awakened by the sound of a stagecoach rattling up the street. I got up heavily and went to the window. The sun was setting. The stagecoach pulled up in front of the Bonanza, and a slim man in gunslinger's garb stepped out. Correction—Svetlana stepped out. The costume might have flattened her curves, but it couldn't hide the femininity in her walk. To complete the costume, she wore a Vaquero-style hat with a round, flat brim, and her hair in a French braid. I smiled at how natural she looked in the outfit.

True to form, my associate had chosen the most opulent of the three hotels for her lodgings. The bellboy swaggered up to her suitcases, but when he went to pick them up, his arms nearly came out of their sockets. Good old Svetlana. They went into the hotel.

I freshened up, waited ten minutes, then used the hotel service entrance. The front desk and lobby were empty. I spun the register toward myself, and Svetlana's precise handwriting jumped off the page. She had registered as "Ivana Robalot," which gave me a great idea. I went upstairs to room 302 and knocked.

"Enter," Svetlana said.

I took a breath and went in. She sat at the open window with her legs crossed, gazing at the gathering dusk on Main Street. Lamps were lit around the room. Her hat hung from one of the bedposts. I shut the door.

"*Ivana Robalot?*" I said.

She stood and walked over. "You look tired, Dakota."

"Thanks for noticing."

"And you look like you slept in your clothes."

"Because I did," I said.

"And..." She pinched her nose.

"Yeah, sorry about that."

Svetlana's room wasn't a suite, but compared with my spartan digs over yonder, it was Versailles. I stretched out on a sofa.

"How's our client?" I asked.

"A little better. Her niece is off playing someplace, but Vivian has friends staying over."

"And Louis?"

"The Coast Guard stopped searching yesterday." She unlatched her suitcase. "It appears Louis sailed away."

"And leave all that personal stuff behind?" I said. "I don't buy it. Something is rotten in Denmark."

"Tell me what has happened."

I tried to formulate a logical account of recent events, but I was too exhausted. Chronological order was over-rated anyway.

"Look, I'm just going to ramble and we can make sense of it tomorrow."

"I am used to it," she said.

In the best order I could muster, I told her about everything that had happened and everything I had learned since I arrived. I omitted the snakebite for some reason, and concluded with how it seemed Heather had a boyfriend in Yellowstone.

"Miss Styles says she goes down there on the week-ends," I said. "We need to follow her."

"Come." She beckoned me with a finger.

I went to her open suitcase on the bed. All of the things I'd asked her to get, including the GPS, were there. Then she snapped away a sheet, revealing a pile of foodstuffs that included hard salami, provolone and Italian bread from our favorite *salumeria* on Mulberry Street, and two bottles of sparkling apple cider.

"Didn't McCourt say something?" I said. "I hope he doesn't know who you are."

"He does not. I'm here as a guest, remember? And yes, he tried to stop me. He wanted to 'look over' my suitcases."

I grinned. "And…?"

"I ignored him," she said. "A horse never acknowledges a dog."

"You have no idea how great this is." I picked up the Italian bread and inhaled. "The food here is *so* bad."

Svetlana pulled a folding knife from her pocket and opened it.

"Sit, I make you a sandwich."

I went to a table by the window. A minute later Svetlana brought over some sandwiches, a bottle of cider and two plastic cups. We ate and drank in silence until the light outside was gone. She poured more cider for us.

"So, will you show me around your territory tomorrow, marshal?"

"Sure will, little lady. You loaded the maps on the GPS?"

She nodded.

"Okay, Miss Robalot, listen up," I said. "Tomorrow morning, when the bank opens, you're going to rob it."

"Am I? And what time does it open?"

"Nine."

She pursed her lips. "That early?"

"That early. See Kurt down at the livery first. He'll have a horse ready for you. After the robbery, I'll send a posse on a wild goose-chase." I handed her a resort map and pointed at the southern road out of town. "Go this way, then loop around and I'll meet you at the gallows."

"And why are we doing this?" she asked.

"To create a diversion. There's supposed to be a tour around the sites we need to check out. I want them well out of the way."

She yawned and nodded. This was my cue to leave. I got up and opened the door.

"Sweet dreams, Miss Robalot."

"Good night, Marshal."

37

IVANA ROBALOT

I headed back to my room, and as I crossed the street, I saw that the windows were lit upstairs, which meant Kat was in there. As great a kisser as she was, I couldn't afford to get distracted. Not now, and not with Svetlana staying right across the street. No, if I wanted to sleep tonight, I'd have to improvise.

Quietly I snatched a blanket and pillow from the jail, then went to the livery and bedded down in an empty stall. Sometime in the night, I heard the creak of the barn door, followed by a loud clang. A few hours later, I could have sworn I heard the same two sounds. I was awakened again at first light when Kurt came in. It was cold, and I staggered out of the stall wrapped in the blanket. Kurt poured me a cup of coffee from a big ceramic pot.

"Hope you like it black," he said.

"I do, thanks."

He handed me the cup. "Kicked out of bed last night?"

"Something like that."

As he started to muck stalls, I tossed the blanket aside, grabbed an extra shovel and helped him. I was less weak today but still not a hundred percent, and my snakebitten arm was sore as I shoveled.

"You know"—Kurt pitched a shovelful into the wagon—"seven years I been here, and you and Sidney are the only ones to do this with me."

I leaned on my shovel, took a sip of coffee. "I kind of enjoy it."

"You *like* shoveling horse crap?"

"There's a clear result," I said. "Do it, get a nice, clean stall. *That's* what I like."

He rolled his eyes to heaven. "Like my ma used to say: 'Takes all kinds.'"

We worked for a minute without speaking. As we moved to the next stall, I refilled my cup.

"Hey, Kurt. You didn't happen to come in here last night, did you?"

"Nope. Why?"

I told him about the noises. He shrugged.

"Maybe the place is haunted."

"Maybe," I said. "Hey, thanks for taking care of that snake for me."

"No problem. Like to say 'my pleasure' but there was nothing pleasant about it."

When we finished, I saddled up my horse while Kurt prepared a regal white mare for Svetlana. I choked down a leaden pancake at the Mountain View, and moseyed over to my office.

The place was ransacked. The desk drawers were torn out and smashed, their contents scattered on the floor. The gun rack was splintered, lanterns shattered, mattresses gutted. Even the pillows were ripped open. Somebody had been searching desperately for something.

I grabbed the shotgun where I'd hidden the papers and slid them out. Nobody knew I had them, so they must have been after something else. Something hidden in the jail earlier? Maybe something incriminating, like a garrote?

Annoyed, I grabbed a broom and started to sweep up the place. When I was almost finished, I found a tiny strip of blue calico snagged in one of the floorboards. It had the same pattern as Heather's dress. I remembered that Heather had been in here on my first day, to take me to the story meeting. The fabric may have been here since then and I hadn't noticed it. Then, sweeping under the desk, my broom hit something else: Kat's peacock feather fan. This, too, could be a coincidence. It seemed in Kat's character to come in here looking for me and throw her fan on the floor in disgust.

Had both of them broken in here last night, just one of them, or neither?

I put the broom away and went out on the porch. Down the street, half a dozen guests and actors formed a queue outside the bank. Kat was one of them. I went back inside, grabbed the fan and strolled over. She was chatting in character with a fellow actress.

"Miss Styles," I said. "I believe this is yours."

I gave her the fan. Rather than any guilt, her face showed nothing but scorn. The problem was—and this had been my problem from the moment I arrived—I couldn't tell if the actors were being truthful or if they were acting.

As the bank door opened and we filed in, Kat leaned into my shoulder and whispered, "I waited for you till three, you jerk." Then, just when I thought the situation couldn't get any more uncomfortable, McCourt and Irving sauntered in.

"Marshal Stevens," McCourt said. "I've been looking for you."

"I was waylaid."

"Well, at least somebody was," Kat said.

"Waylaid?" Irving said.

"Yeah, outside of town," I said. "Brigands. Or were they highwaymen? I can never tell."

Kat flapped her fan. "They club you at all?"

"No," I said.

"Too bad."

A guest couple stepped away from the teller, the wife fanning her husband with a stack of play money. They chuckled. At the door they stopped short and backed up. Svetlana walked in with her revolver pointed at the man. A red bandana masked her face. She swept her gun across the room.

"Everybody against the wall! Up with your hands! Now!"

"Excuse me, miss," I said, "but I believe you meant to say, '*Stick 'em up.*'"

She ignored me and tossed an empty feed sack at the teller.

"Fill this," she said.

Irving turned to McCourt. "This wasn't discussed at the meeting."

"I don't—"

"Silence!"

Svetlana aimed at the ceiling and fired. In the tight quarters, it might as well have been dynamite. Kat dug her nails into my snakebitten arm. A new word would have to be invented to describe the pain I felt.

While the teller filled the sack, Svetlana went along the row of customers, dropping our guns on the floor. After dropping mine, she paused and scraped my cheek with her gun barrel.

"You could use a shave, marshal."

"I don't know who you are, lady," I said, "but you won't get away with this."

"Really?"

Svetlana snapped her fingers at the teller and the feed sack, now full, breezed past my head. She caught it in her free hand.

"I beg to differ. Now, be a good boy and make everybody count to a thousand with you."

"He can't count that high, sweetie," Kat said.

Svetlana shoved Kat against the wall. "And you're sure you can, *sweetie*? Now count!"

With our backs to the door, we got to 17 before I heard her riding away. I grabbed my guns and ran outside. A dust trail led south. The guests walked out grinning, followed by Kat, Irving and McCourt, who weren't.

"McCourt!" Kat said. "Who the hell was that, and why don't *I* have that part?"

"I'm as much in the dark as you," McCourt said.

I climbed aboard my horse. "She's heading south. I'll need a posse. Get everyone you can and comb the area south of town. I'll be hot on her trail."

"Okay," McCourt said, "we'll catch up with you."

I snapped the reins and galloped after her.

38

WRONG PLACE, WRONG TIME

I took the long way around, and when I reached the gallows Svetlana was sitting tall in her saddle, reading the GPS. As I pulled up alongside her, she drew her pistol, spun it on her finger and re-holstered it.

"Cute," I said. "Been practicing that for me?"

She batted her eyes. I poured some water on a handkerchief and dabbed my neck. The heat was going to be relentless today.

"So," she said. "Did the posse buy our little ruse?"

"Are you kidding? They're halfway to Idaho by now. Still have the money?"

She patted her saddlebag. "If only it were real."

"Well, darlin', help me solve this case so we can collect our re-ward. Now, lemme have a looksee at that there GPS."

"No more cowboy talk," she said. "You are terrible at it."

Svetlana wheeled her horse around until our stirrups touched. She held out the GPS and pointed at the screen.

"After I loaded the maps, I added the marks from Shaw's map."

She pressed a button. The map scrolled until a group of little triangles with numbers on them appeared.

"Now, here is the interesting part," she said. "The marks are not around Ricochet. They are around the ghost town of Loot."

"What?" I said. "You mean I've been looking in the wrong place?"

"It is not your fault. We only had sections of a map—a map that got waterlogged, I might add—and some blurry photos to go by. You had no way of knowing the sites weren't in Ricochet."

"And you figured this out by?"

"Comparing the elevations," she said. "Once I downloaded the GPS maps, I compared the elevations to the ones on Shaw's map. The contours of both places are remarkably similar, but the hills around Loot were an exact match. These are the spots that had dates on them." She highlighted several triangles on the GPS and handed it to me.

"Which one had the earliest date?" I asked.

"Hmm, perhaps number *one*?"

"Wiseass. All right, let's get started."

We rode for a couple of miles, during which I marveled at Svetlana's perfect riding form and posture in the saddle.

"I didn't know you could ride," I said.

"When I was a little girl in the Ukraine, my grandfather had horses."

"But that was what, ten years ago?" I said jokingly.

Her hat shaded her face. She looked at me with hooded eyes.

"And I took a lesson before I came out here," she said.

"I should have known." I shook my head.

The first location was on a hillside north of Loot. According to the GPS, we were right on top of it, whatever *it* was, and after skirting the woods for half an hour, looking for a way in, we got down and tied off the horses.

"We'll have to go in on foot." I consulted the GPS a final time and put it away. "Make sure you keep talking to me."

"You don't want us to get separated," she said. "How sweet."

"No, I don't want us getting mauled by a grizzly. Most attacks occur when hikers surprise them."

She put her hands on her hips. "I did not sign on for grizzlies. If we see one—"

"Yeah, yeah, I know—you quit. Come on."

The enmeshed tree limbs and underbrush were so thick, I couldn't see more than ten feet in any direction. If we were going to step on a sleeping bear, this was the place. I called out through the trees.

"See anything?"

"You mean besides this giant red 'X' on the ground?"

"What?"

"I see trees," she said. "Lots of trees. What are we looking for anyway?"

"I'll know it when I see it."

"Sayeth the great detective."

I thought back to my plane trip out here, when that builder remarked that the circles on Shaw's map could be locations for perc or soil tests. I couldn't imagine anyone wanting to build something out here. Too isolated. Better for hiding something.

We came together in a clearing filled with pine stumps. Something crunched under my foot. I picked it up. It was the packaging from a pair of D-cell batteries.

"Someone's been here." I handed the plastic to Svetlana. "Last I checked, Duracells weren't a native species."

"We are never going to find anything this way," she said. "We should split up."

"All right, but don't get out of earshot," I said.

"Don't worry, I won't abandon you."

Beyond the tree stumps, the hill dropped off sharply. Cowboy boots with spurs aren't designed for hiking, and my feet kept sliding out from underneath me.

I hadn't gone a hundred feet when a crack echoed through the woods. Svetlana shouted, a note of panic in her voice I'd never heard before.

"Dakota, I'm falling!"

I scrabbled up the hill and spun around in circles looking for her.

"Where are you?"

"Here! Hurry!"

Shielding my face with my arms, I smashed through a clump of thorns and winced as they scratched my wrists.

"Here, Dakota!"

Only her head and shoulders were visible above a pile of pine boughs and loose brush. I was frozen, trying to figure out what to do, when there was another snap.

She was sucked under.

39

QUITE CLEVER SOMETIMES

I could just make out one of her hands in the brush pile. The trap was twenty feet away, and too wide for me to reach her. No sticks handy. There was rope back on the horse, but it would take too long. The entire pile of pine boughs and brush quaked as she slipped another inch. Looking around frantically, I saw a small aspen as far away from her as it was tall.

It had to work.

"Hold on," I said. "Don't even *breathe*."

I threw off my coat and hat and shimmied up the slender tree. As I got higher, it bowed toward the ground and I shimmied along sideways. I kept going until I hung directly above Svetlana. I could see her face through the branches. She was scared.

"Look at me, Svetlana," I said.

I shimmied to the end, until I hovered just above the trap. Carefully, I stretched out my arm, snaked it through the brush, and grabbed her wrist—tight enough to cut off the circulation.

"I've got you," I said. "And I won't let go."

She grabbed my wrist back. "I hope you're as strong as you think you are."

Locking my knee and elbow around the tree, I pulled with all my strength. The tendons in my arm shrieked. My teeth clenched until I thought they would break. But I got her head to the surface. I shimmied backwards on the tree, rested for a moment and pulled again. This time she didn't move.

"I think you're caught on something," I said. "Very gently, move your legs. Make sure your boots are free."

"Okay." She wriggled. "There."

I was sweating and could feel a drop trickling down my wrist, toward our joined hands. I pulled again and some buttons on my vest broke from the strain. Now her torso was out, but a mutiny had begun in my outstretched arm with a painful quivering in the shoulder. I ignored the pain and continued the pattern: pull, shimmy, rest, pull.

Pull. Shimmy. Rest. Pull.

Her legs were out now, but I couldn't tell if we were clear of the trap, so I repeated the pattern one last time.

And then my arm started to give out.

Still holding her, I let go of the tree and we fell into a bed of moss and leaves. I landed on top of her. Panting and trembling, we just stared into each other's eyes as the adrenaline cleared out of our heads. It was a joy to feel her breathing beneath me. She felt softer, more fragile, than I had imagined. Her hat was gone and her normally pristine hair was askew, but even so, this was the closest I'd ever been to this woman and I was overcome. Beautiful was faint praise for her. Our lips hovered inches apart. I wanted to kiss her, and I think she wanted to kiss me, but there are moments, and I ruined this one by speaking.

"You okay?"

"Define okay," she said. "I almost fell into a bear trap."

"Almost." I brushed some pine needles off her face.

"Dakota?"

"Yeah?" I said.

"No offense, but…" She pinched her nose.

"Sorry."

I got up, walked back to the horse, and returned with a coil of rope. Tying one end to a tree and a bowline around my waist, I wormed over to where she had fallen through. It was an eight-foot gap between two rock formations—deep and well hidden. Far below, light leaked in from someplace.

This was no bear trap. It was meant to conceal something.

I retrieved Svetlana's hat, brought it back over to her and untied the rope from myself.

"Let's get a flashlight," I said.

She produced a Mini Maglite from her pocket and shone it in my face.

"How do you always…?" I said. "Never mind."

Noting our location on the GPS, I put my coat and hat back on and led us down the hill. A clump of dead pines leaned against a notch in the rocks. I wrenched one away to create an opening. Svetlana tossed me the flashlight.

"Age before beauty," she said.

I shone the light into the darkness. The ground looked solid, and there didn't seem to be any sleeping grizzlies. We crept inside. Here, the gap between the rock formations expanded to about twelve feet, forming more of a cave. About fifty feet up, sunlight filtered through the enmeshed branches, creating a net pattern on the stony floor. Off to the side was a heap of rocks and heavy timbers. We continued inside.

Finally the gap came to a dead end. Crisscrossed planks were nailed across an opening. I shone the beam around the edges.

"I'll be damned."

Svetlana stepped up beside me. "What is it, a tunnel?"

"A mine shaft," I said. "Probably one of the gold mines from the days of Loot. And by the looks of it, somebody's been in here recently." I pointed the flashlight as I talked. "See that pile of rocks? Back in the day, when a vein dried up, they would seal off the opening so folks couldn't go in and get hurt. Now take a look back over here." I swung the flashlight beam around. "New boards, and notice the nails. No rust. They're also new."

"I must admit," she said, "you are quite clever sometimes."

And then I figured it out: the marks on Shaw's map weren't marks for soil or perc tests; they were the locations of mine shafts. And the person who had reopened this shaft and nailed it shut again? My friend on the four-wheeler.

"It's gold, Svetlana," I said. "The mines, that's what Shaw was interested in. Not the Western theme park crap."

"It makes sense," she said. "He kept saying there was a lot more to the resort. But, Shaw was killed."

"That's right. By a sniper hired by Roman, which means—"

"—that Roman probably knew about the gold as well."

"Exactly," I said. "And those calls from his house suggest he was working with someone out here. My guess is Heather. Which reminds me, she's got the weekend off. We've got to follow her and see if Kat's story about a second boyfriend in Yellowstone is true."

"Oh, it's *Kat* now?" Svetlana said. "Anyway, Gardiner is near Yellowstone, so we should check out Patrick Hollis while we're there."

"Good idea."

A branch fell from the trap above and clattered on the rock pile.

"I think we should go," I said.

"I agree."

40

A Bouquet Slightly
Smaller than a Sequoia

Changed into our 21ˢᵗ century clothes, smelling re-freshingly of shampoo and toothpaste, Svetlana and I followed Heather out of the resort. It was a relief to escape 1885 and to be shaved again. While I navigated the narrow switchbacks, keeping one eye on Heather's pickup and the other on the road so I wouldn't drive off a cliff, Svetlana studied Shaw's map and made notations of the mines we had checked out so far.

"Three recently boarded-up mines," she said. "It could be a coincidence."

"I don't think so. I think we've got a pattern on our hands." I put the SUV into 4-wheel drive as we went into a washed-out turn. "But following Heather is more important right now. You spoke to Walt?"

"Yes." She put the map away. "He is sending back our horses and the stolen play money, but if asked, he has no idea where we are."

"And what did it take to persuade him?" I asked.

"One hundred dollars," she said. "And a smile—from *moi*."

"Half the New York rate. Nice."

At the main highway, U.S. Route 93, our quarry made an unexpected left turn.

"She's heading toward Missoula," I said.

"Perhaps the boyfriend is there," Svetlana said. "Or there may not even be a boyfriend. Women are jealous, gossiping creatures, Dakota. Your little Kat could be spreading lies."

"Maybe."

Svetlana took out her iPhone and tried to make a call. A minute later she shoved it back in her handbag with a huff.

"Who were you calling?" I asked.

"I was trying to check messages, but there is no service around here. I will try when we get closer to civilization."

"Do I detect a hint of city girl snobbishness?" I said.

"Yes."

We snaked through a mountain pass where they were widening the road. The dislodged boulders loomed as big as houses. I stayed two cars behind Heather's through the construction zone, and outside of Missoula she merged onto I-90, taking the exit for Missoula University Hospital and stopping at a florist. I parked in a convenience store lot next door with the SUV facing the road and the engine idling. We watched the florist and waited for Heather to reappear.

"I feel naked out of my coat and hat," I said.

"You do look handsome in them," Svetlana said.

"Maybe I should wear them back in New York. Start a new *Midnight Cowboy* thing."

"Yes, an excellent idea." She rolled her eyes. Digging into her handbag, she pulled out a pair of small walkie-talkies. "As you requested."

"Thanks." I put one in my pocket. "I should call Briggs now."

I checked my phone for service and dialed his number. He picked up on the second ring.

"Stevens? What's up?"

"Just thought I'd let you know," I said, "we're off the resort and following Heather. Let me ask you, do you know anyone at the BLM office in Missoula?"

"Bureau of Land Management? Sure, why?"

"I need some information about the mines on the resort, but tomorrow's Saturday and they'll be closed. Could you get them to open up in the afternoon for us?"

"Shouldn't be a problem. I'll let you know if it is," he said. "Call me back tomorrow and tell me what you find."

"Assuming we find anything."

"Yeah," he said. "Bye."

Heather emerged from the florist with a bouquet slightly smaller than a sequoia. We followed her down Broadway to the hospital, and I parked two rows over from her as she walked inside.

"I'll go," I said. "Probably here to see Boone. Switch on your walkie-talkie and call me if she comes out."

I switched on mine and ran inside. Heather was already past the nurse's station, strolling down the hall with the monster bouquet. She wore a pair of tight white jeans that did her credit. I waited until the duty nurse was facing away from me and hurried after Heather. She ended up in a room in the cancer center wing.

The cancer center? What was going on? Did Boone have cancer?

I stood outside the room, trying to look enthralled with a bulletin board of announcements as I strained to hear what was happening inside. A woman's voice was barely audible above the hospital din.

"It's so good to see you, honey. Can you stay the night?"

"Sorry, mom, but we've got a room at the Old Faithful Inn."

My eyebrows jumped. I went into an empty room and called Svetlana on the walkie-talkie.

"You're not going to believe this one," I said. "She's visiting her *mother*."

"What about Boone?"

"Not sure."

"This is fun," she said. "You like the walkie-talkies?"

"Yeah, they're swell. Bring 'em over to my tree house later."

"Why do I get the feeling you were an angry little boy? Over."

"Over and *out*."

I resumed my post in the hall.

"Be back in a minute," Heather said.

"Where are you going, dear?" her mother said.

"One of the actors is here. Broken leg. I'm just going to pop upstairs and say hello."

I ducked into an alcove, let her pass and waited a moment before following her to the second floor. As I was exiting the stairwell, I heard Heather and Boone talking in the room across the hall. A nurse whisked by. The second she left, I cocked an ear to Boone's door.

"I can't stay," Heather said. "I just wanted to see how you're doing."

"Doing great, can't you tell?" Boone said.

"Listen, it wasn't my fault," she said. "I need to get back to my mother."

"Yeah? What's her problem?"

"She has *cancer*, you jerk. Goodbye."

For variety, I ducked into a bathroom this time. Once Heather's footsteps had faded, I strolled into Boone's room. He was flipping rapidly through channels on the TV.

"What are *you* doing here?" he said.

"I'm really sorry about your leg, Boone."

"All right, you're sorry." He flipped channels. "Now get out."

"Can't," I said. "I need to ask you a couple questions."

"You're not asking me shit."

He paused on a sports news program and began flipping channels again.

"You tore my ACL, you sonovabitch," he said, staring at the TV. "It's gonna take months of therapy just to walk right again."

"Why'd you attack me?" I said. "Who put you up to it?"

"Look, Kat told me to play it aggressive. She said it was McCourt's idea."

"Why don't I believe you?"

"All right, so I got a little physical? I'm not the one who blindsided somebody with a friggen chair." Boone shut off the TV. "Look, what do you want?"

"It was Heather, right?" I said. "I was getting too close. She needed you to warn me away."

"Too close to *what*?"

"Sidney's murder," I said. "Be honest and I'll put in a good word for you."

"Are you a cop?"

"Did she promise you some of the gold? Talk to me, Boone."

"Gold?" he said. "What are you talking about?"

I had been studying his eyes. His responses seemed genuine. Then again, he could just be a better actor than I thought.

"Okay, I'll play along—for now," I said. "But when I come back, I'll be expecting answers."

Outside at the SUV, Svetlana had slipped behind the wheel, which was fine by me. In two years, she'd become excellent at tailing people. Besides, we knew where Heather was going and I was tired.

"How'd it go?" she asked.

I raked my hands through my hair and moaned.

"That well?" she said. "FYI, there isn't a room available at Yellowstone anywhere."

"We'll check once we're down there," I said. "Something will open up."

"There is something else," she said.

"What?"

"I checked messages and there were half a dozen from Vivian. She wants a report."

"Damn it, I told her I'd be in touch when I had something definitive," I said. "What am I supposed to do, call her and say I'm more confused now than when I started?"

"Perhaps I should call her," she said.

"No, I'll call her—*when* we have something."

Just then, Heather came out, pausing at her truck to dab her eyes and blow her nose. As soon as she regained her composure, she sped out of the parking lot. Svetlana started the engine and followed.

41

OLD FAITHFUL

During the long drive to Yellowstone, Svetlana kept a perfect two-car buffer between Heather's and ours. Once inside the park, however, an RV the size of a blue whale somehow slipped between us, and then we were stopped by a bear-jam and waited half an hour for it to clear. We lost Heather briefly on the Grand Loop Road and caught up to her just as she parked in front of the Old Faithful Inn. She carried her overnight bag to the geyser viewing area and sat on a bench. I got out while Svetlana parked, and we met at the hotel entrance. The evening sun was dipping beneath the treetops.

"Looks like she's here for the night," I said. "See if you can get us rooms, and meet me on the observation balcony."

Although I'd been here before, I took my time going inside so I could admire the lobby. Four stories of lodgepole balconies and treehouse-like catwalks rose to the roof. Even worldly Svetlana was awed. I went upstairs, bought two club sodas and secured a pair of Adirondack chairs on the balcony outside. Couples crowded at the rail. I handed Svetlana a drink when she sat down.

"When's it go off next?" I asked.

She checked her watch—a slim, diamond-encrusted deal given to her by a male chess admirer.

"Two minutes," she said.

Heather was on her bench when a man in a ranger's uniform approached her and said something over her shoulder. She jumped up and threw her arms around him. He looked like the tall young man I'd seen in the photos in her room.

"That appears to be the boyfriend," I said.

"There are no rooms," Svetlana said. "Not in the whole park."

"We'll figure something out."

I watched Heather and the boyfriend. He was very tall—6'5" was my guess—but much less brawny than Boone.

"Thar she blows!" a man yelled behind us.

As always, the geyser was impressive. Svetlana had never been here before, and I enjoyed watching her usual intensity morph into wonder.

"It sounds like popcorn popping," she said.

"Right? First time I saw it, I thought it'd be more of a hissing." Down at the viewing area, Heather and the boyfriend were headed inside. "Heather didn't see you in Ricochet, did she?"

"No."

"Okay. Follow her and see what room she's in. Meet me in front of the fireplace downstairs."

"We'll *meet* in the restaurant," she said. "You're buying me dinner."

In the restaurant, I got a corner table with a view of the entrance, ordered shrimp cocktail, and waited. At first I suffered the pitying stares of couples who thought I was dining alone. However, I was amply vindicated when Svetlana sashayed in and every man in the place choked on his bison burger. I knew that catwalk gait of hers well. It was the same one she used whenever she left chess tournaments with the championship purse.

"Well?" I said.

She sat down, spread the napkin on her lap and ate a shrimp before tossing a plastic room key on the table.

"What'd you do, mug them?" I said.

"I wandered into the staff locker room. One of the housekeepers left her locker open, and she had two, so—"

"You borrowed one," I said.

"Correct. And now…"

She snapped her fingers and the waiter materialized at her elbow.

"I will have a Virgin Mary and the prime rib," she said. "*Rare*. Simply coax the cow into a warm room."

"Very good, miss."

"Miss." She rested her chin on her fist. "Did you hear that Dakota? Such a smart young man. Make sure you tip him well."

I strummed the room key across my fingers like a guitar pick. "Have I ever told you how much I love your situational ethics?"

"No, but you may fawn over me while I eat these shrimp."

After dinner Svetlana commandeered a housekeeping smock, and as soon as the lovebirds left for the restaurant, she entered their room. I kept watch on the restaurant doors from the balcony in the lobby. There was a distinct dearth of attractive, single women my age, and I got bored watching male retirees wander around with fanny packs. I called Svetlana on the walkie-talkie.

"Anything yet?"

"Yes, a written confession," she said. "Go away."

Ten minutes later, I knew Svetlana was coming because a man looking down the hallway tripped on one of the fireside rocking chairs. She came upstairs and leaned over the rail beside me.

"What, no smock?" I said. "I wanted a picture of you in one."

"Speaking of." She dipped into her handbag and whipped out a Nikon SLR digital camera with a zoom lens.

When Heather and her companion walked out of the dining room, they paused in the lobby to smooch. Svetlana snapped several photos before they strolled outside, swinging their clasped hands.

"So," I said, "whatcha get?"

"Well, for starters, the woman uses almost no makeup."

"Somehow I don't think that's going to win a conviction."

"And," she said, "since he left his wallet in the room, we know that the boyfriend is Patrick Hollis and that he lives at thirteen Elk Rest Lane, Gardiner, Montana."

"Nice work, Champ. Gardiner's just north of the park. We can check it out in the morning."

"I will talk to the concierge again," she said. "Perhaps a room has opened up."

There were no rooms. Not at the Inn or the other hotels in the park, not in West Yellowstone, Jackson Hole, or Gardiner. However, there was one campsite still available. Once I convinced Svetlana of the merits of this option, we checked in, paid the fee and drove over to West Yellowstone. Mercifully the sporting goods store in town stayed open late for tourists like us, and I went inside to buy equipment while Svetlana ate a Rocky Road ice cream cone in the car. I purchased a tent, a double air mattress, and, because they were out of individual ones, a sleeping bag made for two—a fact I concealed until the last minute.

"What do you mean for *two*?" She paused eating her ice cream cone.

"Meaning two people get in it." I parked in the campsite and shut off the engine. "Hey, who saved your life today? I think you can trust me."

She looked at me askance.

"Look," I said. "I'll keep all my clothes on."

"As well you should," she said. "I understand the nights can be quite cold around here."

Even in the dark, I had the tent set up and the mattress inflated in twenty minutes. Gentleman that I am, once she returned from the bathroom, I waited for her to go in first and get settled. Once she gave me the all-clear, I went in, put on my fleece and curled into a pathetic ball on the edge of the air mattress. It was uncomfortably quiet until she spoke.

"Dakota, do you think we're on the right track?"

"Not sure."

I rolled onto my side. I could just make out her profile in the dark.

"So far, the Heather-Boone hypothesis is the only one that fits the facts," I said. "Still, this new theory about the gold has thrown me for a loop. What do you think?"

"I think we don't know the exact nature of Heather's relationship with Sidney," she said. "It might have been Platonic. Did anyone actually catch him and Heather in bed together?"

"No, but that wouldn't prove anything either. What if somebody found us like this?"

"Touché."

"You raise a good point though," I said. "Tomorrow we'll check out Patrick's place, see what else we can learn."

"Very well. Goodnight."

"Goodnight, Champ."

We rolled our separate ways and were silent for a while. Footsteps crunched past our tent, and when they faded, the sounds of the night woods rose up again to fill in the void.

The music of Yellowstone.

Then the air mattress jostled beneath me and there was the whine of a zipper.

"Fine, get in," Svetlana said.

I slid into the sleeping bag. It was cozy with her body heat.

"This is only because of what you did today," she said.

"Of course."

I was gazing out the rear vent at the clearest night sky I'd ever seen when her hand brushed my shoulder.

"I never thanked you for today." She sounded tired. "That's the second time you've…"

"Shhh," I said. "It's okay. Go to sleep."

The wind rustled the pine trees.

I drifted off to the soft breathing of my Ukrainian partner.

42

THE NICEST DOUBLE-WIDE

The tent was heavy with condensation when I awoke. I tried to rouse Svetlana, but she growled at me. Actually growled. Being a fairly astute guy, I took this to mean she wasn't interested in detecting at this hour. Quietly, I got out of the sleeping bag, put on my shoes, and set out alone.

Driving across the park at sunrise with the windows down was beautifully serene. I saw a mama buffalo and her calves crossing the road. As I passed Mammoth Hot Springs, the steam rose in the thin morning light and the air was heady with sulfur. I drove on, beneath the great stone arch at the north entrance, and through the sleeping village of Gardiner.

Patrick's address, 13 Elk Rest Lane, was a trailer on a large open lot. Nestled at the foot of a mountain, it was the nicest double-wide this detective had ever seen. The driveway was empty. I parked up the road, jogged back and knocked on the door. Just one of Patrick's buddies dropping by for a friendly 7:00 a.m. visit. When no one answered, I slipped on some latex gloves and tried the door. It was open. Patrick was either very trusting or he didn't have anything worth stealing.

Like other trailers I'd been in, it opened into the living room. Right away I was struck by how tidy the place was. The pillows were symmetrically arranged on the sofa. The rug had been vacuumed. Even the kitchen floor was scrubbed.

While I didn't expect to find a smoking gun, I did hope to establish some kind of connection between Patrick, Heather and Sidney. It didn't take long.

In the first bedroom I found a long table with a magnifier lamp mounted on it. A dozen Indian-style necklaces in various states of completion festooned the tabletop. A dozen more naked rawhide braids hung from hooks. One of these innocent pieces of jewelry could have been fashioned into a garrote, making it possible that *Patrick* killed Sidney. Then again, he could have just supplied Boone with a tool to do the job.

In the master bedroom, on a small bill-paying desk, I found a copy of Sidney's will and the stubs of two plane tickets to New York. The dates would have put Patrick and Heather in New York during Sidney's funeral and Roman's murder. I turned my attention to the bureau next. Buried in the bottom drawer, under a Bozeman High School football jacket, was an "I ♥ NY" T-shirt with something hard wrapped inside.

The something hard was a gun.

It was a nickel-plated Beretta Bobcat .25 auto, an unusual firearm for a man Patrick's size. Designed to be a lady's gun, it fit in the palm of my hand. Most of these just sit in a drawer or a woman's purse unfired. I turned the gun over and examined the end of the barrel. Little black pinwheel marks coated the end of the muzzle, which meant the gun had been fired. Not necessarily recently, but it had been fired. I pulled out the magazine. The bullets were hollow-tipped—the type that made small entry holes (like the one I'd seen in Roman's head) and expanded on impact.

There were several possibilities with the gun. It could be the weapon used to kill Roman, it could be a coincidence, or it could be a plant. I replaced the magazine, wrapped up the gun and stowed it back in the drawer. If removed without a warrant, it would be worthless as evidence.

Finally, deep in the closet, behind a spare ranger's uniform, I found something odd—a set of pink nurse's scrubs. I double-checked to make sure nothing was out of place, then walked to the door pleased with what I had discovered.

I'd found a smoking gun after all.

43

A SCHEME DEVELOPED

Svetlana and I were in the Mammoth Hotel dining room with a unique window view: a herd of elk lying on the grass in front of the park administration office. While Svetlana pecked at her *huevos rancheros*, I excitedly told her about my findings at Patrick's. For the first time since this case began, the solution seemed in our grasp. Svetlana wasn't quite as confident.

"Isn't it all circumstantial?" she said.

"I realize that."

I sawed through a stack of huckleberry pancakes. Svetlana gestured with her fork.

"So," she said, "you believe Patrick accompanied Heather to New York to kill Roman?"

"Yeah. But ask me again in five minutes and I'll give you a different theory."

"Assuming your theory is correct, *why* would Heather need to kill Roman?"

"Theoretically speaking, of course," I said.

"Of course."

"Because she contracted with him to have Shaw and me killed. As long as Roman was alive, there would be someone to tie her to Shaw's death."

"But the gun you found," she said. "We don't know it's the one that killed Roman."

"Nope. Which is why you're going to call my buddy, Brian Sutherland, with the New York State Police, and ask him in your flirty, Ukrainian way to—"

"—find out what caliber gun was used to kill Roman?"

"Exactly," I said.

"Why me?" she said. "He's *your* friend."

"You have nicer legs."

"True. Okay, I do it."

She put down her fork, pushed her plate away, and peered at me over her Dolce & Gabbana sunglasses.

"So," she said, "what is your plan?"

"Plan?"

"Yes," Svetlana said. "A scheme developed for the accomplishment of an objective. A plan. "

"Oh, one of them things. Well, little lady, I reckon I'll just round up the suspects and beat 'em with a rubber chicken till one of 'em confesses."

Her lips tightened up. She almost laughed.

"Oh, come on," I said. "That was kind of funny."

"Seriously, Dakota, my chess students are better at devising plans than you."

"That's only because teacher scares them."

She smiled and sipped her coffee.

I ate the last of my pancakes and washed them down with a tall glass of milk. Days of bad Ricochet food had left me starved. I patted my mouth with my napkin and leaned across the table. I had taken Svetlana's comment as a challenge.

"You want a plan?" I said. "Okay. First, we're checking out R.C. Development Corp. Then we're going to the BLM in Missoula and find out if anybody's been poking around in the records for the mines on the resort. After that, we'll pay Heather's mom a visit at the hospital. She needs to know that Heather could be in deep trouble unless we find out what really happened to Sidney. And when we get back to Ricochet, no more sneaking around. I'm letting it be known that I'm a gen-u-ine deputy sheriff looking into Sidney's murder. Once the cat's out of the bag, the murderer might slip up." I pounded the table. Patrons stared. "*That's* my plan, sweetheart."

Svetlana was silent while I signaled for the check. Outside, the elk were standing now, grazing on the lawn.

"So," I said. "My plan—what do you think?"

She reached across the table and patted my hand.

"I think the rubber chicken one was better."

44

CALL DALE!

The second we pulled into the address for R.C. Development Corp., my keen detecting instincts told me something was awry. Perhaps because the alleged development company was an abandoned filling station in the middle of nowhere, complete with hip-high weeds and torn-out pumps.

"Charming," Svetlana said.

We got out. The front door was solid steel with a mail slot. It was locked. I went to the big picture window, wiped away some of the grime and peeked inside: a desk with a phone, and a wastebasket with junk mail overflowing onto the floor. I could pick the door lock, but I preferred to find a less exposed way in.

"Keep an eye out," I said.

Svetlana looked around. "For what? Tumbleweed?"

There was a garage door, but the lock was filled in and the door felt welded shut. I went around back. The entire building was cinder block. Short of smashing the picture window, the only way in was through the front door. I returned to the SUV, where Svetlana leaned on the bumper watching the road.

"I'll have to pick the lock," I said.

"Maybe not." She was on her iPhone.

"Who are you calling?" I asked.

"Dale."

She pointed to a real estate sign. It was for Big Sky Realty with a picture of a balding, smiling man and a message to "CALL DALE!"

When Dale got on the line, Svetlana explained she was in the market for a commercial lease and had stumbled upon the gas station. Could he drive out and show it to her and her assistant? Yes? Wonderful. She hung up.

"So what's our business?" I asked.

"Florist."

"And I suppose I'm your assistant."

"You suppose correctly."

She sat in the passenger seat with the door open and one of her long jeaned legs dangling out. She put on lipstick, blotted it with a napkin and produced a silk scarf from the back seat. Once it was fastened around her neck for maximum chicness, she grabbed her Gucci bag and waited outside with me.

Ten minutes later, a shiny red Ford pickup rolled into the dusty lot. A man in a dress shirt and bolo tie got out. He shook Svetlana's hand.

"Dale Winters."

"Svetlana Krüsh."

"That German or something?"

"Close," she said. "Ukrainian."

"So, where you folks from?" Dale sorted through keys on a large ring.

"New York," Svetlana said. "I own a chain of florists and I'm considering starting one out here."

I stifled a grin. Dale opened the door and we went inside.

"Sorry about the mess," he said. "Last tenant ran out on me. Haven't had a chance to clean her up."

"What happened to them?" Svetlana asked.

Svetlana, the sympathetic florist.

"Don't know, tell you the truth," Dale said. "One day the rent checks just stop coming, so I give them a month. Didn't hear anything, so I changed the locks."

"Really?" I said. "What kind of business were they in?"

"Only met one guy. Indian fella—didn't tell me much—said they did property development. Asked what properties and he said they were all in Canada. Should've done more of a check, but it was the middle of winter and the place was just sitting here."

"Hard to believe," I said.

Svetlana frowned at me. Dale walked into the center of the crumbling Linoleum floor and gave his spiel.

"Won't kid 'ya, the place needs work, but maybe we can make some kind of sweat-equity deal." He went to the window. "You got plenty of parking, and lots of traffic."

We'd been here for an hour and Dale's was the first car I'd seen.

"Dale," Svetlana said, "perhaps you could show me the garage while my assistant measures for the counters and refrigerated cases."

"Sure, follow me," he said. "Got a nice sized Dumpster outside, too."

"Now, Dale, no teasing."

As soon as the door shut behind them, I sifted through the pile of mail. A lot of the usual junk, including store circulars and free community classifieds. I grabbed the wastebasket. There was no time for niceties, so I dumped it right on the desk. Most of the trash was comprised of untouched R.C. Development letterhead. Mixed in with the paper were about a dozen envelopes that had been torn open. None of them had return addresses, but the postmarks were legible: Orlando, FL and Martha's Vineyard, MA.

Shaw. The last postmark, from Martha's Vineyard, was three days before his death. I pocketed the envelopes and slid the rest of the paper into the trash. Just for giggles, I picked up the phone and got a dial tone. I pressed the redial button and a woman answered.

"Bison Construction," she said.

I hung up and rifled through the desk. All I learned was that somebody had a fetish for mustard packets. I was closing the desk drawer when Svetlana and Dale walked in. Svetlana shook Dale's hand.

"Thank you. I'll be in touch."

We went outside. Dale locked the door.

"Any idea when?"

"Unfortunately, no," Svetlana said. "We are considering other locations."

"Well, don't wait too long."

We got in the SUV and drove away. A mile down the road, Svetlana sighed.

"That poor man."

"Poor man, my ass," I said. "You made his day. Besides"—I handed her the envelopes—"now we've got a solid connection between Shaw and the reservation."

She inspected the envelopes. "What do you think was in them?"

"You tell me. What would make somebody tear them open like that?"

"Money," she said.

"That's what I think. Carries Bison was getting checks from Shaw."

"For?"

"My guess?" I said. "Building the casino. Now the question is, why?"

45

THE LEGEND OF LOOT

The Missoula Field Office of the U.S. Bureau of Land Management resided in a low-slung cement building that looked more like a strip club than an office of the federal government. We parked, went inside and followed the signs to "Claims & Mining Records."

Shelves full of archive boxes stretched to the far end of the room, but something in the foreground grabbed my attention: an attractive woman. With glossy blonde hair and pillowy lips, she looked like a Hollywood starlet who'd been vacationing in Montana and developed amnesia. She typed on a computer with her profile to us. I read the nameplate on her desk and handed her a business card.

"Hi, Jennifer. We have some questions about mining claims. Could you help us?"

"Ah, Mr. Stevens," she said, examining the card. "You're lucky we like Sheriff Briggs as much as we do."

Her eyes flicked to Svetlana, and stayed there.

"I'm interested in Loot, Montana," I said. "It's part of Ricochet now. I need to find out if there have been any recent inquiries about the property."

Jennifer eyed Svetlana's trim and denimy thighs the way a kid does a piece of taffy.

"Yeah, no problem." She called over her shoulder. "Carl? Pull the Loot file, will you?"

Somewhere deep in the stacks, a chair screeched. A moment later, a round-shouldered milquetoast scissored into view at the end of the aisle. He stared at Jennifer with his arms at his sides.

"Loot, Carl," she said. "Please."

He nodded crisply and scissored back into the shadows.

"He okay?" I asked.

"Carl? Yeah, he's fine."

While we waited, I concluded that my charms would be wasted on Jennifer, especially when Svetlana yawned and stretched, and Jennifer just about swallowed her own tongue. Behind her, Carl approached carrying a banker's box with "LOOT, MT" printed on the side. He plopped it on a table.

"It's all there. Few pages torn out of a journal, but otherwise the stuff's in good shape."

"Pages torn out?" I said.

"Yeah, a journal kept by the original mine office in Loot," Carl said. "I noticed the damage last year."

"Do you keep a log of who examines the file?" Svetlana asked.

Carl opened the box top and slapped its back. Taped to the cardboard were several sheets of lined notepaper with names and dates on them.

"Right here. But we only keep records going back a year or so."

Jennifer pulled out two chairs at the table. "Mr. Stevens, Miss—"

"Svetlana," she said.

"Svetlana, can I get you something to drink?"

"Water would be fine. Thank you."

Jennifer smiled and walked away.

"Know what you're looking for?" Carl asked.

The guy didn't look you in the eye when he talked. He gazed over your shoulder, like he expected a hit man to walk in behind you at any moment.

"Not exactly," I said.

He sighed. "Please tell me you're not treasure-hunters."

"What?"

I knew what he was talking about, but once you got knowledgeable people talking, it was usually a good idea to let them go.

"You know about the legend, right?" he said.

I remembered McCourt telling me about the gold legend and dismissing it as "a fool's errand." I was about to say so when Svetlana reached out and touched Carl on the arm.

"We'd love to hear it," she said.

Carl's posture instantly straightened, like a leper cured by Jesus.

"Well, if you really want to know." He put his hands in his pockets and began.

"In 1884, five miners made a big strike," he said. "They were McCarthy, Manning, Hilkert, Smith and Birch."

"Sounds like a law firm," I said.

Carl frowned.

"Poor joke," I said. "Go on."

"They found tons of mineral gold but didn't have the right equipment to haul it out," he said. "Missoula was the closest place that had the equipment. Unfortunately it was November and the passes were closed."

"What happened next?" Svetlana said.

"A big mistake, that's what happened," Carl said. "They set out anyway and made all of their laborers come with them. In the meantime, they'd hidden the gold someplace around Loot—in a couple of the mines, according to the legend. Left without telling anybody where it was hidden, not even their wives."

Jennifer placed a tall glass of water with lemon in front of Svetlana. I didn't get any.

"Keep going, Carl." Jennifer leaned into Svetlana's shoulder. "He's so cute when he gets on this stuff."

"Well, they hadn't been gone two days when there was a terrible blizzard. Never made it to the trading post. Search party went out in the spring. Didn't find a single body."

"So, how do we know the legend isn't true?" I asked.

Carl shrugged. "Maybe because so many people have looked, including experts, and nobody's found a single nugget."

"Carl really knows what he's talking about, Mr. Stevens," Jennifer said.

"What people are most interested in this information?" Svetlana asked.

"That's easy," Carl said. "Treasure hunters mostly. But now and then we get a researcher."

"Thank you, Carl," I said.

He nodded and drifted back into the stacks someplace. I scanned the list of names on the box sign-out sheet. One person had signed out the file four times in the past year: Dr. John Todd. I turned to Jennifer, who was admiring my associate.

"This Dr. Todd." I pointed at the list. "Do you remember him?"

"Of course. He's a professor at the university. Geology."

"The one here in Missoula?"

"Yes," she said. "He's like a historical geologist, or a geologic historian. I don't know what you'd call it. Writes books about mining communities."

"Thanks."

She pointed with a pencil. "I'll be over there if you need anything."

I dug into the box, separated the folders into two stacks and pushed one toward Svetlana.

"Let me guess," she said. "We'll know it when we see it."

"Are you making fun of my methods?"

"Yes."

For two hours we examined folder after folder of official claims documents, land surveys, deed transfers and photos of mine entrances. When one of us finished with a folder, we traded off. I skimmed the tattered journal Carl had mentioned, but all I learned was that mining was brutally hard work, that there were cave-ins, and that promising shafts often amounted to nothing. After the last folder, Svetlana and I just looked at each other shaking our heads.

"Well, *that* was fun," she said. "I'm going out for some air." She grabbed her handbag and marched out.

"Nice to meet you, Svetlana," Jennifer said.

Jennifer was crestfallen. I signed the box sign-out sheet and brought the box over to her.

"Don't worry, she's just shy." I nodded at the business card I'd given her. "If you're ever in New York, look us up. Thanks for your help."

I had just walked outside and was about to call Briggs when my cell phone rang. It was Briggs.

"Where are you?" he asked.

"Missoula, the BLM," I said. "Why?"

"Get over to the hospital. Emergency room."

He hung up.

46

REVERSALS

The hospital parking lot brimmed with police cars—cruisers from the state police and the Missoula city cops, and Sheriff Briggs's SUV. We went inside. Briggs was drinking a cup of coffee and talking to another cop. The cop wrote in his notebook and walked away.

"What happened?" I asked.

"I'd ask you the same thing," Briggs said. "What happened between you and Boone?"

"We disagreed about acting technique. He was too method for my tastes."

"Yeah, well he's dead."

"What?"

"Relax, had nothing to do with his knee." Briggs adjusted his cowboy hat. "Coroner did a preliminary blood test in the lab here. Looks like somebody injected him with a syringe full of sedative. Heavy-duty stuff, like for cattle." A gurney rolled by carrying a large body bag. "Poor bastard went to sleep and nobody noticed till the shift change."

"Any witnesses?"

"Sort of," he said. "One of the janitors saw a nurse exit his room and slip down the back stairs. We've been questioning all the staff. So far everybody's accounted for. We're thinking it was somebody from the outside in nurse's scrubs."

"What color scrubs?" I asked.

"Pink, why?"

"No reason."

I thought of the set in Patrick's closet. Svetlana must have noticed my expression change because she squinted at me as if to say, *"What are you hiding, Dakota?"*

"Any other description by the janitor?" I asked.

"He said the nurse had blonde hair and a…uh…nice chest."

"A remarkable eye for detail," Svetlana said.

"How he remembers it, Miss Krüsh." Briggs dropped his cup in the trash can.

"What about cameras?" I pointed at the ceiling. "Doesn't the hospital have them?"

"Updating the system," Briggs said. "Only in maternity right now."

Svetlana picked an invisible piece of lint off her sweater. "Do you suspect somebody from the resort?"

"Maybe," Briggs said. "A couple of state detectives went over to Ricochet to get statements. Seems the only two women unaccounted for are Heather Van Every and that crazy gal, Kat Styles."

Svetlana gave me a look.

"I don't know about Kat," I said, "but last we saw Heather, she was with her boyfriend at the Old Faithful Inn."

"Boyfriend?" Briggs said. "I thought Sidney was her boyfriend."

"Second boyfriend," I said. "Patrick Hollis. He's a park ranger down at Yellowstone."

I purposely didn't mention his address so Briggs wouldn't know I'd been there. Briggs wrote the name on a pad.

"Find anything at the BLM?" he asked.

"Maybe," I said. "Nothing solid yet. What about that Molotov cocktail bottle I sent you? Any prints?"

"Zip. Must've been wearing gloves."

"Aren't they always."

"Well, you've got my number," he said. "Keep me posted."

Briggs tipped his hat to Svetlana and sauntered away. The automatic doors whirred open. Once he was in the parking lot, Svetlana turned to me with her arms accusatorially crossed.

"What aren't you telling me?"

"The nurse's scrubs," I said. "I found a set this morning in Patrick's closet. Pink ones."

"It could be another coincidence," she said, "but still—this does not bode well for Heather."

"No, it doesn't. We need to speak with her mother. Hopefully she can shed some light on this."

We followed the signs to the cancer center. A plain-clothes cop was seated outside her room, waiting for Heather in case she returned. I told him we were friends of the family and he let us pass. Heather's mother was knitting when we walked in.

"Hello, ma'am," I said.

She smiled. Her face hinted at the beauty she once was, before the cancer had sapped her skin of its luster.

"I'm Dakota Stevens, and this is my associate, Svetlana Krüsh. We know Heather from the resort. We need to talk to you because Heather is in a lot of trouble, ma'am. We might be able to help, but we need to know where she is."

"Are you with the police?" The outline of a body was barely discernible beneath the covers.

"We're private detectives," Svetlana said. "We've been working on a case at the resort."

"If this is about Mr. Boone," she said, "I already told them—Heather hasn't been here since yesterday. She's down in Yellowstone seeing her boyfriend."

"This isn't about Mr. Boone, ma'am," I said. "We have reason to believe that Heather may have killed her other boyfriend, the owner of Ricochet, Sidney Vaillancourt."

With visible effort, she lifted her head off the pillow. "Did you say *boyfriend?*"

"Yes, ma'am."

She broke into a laugh that morphed into a hacking cough. A nurse passing by outside stormed in.

"What's going on here?" the nurse said. "She can't be upset like this."

After coughing into a tissue, she was cadaver-still on the bed, her forehead perspiring and a smile on her face.

"It's okay, nurse," she said. "These two just said the funniest thing I've heard in a long time." She fixed her eyes on me. "Sidney wasn't Heather's boyfriend, Mr. Stevens. He was her father."

47

SABBATICAL

After the revelation about Heather and Sidney's relationship, and after corroborating Sidney's paternity with the hospital copy of the birth certificate, I spent most of my time at dinner and in my motel room chastising myself for missing something that now seemed so obvious.

At 4:30 a.m., I sprang awake, gasping. I went into the bathroom, drank two glasses of tap water, and studied myself in the mirror. Maybe it was my imagination, but I seemed to have aged since the beginning of this case. I needed oxygen. In one of the free local guidebooks, I had read about Mount Sentinel, a small mountain right in town with a giant white "M" on the mountainside that people jogged to. A physical goal—something clear and attainable—was exactly what I needed. I changed into running clothes and hit the road.

The sun hadn't made it over the eastern hills yet, but you could already tell it was going to be a scorcher. My footfalls echoed on the empty streets. Light from a cafe splashed the sidewalk. I picked up a nature trail that ran along the Clark Fork River, and as I settled into a rhythm, my head began to clear out. I began to believe I could still solve this case.

At the foot of Mount Sentinel, I stopped and stared up at the giant "M." It seemed so close, but if I'd learned anything about the West, it was that things were a lot farther away than they appeared. Like solutions to murder investigations. The path—a series of 11 switchbacks—zigzagged up the mountain. I started up.

So, Heather was Sidney's daughter. In fairness to myself, I had been suspicious of the rumors of hanky-panky because no one had ever caught them in the act. Still, daughter or not, she had the most motive: $100 million and control of the resort. The circumstantial evidence against her was strong, and even stronger in the deaths of Boone and Roman.

I'd forgotten how much thinner the Rocky Mountain air is than in the East, and I struggled to catch my breath. The path was steep. My side ached. I clutched it in my fist and kept running.

What about finding Kat's fan in my office? What if she had orchestrated this entire thing?

My chest burned. My legs throbbed.

According to Briggs, Kat was unaccounted for yesterday afternoon. Maybe she was a lot smarter than I gave her credit for. Maybe she killed Sidney *and* Boone, and framed Heather to take the rap.

I reached the "M" and collapsed on the grass, panting. As I caught my breath and the buildings of Missoula University shone in the rising sun, I thought about Professor John Todd and his recent interest in Loot, and wondered if I should go down there and poke around. I was debating it when I thought, *"What would Jim Rockford do?"*

I got to my feet and started down the hill.

In the student center, I found a campus directory. The geology department was on the third floor of the Science Complex. When I got there, the department door was wide open and Todd's office was at the end of the hall. An undated note hung on the door:

Students:

It is with tremendous pleasure that I undertake a year-long sabbatical to complete the research for a new book. If you have an issue that requires immediate resolution, please see either Professor Lawton or Mrs. Hayden.
See you next fall.
Best regards,
Professor Todd

His door was locked. I was about to leave when I spied the faculty mailboxes. Todd's box was fetchingly full. *"Act boldly and mighty forces will come to your aid,"* some philosopher once said. I snatched all of Todd's mail and hurried out of the building.

Somehow I wasn't surprised when I ran into Svetlana on the steps. She wore a new buckskin jacket with fringe on the sleeves. When she put her hands on her hips, the fringe quivered.

"You stole his *mail?*"

"I know, I know, it's a federal offense," I said, "but we'll mail back anything that isn't useful. Right now I could do with some breakfast."

"No, right now you could *do* with a shower."

"You know, Svetlana, with all the languages you speak, how you didn't become a diplomat I'll never know."

Twenty-Twenty

After checkout and breakfast, we headed back to the resort. The mail ended up being a dead end. A lot of scholarly journals with prose so stultifying I thanked God I wasn't an academic. We dumped them in a mailbox on our way out of town.

The road seemed longer and straighter than it had the day before. I stared at the horizon in the direction of Ricochet. It was threatening rain. Ahead, a fence had fallen down and a few dozen cattle stood in the road. Men on horseback were driving them back in. We stopped. I nodded at the scene.

"How would you feel if I quit all this detective stuff and became a cowboy? Wanna join me, help me work them cows?"

Svetlana lowered her sunglasses. "No."

One of the cowboys spied Svetlana in the passenger seat. He touched his hat. She returned the gesture with an unusually friendly finger-wave.

"So," she said, "Sidney was Heather's father, and Boone is dead. What excellent progress we're making."

Something about Boone's death stuck in my craw. Heather just walked in there, pumped him full of cattle sedative and walked out? It didn't ring true. I pulled out my phone.

"Who are you calling?" Svetlana asked.

"Briggs."

The cowboys yelled and waved their coiled-up lariats. The cattle didn't appear to move any faster. Briggs picked up.

"What?"

"And good morning to you, sheriff," I said.

"Rancher's missing some cattle. Make it quick."

"Maybe they're the ones I'm looking at."

"What?" Briggs said. "Where?"

"A road south of Missoula."

"Cut the bull, I'm busy."

"Quick question," I said. "How was Boone's eyesight?"

"Twenty-twenty. Why?"

"How do you know?"

"Got his medical file from the resort," Briggs said. "All the actors have to pass an annual physical. You know, insurance stuff. What's your point?"

"You took a statement from the nurses, right?"

"No, the state guys did, but I was there."

"Did Boone cry out for help or try to hit his call button?" I asked.

Svetlana looked at me.

"Not according to the report," Briggs said.

"Doesn't that strike you as odd?"

"No. Woman hit him with a hell of a lot of sedative."

"I realize that," I said. "But here's the thing. If somebody I knew—somebody like Heather—walked in wearing a nurse's uniform and carrying a syringe, I'd put up a fight, scream, hit the panic button, anything. I would have known she was up to no good."

"Maybe he didn't recognize her," Briggs said. "Hell, maybe he was taking a nap."

"During the shift change?" I said. "I don't know about you, Briggs, but the couple of times I've been in the hospital, there was always someone coming in to do something. I think the reason Boone didn't call out is that he didn't recognize the person. As far as he knew, she was just another nurse, doing her thing."

Svetlana smiled faintly. The road was almost clear.

"Now that you mention it," Briggs said, "a cafeteria worker claimed Boone was awake when he delivered lunch. We put that about ten minutes before Nurse Death. Shoot, you might be on to something. Why don't you drop by my office so we can kick this around?"

"Can't. Need to get back to the resort and see if Boone's death has stirred up anything."

"And I'll see if I can find Mr. Kittredge's livestock."

"That happen much?" I said. "People stealing cattle?"

"Bad economy, more than you'd think," Briggs said. "Call me when you get something new."

"Well, Svetlana's buckskin jacket is new. Does that count?"

"Goodbye, Stevens."

I hung up and tugged on a piece of fringe on Svetlana's elbow.

"You do look nice in that, by the way."

"I know," she said. "That is why I bought it."

The road was clear now. We drove away. Svetlana patted my arm.

"Smart, Dakota—about Boone not calling for help."

"Thanks."

A logging truck turned onto the highway in front of us. I passed it on a double-yellow. I was eager to get back and clamp down on this case.

"What if the muscle wasn't Boone?" I said.

"Patrick then?"

"Possibly. He's tall enough. I keep thinking about all of those calls Roman made to Yellowstone and Gardiner."

"Okay," Svetlana said. "Roman hires Patrick. Then who kills Roman?"

"Patrick maybe," I said. "Or Louis."

"And who killed Boone?"

I shrugged. Svetlana leaned her seat back and assumed a catnap position.

"I am confused," she said.

"So am I, darlin'. So am I."

49

Tall, Blonde and Evil

Back at Ricochet Depot, Svetlana and I boarded the train and took a seat in the passenger car. A pair of burly characters got on with us and sat outside on the flatbed. They weren't CEOs. The conductor read a newspaper at the other end of the car, and there were no other passengers. Svetlana and I sat across the aisle from each other with our feet up.

"So," she said, "you spoke to Walt back there?"

"Yeah. I described Roman and Patrick. Asked if anybody matching their descriptions visited around the time of Sidney's death. He said no."

"Perhaps they wore disguises."

"Perhaps," I said.

"So, now what?"

"They're holding a memorial service for Boone. Oh, and Kat and Heather are back. They came in on an earlier train."

I looked out the window. Across the plain, a purple front was moving in.

"Let's get some air," I said.

We went outside on the flatbed car and stood near the rails. The men who had boarded with us sat on a far bench, passing a flask back and forth. They ignored us. Underneath their frock coats, trapezius muscles bulged. I'd had enough experience with tough guys to know them when I saw them, and I sensed these two weren't here for an Old West vacation. I kept an eye on them while Svetlana admired the landscape.

"It is lovely, Dakota. I will miss it, *if* you ever solve this case."

"I'm working on it," I said.

The train wound through the ravine and climbed the grade. I gestured at the tailings piles.

"They really should get rid of those."

"I don't know," Svetlana said. "They add a certain *Je ne sais quoi.*"

We were approaching Loot.

"Did you get the nickel tour when you came in?" I asked.

"If you mean McCourt rambling on about nine-ty-nine *thousand* acres, then yes."

I was gazing at the Hotel Meade when something moved in one of the upstairs windows. Just like the first time.

"Hey, did you see—"

"Movement in the top floor window of that brick building?" she said.

"Damn, you *do* have predator eyes," I said.

"I am the mighty huntress."

"Well, huntress, get ready to do some hunting. We're checking that out."

In Ricochet, Svetlana went to the livery to fetch our horses while I walked down to the church and slipped into a pew in back. Two gigantic bouquets of lilies and a headshot of Boone rested on an altar. McCourt and Irving sat onstage while one of the actors waxed nostalgic about Boone. Kat and her half-dozen ladies-in-waiting huddled together in the front row, dabbing their eyes with handkerchiefs. I couldn't tell if they were really crying. When the actor finished his speech, I started down the aisle.

"Thank you, James," McCourt said. "I'm sure we all—"

The second McCourt focused on me, the entire congregation turned around. Benches creaked. Clothes rustled. I could feel their eyes on me like red-hot lances.

"Marshal," McCourt said.

"I have an announcement." I went onstage. "Sorry to interrupt, but it's time you all knew something. My name is Dakota Stevens, and I'm not an actor. I'm a private detective from New York."

Kat glared at me, as though my subterfuge had been a personal affront to her alone.

"I was hired to find the killer of Sidney Vaillancourt," I said. "I have reason to believe that Mr. Boone's death is connected to Sidney's. Now, most of you don't like me and that's fine. You don't have to like me. But you do have to cooperate with me."

"You have no authority here," said one of the actors. His buddies mumbled in agreement.

"Actually, I do," I said. "I'm a sworn deputy with the county sheriff's office. Call Sheriff Briggs and check it out if you like."

Svetlana entered the church and stood in back.

"I've spoken to some of you already." I glanced at Kat and Heather. "As for the rest of you, I or my associate, Svetlana Krüsh, might speak with you." I gestured to her. "Just go about your regular schedules and we'll catch up with you. Have a nice day."

I marched down the aisle and met Svetlana out on the street. The wind had picked up, blowing dust around. She tossed me the reins to my horse.

"Have a nice day?" she said.

"All right, so I'm not Winston Churchill."

"No, you're not."

By the time Svetlana and I arrived at Loot, storm clouds had rolled in and engulfed the resort. We left the horses tied up in the woods and were sneaking around a barn when I spotted four-wheeler tracks at the barn door.

"*Hello*, what have we here?" I drew my Peacemaker. "Let's have a look, shall we?"

I edged inside with Svetlana right on my heels. Faint light seeped in through holes in the roof, illuminating tire tracks on the dirt floor. Under a small hayloft, several new shovels and pickaxes leaned against the barn slats.

"It appears someone has been busy," Svetlana said.

Rain began to patter on the roof, and a few drops got me on the neck. I holstered the gun.

"The rain should bring this guy back soon," I said. "Come on, I have an idea where he's staying."

We ran across a meadow to the Hotel Meade. The front door was locked, so we went around back. Eight feet off the ground was an open doorway; the stairs had long since rotted away. The rain picked up. I jumped for the sill, missed it, and landed in sagebrush up to my thighs.

"It appears someone needs to visit the gym," Svetlana said.

I focused on the sill, jumped again, and this time pulled myself smoothly up. Svetlana glanced at her nails and the rough wood at my feet. I straightened my hat.

"I'm tempted to leave you," I said. "All right, here."

I lowered my hands to her. My arm still ached from the snakebite and the pit incident, but Svetlana had laid down the gauntlet. Ignoring the twinge in my arm, I heaved her up to the landing.

"You were saying something about the gym?" I said.

"How else did you expect me to motivate you?" She snapped her frock coat into place. "You pride yourself on being strong."

"And dashing."

I brushed a raindrop from her cheek. She pushed my hand away.

"Go on," she said.

We crept down the hall, our every step echoing through the building. The first floor was empty. We went upstairs to the top floor. At the end of the hall a door was open. It was the room where we'd seen the movement in the window. I drew the Peacemaker.

Inside was a cot with a sleeping bag, a Coleman stove, pots and pans, bottled water and canned goods. A small chemistry setup rested on an overturned crate. A curtain fluttered in the window. Somebody had made himself right at home.

The sky rumbled. The rain accelerated to a downpour. I holstered my gun and glanced out the window.

"Excellent," I said. "This should bring our friend back very soon."

Behind me, Svetlana muttered, *"Shchto tse ye?"*

She was rummaging through a crate of paperbacks. They were pulp fiction works with scantily clad women on the covers and titles like *Pajama Party* and *Tall, Blonde and Evil.*

"Oooh, here's a piece of literature." Svetlana held one up to the window and read aloud. "*Snow Bunnies.* 'On the ski-lodge circuit, the colder the weather, the hotter the action!' *Please.*" She dropped it in the crate.

"Put those aside," I said. "You know, evidence."

"Smut."

"What do you expect? Kinda tough to get Cinemax out here."

She looked around the enchanting abode and made a face.

"Now what?"

I listened to the rain. The drops were fat and slapped on the windowsill.

"We wait."

50

WAITING

We sat on the floor. Svetlana opened a stylish leather musette bag and produced a package of chessmen cookies. She tossed me one.

"A *pawn*?" I said. "Give me a knight at least."

"They taste the same."

While I ate the cookie, Svetlana pulled out her iPhone and began to play chess. I wanted something to do to pass the time, so I grabbed one of the paperbacks: *Daddy's Girl*. On the cover, a vampish blonde hugged a man while pickpocketing him. I flipped to a random chapter and read:

> Suzy swung Daddy's Packard up to the curb in front of Bayside Court apartments. She cut the engine. Jimmy sulked in the passenger seat as she applied new lipstick and unbuttoned the top two—*no, better make it three*—buttons on her blouse.
>
> "I don't like it, Suze," Jimmy said. "Why can't I just do it?"
>
> "'Cause you don't have the spine, baby."
>
> "Yeah? What if this guy turns on us? What then?"

She puckered her lips in the mirror and snatched the car keys. "We'll burn that bridge when we come to it."

"Maybe I should come."

"Not a chance."

Suzy slid out of the car, torched a Lucky.

"Give me ten minutes," she said. "Any longer and I had to go to Plan B."

"What's Plan—"

She slammed the door on Jimmy's question and strutted up to the gate. It was open.

At apartment 2D, she flicked the cigarette off the balcony and rapped on the weatherbeaten door. Jazz saxophone sprayed out of the keyhole. Suzy bent over and peeked inside. A man approached, stripped to his briefs. When the door breezed open, Suzy took her time standing up. Behind him, the music was prominent. So was the banana in his shorts.

"Nice," she said.

"Nice what?"

"The horn. Coltrane, right? Whatcha' think I meant?"

He wagged a finger at her, making his chest muscles bounce.

"You're that doll from the other night. Whaddaya want?"

"Cold out here."

He waved her inside. She squeezed by and sashayed across the room to his Hi-Fi. The apartment was shabby, but his record collection wasn't. He grabbed her wrist.

"You didn't come over here to talk jazz."

She jerked her arm away. "Get a girl a drink."

"Yeah," he said, his eyes probing her cleavage.

Suzy smiled to herself. This guy would be a cinch.

Leaning against the doorjamb, she parted the leaves of her blouse.

He returned with two highballs, gave her one. The first half went down easy, the second even easier.

"I'm waiting," he said.

She put down the glass, moved into him and drew hearts on his chest with a fingernail.

"I want you to ice somebody for me."

"This a gag?"

His mind might have been suspicious, but another part of him was curious. Very curious.

"No joke," she said.

"You nuts or something, girlie?" He stared at her for a second. "What do I get?"

"Dough, baby. Lots of it. Plus..." She ran her fingernails down her ripe body.

"S'pose I already got me some of that." He stepped into her.

"Not like this you don't."

He was strong down there. It drilled into her stomach like a vacuum cleaner handle.

"I want a grand first," he said. "You know, like earnest money."

"Don't have it. Yet." She flopped backwards onto the bed and smiled up at him through tousled hair. "I was thinking about more of a layaway plan..."

I was vaguely aware of Svetlana shaking my arm. I pocketed the book.

"Listen," she said.

At first all I heard was the rainstorm. Then, faintly, the flatulent sound of a four-wheeler.

"Do you have your flashlight?" I asked.

"Yes." She reached in her bag.

"Good. When he walks in, hit him with it. He'll freeze up like a rabbit."

The sky outside darkened, cloaking the room in shadows. The rain slowed and quieted. As I drew the Peacemaker and stood in the corner, there was a bang from downstairs, followed by footsteps slogging up the staircase.

Svetlana aimed the flashlight at the doorway. The sound of boots echoed in the empty hall. I took shallow breaths and tightened my grip on the gun. I was pretty sure who this was, but I'd been wrong before.

The second the person stepped over the threshold, Svetlana switched on the light. I spun out of the corner with my gun raised.

"Dr. Todd, I presume?"

"Who are you?" he said. "What is this?"

"You're trespassing," I said.

"This is assault! I'll have you—"

With my free hand, I gave him a modest punch to the solar plexus. He lost his voice and doubled over as if looking for it on the floor.

"Now, listen carefully," I said. "You're coming into Ricochet and sit in a jail cell until you answer my questions. If you don't cooperate, I'll be forced to tell the university about your illegal skulking around private property. Not to mention your penchant for sex-laden dime-store novels."

Svetlana, still shining the flashlight in his face, stepped forward.

"Really, professor—*Snow Bunnies?*"

51

FILL IN THE BLANKS

B ack in Ricochet, Svetlana arranged for dinner to be delivered to the jail while I built a fire in the jailhouse stove. The two of us ate a bad meal by lamplight at my desk. We had locked the professor in the cell, and every now and then he called out something about his being innocent, but we ignored him. Afterwards, we went in and sat down on the bunk across from him.

"Okay, professor, here's the situation," I said. "Four people and a horse have been murdered, so I'm in no mood for games. I suggest you save us all time and tell us what we want to know."

"Exactly who are you?"

"Dakota Stevens. I'm a deputy sheriff."

His shoulders deflated. "Have you anything to eat?"

"I think we can scare up a sandwich for you."

I looked at Svetlana. She nodded and left.

"Now," I said. "Who hired you?"

"Nobody. I'm a geology professor at the university."

I leaned forward with my forearms on my knees.

"Professor, remember that punch I gave you earlier, how you couldn't breathe? Imagine what I could do with a full one."

"That's police brutality, young man, and I refuse to be intimidated," he said. "I won't say another word until I retain counsel." He clamped his mouth shut and looked at the wall.

"Fine, we'll take another approach. I'm going to tell you what I know, and you're going to fill in the blanks."

I stood up and paced across the cell.

"Sometime last year, you were contacted by Randy Shaw, CEO of Orlando Fantasy Group."

Todd's eyes flicked in my direction.

"He hired you to dig around the resort," I said. "I believe this is yours, by the way."

I pulled out the rock hammer and tossed it on his bunk. He avoided looking at it.

"It had to be very hush-hush," I said, "because you didn't have permission, and you were looking for gold. You'd always thought the gold was a myth, but when you visited the claims office in Missoula, you started to believe Shaw was on to something."

Todd shook his head in disbelief.

"Yes, professor," I said, "we found your signature at the BLM."

Svetlana returned with a sandwich wrapped in wax paper. She handed it to the professor.

"What is it?" he asked.

"Chicken," she said. "Allegedly."

He frowned and unwrapped it.

"So, there were meetings," I continued. "You and Shaw met at Yellowstone to form a plan, and when you got your sabbatical at the university, you moved into the Meade Hotel and started checking the mines. At that point, the two of you met once a month to discuss your progress." I turned to face him. "How am I doing so far?"

He stopped eating, stared at the floor, and nodded.

"But," I said, "earlier this month the meetings suddenly stopped."

Todd froze in the middle of his next bite. "I haven't heard from the man in weeks. Where is he?"

I turned to Svetlana. "Care to tell him?"

She shrugged, looked at Todd. "He's dead."

"But the man owes me a great deal of money."

"Take it to probate court," I said. "Now, time for you to start filling in the blanks. How much gold have you found?"

"Just traces." His hands trembled as he put his sandwich on the bunk. "Certainly nothing to support the veracity of the legend."

"And what is your relationship to Carries Bison?"

"Who?"

I gave him a modest kick in the shin.

"Ow!"

"Let's try that again," I said. "Carries Bison."

"Honestly, I don't know who you're talking about." Todd lifted his pant leg and rubbed the bone. "From the name, I assume you mean one of the Indians on the reservation. I buy gas for the ATV over there, but that's it."

"And they just let you, the whitest of white men, parade through there on your four-wheeler?"

"I thought it strange myself. But Mr. Shaw said he spoke to them about me."

"Svetlana," I said. "Any questions?"

"Yes." She crossed her legs and bored into Todd with unwavering eyes. "How is it you have been driving around exploring mines and no one has learned of your presence?"

"But someone has," Todd said. "At first I collected most of my samples at dawn or dusk and no one bothered me. It became too much, though, and I started working during the day. There were a few incidents. A weakened support beam, a pit someone had camouflaged." Svetlana and I shared a look. "Quite unnerving."

"And did you tell Shaw about these incidents?" Svetlana said.

"Of course," he said. "I told him I needed protection, but he refused. He insisted my work remain secret. So, I've been working alone."

"Any idea who's behind these incidents?" I asked.

"No. None whatsoever."

"And the chemistry set?" I said. "For nitric acid tests on samples?"

"Yes."

I stood up. "All right, Svetlana. The professor needs his beauty rest. He has a long day tomorrow. Of doing nothing."

We went out, locked the cage behind us and barred the heavy wooden door to the cell. Out in the office, I collapsed into my chair.

"Damn it," I said, "why won't this get any easier?"

Svetlana sat on the edge of the desk. "I think you are close, Dakota."

"Sure doesn't feel like it."

"You've had cases that seemed impossible before." She shook my shoulder. "You can do this."

We stared at each other, and just when it ceased to be uncomfortable, and I found myself admiring her eyes, she got up, donned her hat, and was gone.

52

GHOST TOWN

The next morning, Svetlana and I met in her room and sat at her window discussing the clues.

"So, Chess Girl," I said. "Do you detect any patterns?"

"Only if you consider the absence of one to be a pattern."

"I see your point," I said. "Each clue points to a different group of suspects. We haven't found the hub yet."

She put all of the papers in a folder and buried it in one of her suitcases.

"So, what is on today's agenda?" she asked.

"Well, I want to visit the reservation again. I'd like to get a look inside that construction trailer."

"And?"

"I need to talk to McCourt," I said. "And I was going to question Heather and Kat again. Care to join me?"

"Hardly," she said. "Besides, I have arranged a phone call with your New York State Police friend about the gun used to kill Roman. Since you warned me about possible eavesdroppers, he will give me a simple yes or no. Also, some of the lesser actors—"

"I think they prefer *supporting* actors."

"They volunteered to give me their statements. I have them visiting one at a time this morning. They might know something."

"They might," I said. "Just make sure they're not acting."

I pulled back the lace curtain. Svetlana's room, at the corner of the hotel, provided a great view of the "T" where Ricochet's two streets converged. The pinched feeling under my navel told me one thing loud and clear: *trouble's coming.* The town itself seemed to sense it; the storefronts, the sidewalks and the streets were empty.

"This place is turning into a ghost town," I said.

"You tend to have that effect on places."

I stood up. "Take care of the professor, would you?"

"I'll bring him a box lunch from the hotel," she said.

"Good. He should suffer with the rest of us." I adjusted my hat. "See you later."

"Wait. Where's your badge?"

I opened my frock coat to reveal the tin star. She removed it from my vest and fastened it to the outside of my coat.

"There." She patted her handiwork. "Go get 'em, marshal."

The loudest thing on the street was the wind, blowing in cool and bracing behind yesterday's storm. I crossed the thoroughfare and headed toward McCourt's house on the far end of town. The two roughnecks from the train lounged on rocking chairs in front of the Ricochet Manor, their legs stretched out across the wooden sidewalk. Their necks strained their shirt collars. The one closest to me had such severe acne scarring, it looked like candle wax that had melted on his face and re-hardened. The other one had slicked-back hair and kept glancing at his reflection in the hotel window. I could have sworn I recognized him from TV someplace. They turned to face me.

"Gentlemen," I said.

They pulled their boots out of the way, but at the last moment Waxface shot one back out, almost tripping me. Luckily I have the reflexes of a mongoose, and sprang over it. They got up snickering and sauntered into the hotel. I had the uneasy realization that I was going to have to deal with those two at some point, but thankfully not this morning. I continued down the street.

This was my first time calling on McCourt. His door had a metal knocker, and after knocking and waiting with no answer, I tried again. The door swung open and McCourt stepped into the doorway in a robe and slippers. I smelled traces of citrus fragrance on him. Cologne? Perfume?

"Mr. Stevens," he said loudly, "what brings you here?"

I couldn't place it, but something was different about McCourt's face. It was less pinched than usual.

"You look good, McCourt. What's your secret?"

"Not talking to people longer than I have to. What do you want?"

"That's better. I was beginning to wonder if you were the same guy." I pointed west, in the direction of Loot. "Made an interesting discovery yesterday. Local guy living in the old hotel in Loot. He's been poking around the resort, looking for gold."

"God, not another one," McCourt said.

"Another what?"

I was tired of standing on the stoop, but McCourt wasn't inviting me in. He leaned against the doorjamb.

"At least once a year Sidney had to deal with one of those treasure hunters," he said. "We'd give them a warning and they'd leave, but a few times Sheriff Briggs had to take them out. College kids."

"Well, this one's a college *professor*," I said. "And he had some pretty serious backing."

"Who?"

"I don't want to say yet because it might be connected to the murders."

"Where is he now?" he asked.

"In the jail."

"I take it he didn't find any."

"Find any?" I said.

"Gold," he said. "I'm sure he didn't, but you never know."

"According to him, just traces."

McCourt gave a decisive nod. "I always knew those legends were bunk."

"Listen, about yesterday," I said. "I thought it best if we got everything out in the open."

He waved a hand. "Personally, I think it's a mistake. The guilty parties will certainly clam up, but if you factored that into your decision."

"Glad you understand."

"Anything else, Mr. Stevens?"

"That's it for now. Appreciate your time."

The door clinked shut. McCourt obviously had someone inside that he was anxious to get back to. I stood there for a moment, then spun on my heels and walked back into town. Now I had to choose between two women who didn't want to talk to me: Kat or Heather. I had no idea how pliable Kat would be at this time of day, but if I brought coffee and smiled gallantly when she opened the door…

By the chime of the saloon clock downstairs, I appeared at Kat's door at ten o'clock sharp, balancing a tray of coffee. I kicked the door with my boot.

"Get lost," Kat said. "Read the schedule. I'm off today."

"Kat, it's Dakota. Open up."

There was the slap of angry feet. She whipped the door open wearing nothing but a loosely tied floral silk kimono. The outfit, or lack of one, was decidedly arousing.

"Go away," she said.

"We need to talk." I lifted the tray. "I brought coffee."

Kat flicked the door open the rest of the way, revealing her bed with one of the younger actresses on it. She was a petite brunette who looked about ten minutes out of Scarsdale High School.

"Guess I should have brought three cups," I said.

"I'm occupied. What is it?"

The girl slipped out of bed wrapped in a sheet. Behind her the morning sun was strong in the window and backlit her lithe figure nicely. She blinked. Her eyes were a glistening coppery brown and she fixed them on me as she cupped a hand to Kat's ear and whispered. Kat's mouth curled into a wicked smile.

"Amber wants to know if you'd like to come in and play with us."

"Tell Amber she's adorable, but she's lucky I don't take her over my knee and call her mother." I stared at Kat. "Five minutes. Downstairs."

The saloon was empty. I took a seat at one of the poker tables and poured myself some coffee. A door slammed. Kat appeared on the balcony, her kimono tied tight. As she stomped down the stairs, I filled a cup halfway with coffee.

"How do you take it?"

"Light," she said.

I filled the rest of the cup with cream and handed it to her.

"Corrupting the youth?" I jerked my head upstairs.

"I'm her mentor."

"Yeah? How's she coming along?"

"Amber? Oh, she's coming just fine." She cradled her cup in both hands. "Now what do you want? Because unless you plan on keeping us company, I don't have much to say."

Two small piles of chips sat on the green baize in front of us. I tossed a couple of mine into the center of the table.

"Tell me why you spread rumors about Heather and Sidney."

"Rumors?" she said.

"You never caught them having sex."

"No, but they went into Missoula together a lot. And where there's smoke, baby, there's fire."

"Not necessarily," I said.

Kat squinted at me. "Look, Mr. Detective Man, you don't know anything about the acting world, so let me enlighten you." She tossed a chip onto the pile. "Besides being good at your craft and good in the sack when necessary, in this business you've got to give good gossip. Actors feed on it. And if you don't have anything to put in the kitty"—she tossed in more chips—"*you* become the one they gossip about. Like they say, the best defense is a good offense."

"How do I know you're telling me the truth?" I drank some coffee.

"You don't," she said. "But I have no reason to lie. Hell, *you're* the one who should be explaining himself. I'm not the detective who's been pretending to be an actor."

"Kat, I'm not playing games here. Heather is the prime suspect in two murders, and while this might please you, I'm not sure she committed either of them. I need to know if everything else you told me is the truth."

She put down her coffee. "Everything else about what?"

"Let's start with your whereabouts." I pushed all of my remaining chips into the center of the table. "On the night of Sidney's death, where were you?"

"In Missoula," she said. "Sidney gave me the night off."

"What about two days ago, when Boone was killed?"

"I was in Missoula then, too. With somebody."

"Who?" I asked.

She shoved all of her chips across the table. "None of your business."

"You realize this makes you a suspect," I said.

"So? I didn't do it."

"Just tell me who you were with."

"Who's that chick with *you*?" she said.

"You ought to ask her."

"Maybe I will."

"Good luck with that," I said.

"You know what?" she said. "I don't have to put up with this shit. If you want to ask me more questions, you're going to have to get a warrant or whatever it is you detective pukes get."

"I think you mean a subpoena."

"Screw you, jerk. Goodbye."

She stomped upstairs and slammed the door. I sipped my coffee for a moment, then put the tray and cups on the bar and walked out. The saloon doors were still creaking behind me when I stopped cold.

Slick and Waxface stood in the street twenty feet away, twirling axe handles.

53

Showdowns

"Ah, gentlemen," I said. "Playing a little stickball?"

"Yeah," Slick said. "With your fuckin' head."

His accent was Brooklyn. Queens maybe. He choked up on the axe handle and slapped the end into his palm. Waxface was chewing gum.

"Get ready for some hurtin'," he said.

"Clever," I said. "Been waiting to use that, huh?"

"Shut up."

Slick took a wrestler's stance with the axe handle. Now I realized where I'd seen him. He was a challenger on *Ultimate Fighting Championships*, that TV sport with no-holds-barred brawls in a caged ring. Waxface looked like a failed understudy. Somehow I doubted they were the type to honor Marquess of Queensberry rules. I eased down the stairs and faced them, not in the least surprised by the situation. I'd already tussled with Indians and a rattlesnake in this fantasy Western town; a showdown in the street seemed inevitable.

Behind me, the saloon doors creaked and footsteps rumbled on the wooden sidewalk. More spectators gathered across the street. In my periphery to my left, I noticed Svetlana; her regal carriage was unmistakable in a crowd.

The tough guys fanned out, slowly swinging the axe handles. The only sounds were the whoosh of the handles through the air and the scratch of their boots in the dirt. They tried to get on either side of me, but I kept backing up in a circle so they couldn't. Then their swings accelerated, the axe handles swiping inches away from my arms, my legs, my head. If I stepped into one of the handles to block it, the other guy was poised to club me from the rear. These two meant me serious harm, and there was no way I was getting out of this without fighting.

As I realized this, a tightness, a volcanic pressure, began to build in my chest and crawl up my throat. It wasn't a heart attack. It was the quiet seething I'd felt in the Bentley at the start of this case. Feeling the adrenaline kicking in, I took a few deep breaths and realized I was angry. Angry about being dragged into this case in the first place. Angry about Sidney's murder, Shaw's murder, the horse's murder, and my own near-murder. Angry about Roman's murder. Angry about Boone's murder. Angry about getting beaten up by Indians. Angry about the snakebite, the pit incident, the crazy rich people, the self-important actors and now these two clowns.

I threw back my frock coat and stepped sideways until there was nothing but empty street behind them. As the firearms instructor at Quantico drilled into us: Be sure of your target and what's beyond and around it.

"Guys," I said, "I'm giving you five seconds to turn around and go home."

Slick twirled his axe handle. "Look, assh—"

I snapped out the Peacemaker, thumbed back the hammer and shot him though the shoulder. He whirled backwards and landed hard on the dirt. Waxface froze. This was supposed to be a battle of tough guys and I'd cheated.

"Don't shoot!" He dropped his axe handle. I holstered the gun.

Slick lay on the ground clutching his shoulder. Not crying out, not whimpering, not even breathing heavy. The guy *was* tough. It was a good thing I'd shot him; in a street fight he could have killed me. There was a respectable smear of blood on his hand, but the injury didn't look life-threatening. Keller walked over aiming a shotgun at the two of them and took their axe handles away.

"How about I have the doctor patch him up and put them in jail?" Keller said.

"I'd appreciate that," I said.

I staggered through the crowd with actors, guests, support staff—the entire town—staring. The crowd parted, and there, blocking my way to the sidewalk, stood the silver-haired gunslinger. My hand instinctively hovered over my pistol, but he made no signs of reaching. Still, he was in my way. I walked straight toward him. At the last second, he stepped aside.

"Hey," he said behind me. "Aren't you even a little curious who I am?"

I turned around.

"You're a P.I. working for somebody related to this case. I'd ask who, but you wouldn't tell me."

"How'd you know?"

"One of us can always spot another," I said.

"Ain't that the truth." He thumbed his chest. "Jim Slade. Jackson Hole, Wyoming."

"Dakota Stevens. Manhattan."

"I know," he said.

Svetlana met me on the sidewalk and led us back to her room. Heather was there, sitting in a wingback chair near the window, twisting a pair of kid gloves in her hands.

"What's going on?" she said. "Who are those men? You shot one of them, didn't you?"

"Miss Van Every," Svetlana said in a crisp, headmistress tone, "you are in no position to be asking anything. We will be asking the questions."

I was glad that Svetlana had taken charge. I was nauseous and my legs had the jimmies from the adrenaline dump during the fight. I collapsed into a chair.

This never happened to Clint.

Svetlana went to a sideboard, removed a vintage bottle of Jack Daniel's and two shot glasses. She poured me one.

"But—"

"You just shot a man," she said. "Take it."

I drank the liquor. Svetlana corked the bottle and put it on the table.

"Would you prefer the good news or the bad news first?"

"There's good news?" I said.

"Actually, no."

I poured myself another shot.

"According to the New York State Police," she said, "the gun used to kill Roman was a twenty-five caliber Beretta, exactly like the one you found in Patrick's trailer."

Heather sprang out of her seat. "Patrick? *My* Patrick? You broke into his trailer?"

"Sit down!" Svetlana said.

Heather shrank back into her chair.

"There is more." Svetlana poured a shot for Heather.

"No, thank you," Heather said.

"*Drink*," Svetlana said.

"Fine."

She threw back the liquor with sorority girl efficiency. Svetlana looked at me.

"Sheriff Briggs called," she said.

Knowing what was coming, I downed my second drink.

"The police searched Patrick's trailer," she said. "They found the nurse's scrubs and the gun, as well as a great deal of rawhide—the same material believed to be used in the garrote that strangled Sidney."

"Nurse's scrubs? Rawhide?" Heather said. "I don't understand."

"They have arrested Patrick," Svetlana said. "Dakota, you are supposed to bring Heather to the depot on the next train. Sheriff Briggs will be there to take her in."

Heather gazed beseechingly at us. "But we—I didn't kill anybody."

I gritted my teeth. I was sick of hearing everybody's version of what they didn't do, especially when the evidence contradicted them. Like Heather here.

"Why didn't you tell anybody Sidney was your father?" I asked.

"Who told you that?"

"Doesn't matter. Why?"

"I didn't want people thinking I got this job because of nepotism," she said. "So we kept it a secret."

"Were the two of you close before you started working here?" Svetlana asked.

"Yes," Heather said. "We had a part-time relationship. He and my mom couldn't make it as a couple. Sidney took care of us financially, and he visited occasionally. I took my stepfather's name because Sidney was concerned what his parents would think."

"Did you ever meet your grandparents?" I asked.

"No, but according to Sidney, they were obsessed with status. They would have had a stroke if they found out he'd fathered a child out of wedlock."

Heather started to cry, dabbing her eyes with her dress sleeve until Svetlana gave her a handkerchief. She sniffed.

"I can't believe he's gone. And now they think *I* did it. I could die."

"Did anyone know you were his daughter?" Svetlana asked.

"Just my doctor. And McCourt. That was a 'next of kin' thing. You know, for emergencies."

"Wasn't Sidney concerned he'd say something?" I asked. "Or use it against him somehow?"

"Sidney said the two of them had an arrangement," she said. "I didn't care so long as the truth never got out, and it never did. McCourt kept his word. Believe me, I won't forget it."

"What about your inheritance?" I asked. "Who else knew about that?"

"Oh, I see where this is going," she said. "Since I was getting all that money, I had motive to kill him. Well, I hate to disappoint you, Mr. Stevens, but I never knew about the will. Not until the reading in New York with Sidney's lawyer."

I stood up and looked out the window. The street was empty again.

"And while you were in New York," I said, "where was Patrick?"

"He came along and did some sightseeing. I went to the services alone." She straightened up in the chair. "Now I want to say something. I think Kat is involved in this somehow. She had a good enough motive anyway."

"What's that?" I said.

"Sidney was planning on getting rid of her."

"What for?"

Heather's eyes glinted with revenge. "For taking her role as a prostitute literally."

"Meaning what?" I said.

Svetlana cleared her throat.

"Need me to spell it out for you?" Heather said. "Kat was sleeping with visiting directors and producers. Basically anyone in a position to help her career." She poured herself another drink and swilled it down. "So, you guys were hired to investigate me?"

"We were hired," I said, "to find out who killed your father."

"But you think I did it."

"At this point, I don't know what to think. However, the evidence is pointing your way."

Heather slumped in the chair. "What's going to happen to me?"

"You'll be arrested," I said. "You might be granted bail, but don't count on it. In the meantime, we'll keep working. And since you're going to have plenty of time to think, try to remember anything that could help us."

"What about a lawyer?" she said. "I've never had so much as a speeding ticket."

"Svetlana will take care of it."

Svetlana rose and pointed to the clock on the mantle. "It's time."

54

STALEMATE

When I returned from delivering Heather, Svetlana and I rode over to the reservation. The construction site was quiet. Once I saw there were no cars around, we tied up the horses and crossed the yard, weaving through stacks of lumber, cinder blocks and shingles. There were literally tons of materials sitting idle. The casino building stood half finished and forgotten in the stark sunlight.

"It's like they're on break," Svetlana said.

"Probably just walked off the job," I said. "Once Shaw's checks stopped rolling in, Bison couldn't pay them." I pulled out my lock-picking set. "Come on, let's get in that trailer."

At the door, I crouched over the lock with a pick and torsion wrench while Svetlana handed me additional picks and kept lookout. Lock-picking is really all about the tension wrench. You continuously have to find the right balance of torque—enough to push the upper pins out of the cylinder while ensuring that pins set and stay set. While there were magicians out there who could do this in five minutes, I managed to get the lock open in fifteen. I was improving.

"Ta-dah," I said. "We're in."

"Dakota…"

I turned around. Bison stood at the foot of the steps with three of his men. They had shotguns leveled at us. I turned to Svetlana.

"What happened to keeping lookout?"

"They snuck up on us," she said.

"We're Indians, we do that." Bison looked at me. "You again. Why am I not surprised?"

One of the men walked up and took our guns. He handed them to Bison.

"Okay, Stevens," Bison said. "I suggest you explain what you've been doing over here. It's been a bad month for me. I need somebody to take it out on and you'll do nicely. Your deputy can beat it."

"No," she said.

"Leave, Svetlana," I said.

"Svetlana?" Bison stepped forward, cocking his head like he was studying a painting. "Not Svetlana Krüsh."

"That is correct," she said.

"*The* Svetlana Krüsh, the chess champion?"

"What is this, *Romancing the Stone*?" I said. "Yes, this is Svetlana Krüsh, U.S. chess champion, international grandmaster and my associate. What's your point?"

Bison removed his sunglasses. It was the first time I'd seen his eyes—they were coal black. He walked to the foot of the steps and stopped.

"It's an honor, Miss Krüsh. I've studied all your published games. That queen sacrifice you made in the third game of the U.S. Championship was brilliant."

"Behave," she said, "and I give you signed photograph."

He stared at her. She stared back. After a tense moment, he smiled.

"Draw?"

"A stalemate," she said.

"It's only because I respect you so much, Miss Krüsh, that I'm not going to beat the hell out of your associate."

"I appreciate that," she said.

I nodded to Bison. "Can we talk?"

"Yeah, might as well. I'd like to know what the hell is going on." He handed our guns back and nodded at his men. "Chill, guys."

We went in the trailer and sat down. Turns out I hadn't missed much: a desk and four chairs, coffee maker, mini-fridge and phone. I felt a twinge of embarrassment for Bison; the Emperor truly had no clothes. We all sat down.

"So," Bison said, "I've figured out you're a private detective. Looking into Sidney Vaillancourt's death, right?"

"Right."

"Well, I didn't kill him," he said. "So, what do you want with me?"

"I know about R.C. Development," I said, "and that Shaw was your backer."

"Go on."

"What tipped me off was the mail," I said. "All those envelopes from Orlando and Martha's Vineyard, and the last one mailed just before his death. I imagine you kept going back, hoping the next check was there."

"All I had was his cell number," Bison said. "One day his wife answers, says he died. I tell her Shaw is our major investor and that we're up the creek without him. She cuts me off, tells me to talk with his lawyer. I worked the guys until the money ran out."

"So what did Shaw want?" I asked. "Ownership of the casino?"

Bison leaned back in his chair. The springs twanged.

"The deal was, if we could encourage Sidney to sell the resort to OFG, Shaw would only take 20 percent of the casino. But if we couldn't, he'd take 60 percent."

"And by *encourage* you mean?"

"Not kill anybody," he said. "Just harass the guests, be a nuisance. Enough so Sidney would sell."

"And you didn't find that suspicious?"

"Which part?"

"Well," I said, "that in exchange for funding the casino, all Shaw wanted was 20 percent and the occasional Indian raid? Doesn't sound like prudent money management to me."

Svetlana leaned forward. "Almost like he knew the casino was a pittance compared to what Sidney's property was worth."

"Exactly," I said.

Bison put his feet up on the desk. "I don't see what you're driving at."

"Have you noticed a guy riding a four-wheeler between here and the resort?" I asked.

"Skinny white guy? Sure. Shaw said he we should 'grant him safe passage.' Geek actually said it like that."

"What if I told you he's a geology professor from Missoula?" I said.

"Geology? What's he—"

"Gold," Svetlana said.

"That nonsense? Come on."

"Shaw didn't think so," I said. "He's had the geologist in there, checking every mine."

Bison put his hands behind his head and stared at the ceiling.

"All right," he said, "so Shaw was nuts and wanted to fund my casino while he looked for gold? So what?"

"Did you give anybody else safe passage?" I thought of Roman. "Maybe a heavyset guy with a crewcut?"

"Yeah, I let a guy like that come through here," Bison said.

"When?"

"Couple weeks ago maybe," he said. "In fact, Sidney called me about it himself, asked if it'd be okay."

"Sidney? You're sure?"

"Positive. Told me if I did this favor for him, he might be willing to cede some of the disputed land. So I said, 'what the hell, sounds easy enough,' and I did it."

"And none of this struck you as odd?" I said.

Bison shrugged. "What can I say? The rich are different."

"That's for sure."

"Hey," he said, "I'm glad you two are enjoying this little puzzle of yours, but I'm up shit's creek here. I owe my crew three weeks' pay, and I've got a multi-million dollar project rotting out there, so unless—"

"We might be able to help," I said. "Right now, the primary suspect is Sidney's daughter. She's due to inherit a hundred million dollars and control of the resort. If you helped clear her, she might be persuaded to invest in your casino."

"What do you need from me?" Bison said. "Name it."

"We'll be in touch."

"When?"

"As soon as we solve this thing," I said.

"Well, hurry up."

Svetlana punched me in the arm. "Yes, Dakota—hurry up."

"Wait," Bison said, "before you go."

He rummaged through a pile of papers on the desk and came up with a copy of Svetlana's chess book, *Krüsh Your Opponents*. He handed it to her with a Sharpie.

"Would you, Miss Krüsh?"

"Certainly." She signed the book.

"And about that autographed photo," he said.

"Maybe," she said. "*If* you are of use to us."

We rode back in silence. While crossing a sunny meadow, I happened to glance at Svetlana. She was gazing at the Bitterroot Mountains in the distance.

"What's up?" I said.

"I will miss this. Our adventure in the Wild West."

"It's been wild, all right. But it's not over yet."

She nodded.

"Good thing you're famous," I said. "You saved my neck back there. Thanks."

"You saved me twice, so I still owe you one."

"You don't owe me a thing, Svetlana."

Bees flitted across the meadow.

"C'mon," I said, "let's get back and I'll buy you dinner."

"I can't wait."

55

Nothing Definitive

Back in town, we stopped by the jail. The place was filling up. According to the doctor, the man I'd shot would be fine and the two bruisers were okay to travel anytime. I thanked him, locked up the prisoners and left.

Since I wasn't pretending to be an actor anymore, I got a room in the Bonanza across the hall from Svetlana's. I lay down and reviewed as much of the case as I could remember. The trouble was, the evidence was spotty at best and pointed to so many combinations of suspects, I couldn't keep them straight anymore: Heather and Patrick, Heather and Roman, Heather and Boone, Kat and Boone—or all of the above. I sensed I was missing something, and that it wasn't to be found in Montana.

The key, I believed, was the connection between Ricochet and New York. If I followed it, it might lead to someone. And I knew just where to start: by releasing the bruisers and following them. Not a bad plan, actually.

I went to the window and looked out on the darkening street. Strolling couples passed in front of lighted windows and disappeared into the shadows. Except for the far away yips of coyotes, the town was dead quiet. There was a knock at the door.

"Come in," I said.

It was the young woman from Keller's store who handled the phone calls. This poor girl spent most of her life scuttling between the mercantile and locations all over town.

"Telephone, Mr. Stevens."

I checked my pocket watch: ten o'clock.

"Who's calling?" I asked.

"Vivian Vaillancourt. She insists on speaking with you."

I yanked my boots on and followed her over to the mercantile. A lamp flickered next to the phone. I sat down and said hello to Vivian.

"Why haven't you called?" she shouted. "I've been here alone for days, waiting for a report! The agreement was you would check in once a week!"

"No, I agreed to call when I had something definitive," I said.

"Well, have you? Something definitive?"

"There have been some unforeseen developments."

"Such as?" she said.

Maybe I had been remiss in not giving her a report sooner. I reminded myself that I was dealing with an unstable woman who had lost her twin brother.

"Okay, for starters," I said, "Heather Van Every—the woman everyone thought was your brother's girlfriend? She's his *daughter*."

I heard the intake of breath on the other end, and the tinkle of ice cubes in a drained highball. After a few breaths, Vivian hissed back, "Impossible. Sidney never would have kept that from me."

"I've seen the birth certificate," I said. "Sidney was her father."

There was a long pause.

"Well," Vivian said, "did she do it?"

"I don't know yet. Right now the evidence points to her. But on the positive side, if it turns out she's innocent, you'll have yourself a lovely niece."

"I already have one I never see, and I don't need another," she said. "Now, what other *unforeseen developments* have there been?"

I gave her a just-the-facts account of everything that had happened since I arrived in Montana, including the attempts against my own life.

"Well, Mr. Stevens," she quipped, "if you don't start getting results, I might just hire Mr. Roman."

"You can't do that."

"Oh, really? And why not?"

"First, he's not licensed," I said. "Second, he's dead."

"I don't understand."

"He's dead, Vivian. It's too complicated to explain right now." That, and I had weak theories on who did it. "Now, about Roman. Who recommended him?"

"Louis, why?"

"Just curious. I'll be in touch soon."

"One more week, Mr. Stevens," she said. "If you haven't found Sidney's killer by then, expect to be replaced."

I suspected she was the one who had hired Jim Slade to keep tabs on me, but before I could mention it, she hung up, leaving me staring at the earpiece. I took a licorice twist on my way out and chewed it slowly as I shambled back to the Bonanza.

The dining room blazed with light. Inside, Svetlana lorded over a long table with a row of men behind chessboards. The scene reminded me of the moment I first saw her—trouncing a row of men outside the Au Bon Pain cafe in Harvard Square. For some reason, wherever she went Svetlana attracted men who enjoyed being dominated. A man whispered over my shoulder.

"A marvel, isn't she?"

"Absolutely," I said.

Svetlana had captured enough of her opponents' pieces to form two complete sets, while the men had only a handful of her pawns between them. At the end of the row, before she could do a carriage return and tear through these poor saps again, I touched her arm. A murmur rose up among the tables as she followed me out to the lobby.

"They think we're an item," I said.

"They think no such thing." She flipped her hair over her collar. "They're discussing strategy, trying to mount a coordinated attack. It won't help." She stood with her back to the room, focusing all of her attention on me. "Something is wrong."

"What if they start switching pieces around?" I said.

"I have all of the positions memorized, Dakota. What is it?"

"Vivian's giving us one more week."

"Then it is time for you to solve this," she said.

"Yeah."

"She is upset, Dakota. We knew she was temperamental when we took this case."

"You're right." I leaned against the doorjamb. "First thing in the morning, have Keller let those two knuckleheads out of jail. I'm going to follow them."

"What about the professor?"

"Leave him there. I want him to sweat it out a while longer."

"Which reminds me," she said. "Isn't it only quasi-legal what we're doing—holding these men without charging them?"

"Yeah, but I'm only a quasi-deputy, so it evens out."

She shook her head and smiled. Across the lobby, a grandfather clock gonged.

"Go," she said. "I will be here when you get back."

"You sound like Grace Kelly. Say that again."

"No."

I jutted my chin at the dining room. "Go whip their smug asses."

She strode back in, and with cold precision proceeded to fell her opponents like a sickle cutting down grain. Svetlana would be fine. As for me and my ability to solve this case, that was another story.

56

PURGATORY

The next morning at dawn, I rode ahead to Ricochet Depot, changed into street clothes and waited in the SUV for the bruisers to arrive. Just as I'd predicted, they came on the first train, skedaddling out of the resort and driving straight to Missoula International. Without any luggage, I was able to follow them easily through the terminal, and once I determined which flight they were on, I bought a first class seat and waited until the last minute to board. By the time they served the champagne, I was settled in with *Daddy's Girl*, reading about sociopathic Suzy and how she fooled the cops with her sweetness. I continued to read on the Denver–New York leg, finishing the book just as we landed, wondering on my way to the street if I was being similarly fooled by one of my suspects.

From LaGuardia, I tailed the bruisers by cab to the Manhattan Meatpacking District. They stopped at a club called Purgatory. Slick and Waxface entered the club by a side door in the alley. I went after them.

Inside, I eased down a dim hallway. Having come straight from the airport, the best I had for a weapon was the business end of a credit card, so I had to be careful. I heard voices and followed them down the hall until I was on the edge of an empty dance floor. I ducked behind the DJ booth. Slick and Waxface stood at the bar, watching a well-dressed fat man with a long ponytail slice lemons. The lights behind the bar silhouetted him. He waved his knife at Slick's arm, which was in a sling.

"Broke your arm, huh?"

Slick didn't say anything.

"But you busted him up, right?" The fat man sliced a lemon in five seconds. He was very good.

"Guy wasn't the cupcake you said he'd be," Slick said. "Guy friggen *shot* me, Harry."

Harry shrugged.

"What about our money?" Slick said.

"You didn't finish the job." Harry stabbed into a new lemon. "You got half. Be glad you're getting anything."

"Then you can forget about us doing that other thing."

"Whatever," Harry said. "I'll put it on Craigslist. Have fifty guys here in an hour."

"Fuck you, Harry."

Slick and Waxface grumbled to each other on their way out. When the door banged shut, I went over to the bar. Harry glanced up from his lemon slicing.

"Position's been filled," he said.

He looked at me again. This time it clicked. His free hand drifted under the bar.

"Harry," I said, "you better be reaching for a swizzle stick."

He withdrew his hand. "Look, it was nothing personal. I was just the subcontractor."

Still holding the knife, Harry lifted the counter door and squeezed through.

"Who hired you?" I asked.

He grinned, then slashed at me with the knife. I sidestepped him. Poor Harry. He had the right idea, and his technique wasn't bad, but he was slow. And out of shape. After five slashes, he was already winded. A trickle of sweat formed on his upper lip.

"Been watching too many kung fu movies, Harry," I said. "Not so easy, is it?"

He kept swinging and started to wheeze. When he had me backed up against the DJ booth, I decided I'd had enough.

"Harry, quick!" I said. "What's the square root of thirteen?"

In the split second he considered it, I ducked under his arm and punched him in the nerve bundle behind his tricep. He yelped and dropped the knife. Grabbing him by his ponytail, I yanked him, stumbling and flailing, across the dance floor. I tripped him to the ground and cinched his hair to a barstool. Harry looked up at me from the floor, supporting his weight with his elbows. His face was red. I hoped the guy didn't have a heart attack before I got the information I needed.

"Let's try again, Harry. Who hired you?"

"Go fuck yourself."

"Never heard of him," I said.

A bowl on the bar brimmed with lemon slices. They glistened with juice. I snatched up a fistful and held them over Harry's eyes.

"Who, Harry? Or I promise you, this is going to sting like a bitch."

"I'm not telling you sh—"

I squeezed, Harry squealed.

"Okay, stop, stop!" He wiped his eyes. "I don't know who it was, honest to God. I got a note, okay? A note with ten grand and a picture of you. Somebody wanted me to hire a couple of guys to bust you up."

"Who was the note from?" I poised the lemons over his eyes for a second squeeze.

"Don't," he said. "I don't know. It was anonymous. Really."

"Why didn't you just keep the money and not do anything?"

"Because the note said he knew who I was, and that if I crossed him, he'd put a knife through my throat."

"How do you know it was a *he*?" I asked.

"I don't. I just figured."

"You shouldn't do that, Harry."

"Do what?" he said.

"Figure."

Harry winced. Clearly, his elbows were in pain from supporting his weight.

"This note," I said, "when did you get it?"

"I don't know. Few days ago."

"How? In the mail?"

"No," Harry said, "on my desk when I was closing up. Somebody must of slipped in and dropped it."

"Any idea who?"

"No, nobody."

"What about somebody who comes in here a lot?" I asked.

He didn't answer. I kicked the barstool so it yanked his hair.

"Ow! All right. There's one guy, but I haven't seen him in a while. Name's Roman. In here almost every night. Ex-military or something. He might of left it."

Roman? Roman couldn't have left the note because he'd been killed over a week ago. But somebody connected to him could have done it.

"Thanks, Harry."

I grabbed a handful of pretzels from the bar and headed for the door.

"Hey," Harry said, "you can't leave me like this!"

"It's a knot, Harry. Untie it."

Even though Purgatory was across town from my office, I decided to walk, hoping a stroll in the summer evening air would help me sort through the case. It didn't. In the short time I'd been in Montana, I had forgotten how cacophonous Manhattan is: horns, sirens, clattering subways, screeching bus brakes, ring tones and one-sided phone conversations—all while the very pavement throbs beneath your feet. I wondered how I'd ever been able to think in this city.

However, I did have one burst of inspiration. On Fourth Avenue, around the corner from my office, I saw a homeless man rifling through a garbage bag. As I watched him reach in and pull out cans and bottles, a glimmer of an idea came to me. I handed him a ten-dollar bill.

"Thank you," I said.

"You're welcome!"

At the office, I called Ricochet, leaning back in my chair and sorting the mail as I waited for the girl to get Svetlana. Five minutes later, Svetlana was on the phone, her voice brighter than usual.

"You are in New York, I assume."

"Yeah," I said. "Listen, tomorrow morning I want you to ride over to the reservation with Professor Todd. Call my apartment from the pay phone over there. There's something I need to tell him, but we can't discuss it on this line."

"A clue, perhaps?"

It was, but I didn't want any eavesdroppers getting wind of it.

"Yes."

"Understood," she said. "Goodnight."

After dinner, I drove out to Vivian's. Her new house-boy answered the door in an Adidas track suit and led me into a wood-paneled 1950s-style screening room. Hitchcock's *North by Northwest* beamed out of a projection room onto the far wall. It was the scene on Mount Rushmore near the end, and normally imperturbable Cary Grant was looking harried. I could relate.

Vivian glanced at me, but if it registered with her that I was here, she didn't show it. I started to say something and she shushed me. I ignored her.

"Vivian, how much money was in your safe?"

"Please, I'm trying to watch this."

"How much?"

"I don't know, enough for an emergency. Ninety or a hundred thousand."

What kind of emergency was she talking about, a meteor strike?

"And besides money," I said, "what else was in your safe?"

"Nothing whatsoever. Now please, I'm enjoying this."

"You had a gun in there. A twenty-five caliber Beretta, right? And that's not a rhetorical question."

She sighed. "So? I'm a very wealthy woman. It was licensed. I have a right to defend myself."

"You do," I said. "The problem is, Roman was killed with the same type of gun, and another one just like it was found in Heather's boyfriend's place."

Vivian touched a remote control and the movie paused. Eva Marie Saint dangled from Cary Grant's arm off the side of Mount Rushmore.

"So," Vivian said, "you think Louis stole the gun and—"

"Shot Roman and sailed away someplace, then went out to Yellowstone and planted the gun?"

Her eyes shot open. "Is that what you think?"

"Not sure yet." I stood up. "But I'm getting closer. In a few days, I might want you to come out to Ricochet."

"Okay, but remember—"

"Yes, I know—one week," I said. "Enjoy your movie. It's one of my favorites."

I let myself out and walked, hands in my pockets, down the front lawn to the end of the dock, where I had a Gatsbyesque moment staring at a light across Manhasset Bay. I had come back east seeking answers, so what did I know?

Well, I knew that the gun used to kill Roman was the same model and caliber as the one stolen from Vivian's safe. *And who took the gun?* Louis. *And who recommended Roman?* Also Louis. So, maybe Louis had learned about Shaw's scheme with the gold, brought in Roman as a partner, then double-crossed him.

Since returning to New York, I'd also learned that Roman and the person who hired the thugs were probably connected. And since the mystery person had paid with a stack of cash, and since Louis had taken a stack of cash from the safe, maybe *Louis* hired the thugs. It was time to talk to Harry again. I looked up the number for Club Purgatory and dialed it. Thumping dance music blared in the background.

"Yeah?" Harry said.

"*Yeah?* Manners, Harry. The proper greeting is hello."

"You? What do you want? I'm busy."

"Got yourself untied, did you?" I paced along the dock.

"I had to cut my ponytail, you prick," he said.

"Actually, I'm right outside."

"What?"

"Just kidding," I said. "Listen carefully, Harry. Pretty boy named Louis—five-eight, fake tan, shiny teeth. Sound familiar?"

"Congratulations, you just described every guy in this place."

"Well?"

"No," he said. "No Louis."

"You're sure? A Louis never came in with Roman?"

"No. No Louis, all right?"

I swore. The moon was up now, shimmering on the Sound. Harry's voice grumbled out of the phone.

"Look, can I go now?"

"Goodbye, Harry."

I hung up and reared back to hurl my phone into the Sound, but at the last second stopped myself. I moaned across the water. A cabin cruiser whisked past the point and headed into the empty Sound.

There was something about Roman I'd overlooked. One thing was for certain: I wouldn't get any answers standing here.

I set my jaw and strode back up the long, blue lawn to my car.

57

THE MOTHER LODE

Garage door locks are easy to pick, and even wearing gloves I was able to gain entry to Roman's house in five minutes flat. I walked upstairs to the den, yanked the drapes shut, switched on my flashlight, and started to search. The police had gone through the papers on the desk and left them in piles. I sifted through them but didn't find anything new. Desperate, I shone the flashlight on the pictures on the walls. Roman and his hunting buddies grinned mockingly back at me.

No Louis. No Shaw. No Heather. No Kat. No Boone.

Drifting the light across the photos, I stopped at one. It stood out from the others because instead of posing in front of an animal carcass, Roman and his pals stood on a boat holding up bluefish. At least two events during this case involved water: Shaw's death on Martha's Vineyard and Louis's disappearance on the Sound. I sprang from the chair, whipped out my magnifying glass, and read the boat's name on the stern:

PULCHRITUDE
BRONX, NY

Ransacking the desk, I found a phone book and flipped through the yellow pages. To my surprise, and annoyance, there were several marinas in the Bronx. I lined up the listings next to Roman's phone bill and compared the numbers.

Come on, baby, be there.

Persistence pays, because on the last number I got a match: Evers Marina, 1470 Outlook Avenue. My pulse was racing as I put everything away and hurried out to the car.

When I got there, boats bobbed in their slips and floating aluminum walkways gleamed in the dock lights. The night air was muggy and still. Storming around until I found *Pulchritude* wasn't an option; the place was too quiet and well-lit for that.

In front of the gangway down to the boats was a night watchman's hut. The light was on. In New York, one thing you can count on is that guys working low-paying jobs like security will usually bend the rules for a few bucks. But you've got to do it right. You have to make them feel a part of your investigation. I pulled two hundred-dollar bills from my wallet and rapped on the door.

A man that looked like a retired cop put down his *Daily News* and opened the door. His badge read, "FRANK."

"Yeah?" he said warily.

"Sir, I need your help."

"Unless you have a craft in here, I can't let you in. Sorry."

"Please, it's important."

I handed him a business card and explained the gist of the case, making Roman out to be worse than Hitler. Then I laid the money on his desk and told him I needed to see Roman's boat.

"I know this puts you in a tough position, but the man *is* dead. You can come with me if you like."

"I can't show you his boat," he said.

"I just—"

"But I'll show you his plane."

"Plane?"

"Yup." Frank opened up a ledger, scanned it and grabbed a set of keys off a hook. Then he picked up the money and gave it back to me.

"Let's go," he said.

What seemed like months ago, Svetlana had told me that Roman had a pilot's license, but I'd forgotten all about it. It hadn't seemed relevant. Frank led me to the far side of the marina, where a small colony of seaplanes floated forlornly.

"About the last place in New York that still keeps 'em," he said.

At the end of the dock, we reached a red and white single-engine Cessna. The plane rolled gently on the wake of some distant watercraft. Frank unlocked the door and stepped aside.

"Probably shouldn't say it, but I never liked the guy," he said. "Take your time."

"Thanks."

As soon as he walked away, I put on some latex gloves, switched on my flashlight and started my search.

The pilot's seat was clean. So was the door pocket. I prayed this wasn't a waste of time. I crawled over to the passenger's seat, reached behind and groped around underneath.

And that's when I hit the mother lode.

A paper band from a bundle of $10,000, a monogrammed handkerchief with the initials "H.V.E.," and a canvas bag containing wire, blasting caps and C-4.

The handkerchief was obviously a plant meant to implicate Heather Van Every, but the paper band from the money—that was different. Follow the money, they always said. I found it hard to believe that large sums of cash could pop up three times in this case and not be connected somehow.

A paper band from a bundle of $10,000. Ninety to a hundred grand stolen from Vivian's safe. And ten grand to Harry. Harry didn't know who had left the money to hire him, but he was fairly certain that whoever it was, it wasn't Louis.

Then there were the explosives to consider. I slumped down in the pilot's seat and tried to piece together what had happened here. Okay. This was a seaplane, which meant it could take off and land on calm ocean water. Calm. According to the Coast Guard, on the night Louis disappeared the Sound was a dead calm. What about a scenario like this? Louis takes Vivian's sailboat. Then, under power from the sailboat's auxiliary motor, he pilots it far out into the Sound, meets Roman, and the two of them sink the boat with the explosives.

But why? To fake his disappearance? It seemed an awful lot of trouble for that.

No, there had to be another reason.

If Louis didn't hire Harry, and Roman didn't—he was dead by then—someone else did. Therefore, there had to be a third person involved. What if this were a simple case of Louis, Roman and the third person stealing the hundred grand, and the three of them double-crossing each other? The third person could have been on the boat with Louis, or on the plane with Roman. At the meet, Roman and the third person *kill* Louis, take the cash and the gun he stole from Vivian, then sink the boat with Louis's body on board, and fly back.

This hypothesis had legs. If it was true, there was a good chance that the third person also killed Roman, since Roman would have been the only witness. The third person probably hired Harry as well, using the stolen cash.

So, who was the third person?

Thunk...thunk...thunk. The pontoon bumped against the dock as the plane rolled on the waves.

Who was the third person? Who?

I was close, really close, and every cell in me knew it.

I shook my head and came back to reality. This was my one and only chance to search the plane, and I needed to be thorough. Stooping over with the magnifying glass and flashlight, I scrutinized the passenger's seat. There were no hairs, or anything else I could see. I leaned across the cushion, opened the door and examined the side of the seat. I found something.

The plastic guard on the seat adjustment lever was missing, leaving the metal exposed. And there, dangling off the tip, was a piece of white thread.

Pinching the thread in my fingers, I sat up and stared out at the black and rippling water until the enormity of what I'd discovered suddenly hit me. A wave of pleasure and disbelief washed over me. It was as if a heavy veil had been hanging over me through this entire case, and now that veil had been snapped away and everything was clear. It all came down to this piece of thread. All of the other evidence fit now, and this sealed it.

I took the thread with me and put everything else back as I'd found it, then locked up the plane and returned to the hut.

"How'd you make out?" Frank asked.

I smiled and slapped the money into Frank's hand.

"Already told you," he said. "Don't want it."

"I know, but maybe she does." I nodded at his wedding band. "Take her out to dinner or something."

"Find what you were looking for?"

"And then some, Frank."

Crossing the parking lot, I pumped my fist like I'd just won Wimbledon. In the morning I would speak with Svetlana and give Professor Todd his marching orders, then I would follow up on a couple of things Kat had said. If she was telling me the truth, I was about to bust this case wide open.

58

Tons

Three days after Vivian threatened to fire me, I returned to Ricochet. Svetlana met me at the train, and as we rode back into town our horses nuzzled each other.

"They've been lonely," I said. "How about you? Miss me?"

She gave me a tepid smile normally reserved for mailmen.

"I have been too busy organizing tomorrow's picnic," she said.

"What did McCourt say?"

"I don't know. I ignored him."

We came over the rise and there was Ricochet. A pang of sadness lodged in my chest. The town seemed smaller than it had just a few days ago.

"What's Professor Todd up to?" I asked.

"Out digging, per your instructions. He will check in with us this evening."

Trotting down Main Street, I grinned at Svetlana's handbills for the picnic. They were nailed up every six feet on both sides of the road.

"Yeah, I think they'll get the point," I said. "Must have taken you all day."

"No, the men did the work," Svetlana said. "I merely supervised. From horseback."

The street was empty. At the "T," Svetlana steered us down to the church.

"Everyone is gathered for the story meeting," she said. "This won't take long."

Svetlana stayed with the horses while I marched inside. McCourt and Irving stood onstage doing their spiel. The actors sat lifeless in the stifling heat. A few women fanned themselves.

"Reservations are down," McCourt said, "so we all have to—"

I stopped in the aisle. "I have a quick announcement."

"Mr. Stevens, we're rather—"

"I just wanted to remind everyone about the picnic tomorrow in Loot. You've seen the posters. Attendance is required."

"You can't do that," McCourt said.

"Required," I said. "Now, I need to see Kat Styles for a moment."

The actors crooned in unison, *"Oooh, trouble!"*

"Oh, grow up." She slid out of the pew.

The second she stepped into the lobby, I tugged her out of sight and kissed her. Her dress rustled in my arms. When we separated, all traces of her recent bitterness were gone.

"Nice," she said. "But what for?"

"For helping me solve the case."

She flapped her fan. "Little 'ole me?"

I stopped the fan, took an envelope out of my pocket and gave it to her.

"What's this?" she asked.

"A thank-you. Contact info for Theodore Vance."

"The *producer*?"

I nodded. "I got his daughter out of a scrape once, and he said if I ever needed anything—"

"Jesus!"

"There's no guarantee, Kat, but it's a chance," I said. "You need to get out of here."

Tears came to her eyes. It was the first genuine emotion I'd seen from her. I pecked her on the cheek and headed for the door.

"Dakota?"

"Yeah?" I straightened my hat in the doorway.

"I won't forget you," she said.

"Yes you will. But that's okay."

Svetlana and I rode to the livery and left the horses, then went to our rooms for a nap. I felt like I had just fallen asleep when Svetlana knocked.

"Dinner?" she said.

"Sure," I said, or think I said. I might have sworn at her.

I splashed some water on my face and galumphed downstairs. She had reserved us a table in the private dining room so we could meet with Professor Todd without being seen. Our entrees were revolting as usual, so we shoved them aside and made a meal of buttered rolls with a bottle of red wine to wash them down. Yes, we were breaking our no-alcohol rule, but after so many wretched meals, dead bodies and near-death experiences, we deserved an evening's respite.

"This is the best meal since I got here," Svetlana said.

"Tell me about it." I refilled our glasses.

Professor Todd staggered in slumping and bedraggled. He pulled up a chair, gnashed into a fistful of bread and quaffed a glass of water. I raised an eyebrow to Svetlana. She snatched the bread basket away.

"Report, professor."

He looked over his shoulder, dipped into his knapsack, and removed a shirt wrapped around something. When he set it down, the contents rattled like large marbles.

Then he unwrapped it.

A pile of gold nuggets gleamed in front of us. Even though some of them were laced with rock, they shone gaily.

"And there's a lot more," he said.

Svetlana narrowed her eyes at him. "How much more?"

Todd drank some water, put down his glass and stared blankly across the room.

"Tons," he said.

59

RATIOCINATION

At noon the next day, Svetlana and I were already at the picnic site in Loot when the train arrived. The locomotive belched steam as the passengers filed off and crossed the meadow. Fifty yards from the tracks, tables with checkered tablecloths waited in a clearing. Heather was here with Sheriff Briggs, and Vivian couldn't be missed: she wore a big straw hat and sunglasses. Carries Bison, disguised as a guest, sat among a pride of rapacious actresses, while McCourt and Irving were right up front, near the dais. The few lingering guests were peppered among the actors and their cliques. Wait staff breezed around serving drinks.

After lunch, Carl from the mining claims office gave his three-minute monologue on the history of Loot. It was highly relevant to the case, so I wanted the audience to hear it. Carl held them rapt as he described the legend of the gold. When he finished, a few were ready to jump out of their seats and start searching for it themselves.

"And now," Carl said, "Dakota Stevens."

I got a smattering of applause and a couple of boos. I went on the dais, took a deep breath and opened with an attention getter.

"Sidney Vaillancourt was murdered."

Everyone went silent.

"And he was murdered for gold," I said. "The legend is true."

I nodded at Svetlana. She heaved a carpetbag out from under her chair. Inside were the gold nuggets Todd had shown us last night. She went from table to table, everyone oohing and aahing.

"There *is* gold," I continued. "Tons of it. As I speak, state officials are extracting and documenting the find, and provided no counterclaims are filed, it will pass to Sidney's estate."

"Where was it?" Keller asked. "In one of the mines?"

"No, because the miners knew that was the first place people would look. Instead, they left it in the *last* place we'd look—the dregs."

I swept my hand at a row of nearby tailings piles. The audience tittered, as though wishing they'd been smart enough to dig there.

"I got the idea when I saw a homeless man picking bottles out of a garbage bag."

"I'll be damned," Keller said.

"Certain piles around the resort are considerably smaller than others," I said. "That's because they were actually larger piles that had been picked through."

"Enough about the gold, Mr. Stevens," Vivian said. "Who killed my brother?"

"I was just getting to that. Initially my primary suspect was Heather Van Every"—she blinked hopefully at me—"but I discovered something that turned this case on its ear. Heather was not Sidney's girlfriend, she was his daughter."

The actors gasped. A woman in back stood up.

"I'm so sorry, Heather," she said. "We had no idea."

"So you're saying Heather did it?" Keller said. "I don't believe it."

"No, Mr. Keller," I said, "Heather was framed. The person behind Sidney's murder is William McCourt."

"I beg your pardon!" McCourt said.

"You bastard!" Vivian jumped from her chair and had to be restrained by Briggs.

The actors grumbled. I waited for the crowd to settle down, then continued.

"McCourt knew Heather was Sidney's daughter and that she had motive to kill him. She was the perfect patsy. Now, here's how I figured out it was him."

I stared down at McCourt. He was perspiring.

"Your doctoral thesis was on the sociological mores of boom-bust towns in the late 19th century American West," I said. "Mining communities. Researching at the claims office one day, you found the journal entry that hinted the gold was in the tailings piles. So, you stole the entry."

"That's a federal offense, sir," Carl said.

I smiled and kept going.

"When I met you, I wondered why your hands were rough like a mason's and why you were so tired and cranky all the time. I figured out why when I was sleeping in the livery a few nights ago and was awakened twice by clanging tools."

I pointed at McCourt.

"Each night you were going out and digging through the piles. But when you found some gold, you could only smuggle out fifty pounds or so. A little bit each week."

"You can't prove any of this," McCourt said. Perspiration trickled down his forehead.

"But at that rate," I said, "it would take a lifetime to get the gold out. You had an accomplice pressuring you, and to make matters worse, Sidney said he was going to get rid of the piles. That's why you killed him."

McCourt shriveled into his chair. I walked to the edge of the dais and stared down at him.

"Carries Bison, the leader of the Indian reservation next door, had never met you. And as far as you knew, he'd never met Sidney either. So you impersonated Sidney on the phone, asking Carries Bison to allow a *guest* to enter the resort via the reservation."

"That's a lie!" McCourt snapped.

"No, it's not." Carries Bison stood up. "I'd recognize your whiny voice anywhere."

I nodded at McCourt.

"In one swoop, you covered your tracks and snuck in John Roman from New York. The two of you strangled Sidney at the gallows and strung him up so it looked like suicide."

A man in back yelled, "We ought to string *you* up!"

"Nobody's hanging anyone," I said.

When the crowd quieted down, I took a drink of water and continued.

"You made several mistakes, McCourt, but two stood out. First, searching bags for 'contraband'. And second, insisting the food be more 'realistic to the period'—or bad. I asked myself, 'Doesn't this guy realize he's sabotaging the resort?'"

"Why'd he do those things?" Keller asked. "McCourt loved this place as much as Sidney."

"I'll tell you why, Keller," I said. "The gold. As long as Ricochet was successful, McCourt would never have the time or privacy he needed to remove it. He had to drive people away."

Across the clearing, the idling locomotive gave a metallic cough of steam. I turned back to McCourt.

"A couple other details didn't add up. Like when I stopped by your house and you seemed a lot less pent up."

The audience laughed.

"*And* you smelled of fragrance," I said. "So, when you didn't invite me in, I knew you had someone in there."

McCourt sat stone-still with his fists clenched on his knees. I looked at the audience.

"This person is key, because McCourt wasn't the brains behind any of this," I said. "She was."

"Enough suspense, Mr. Stevens," Vivian said. "Who was McCourt's accomplice?"

I pulled out a small plastic baggie containing the white thread, and held it up for the audience to see.

"This white thread came from the mystery woman's clothing," I said. "Actually, I should say what *appears* to be white thread. When I first saw it, I knew who it belonged to, and when I got it under a microscope and saw faint traces of indigo dye, it confirmed my initial suspicion. The mystery woman is—"

One of the waitresses put down her tray and stepped forward pointing a gun.

60

REAL OR DINNER THEATER?

"Hello, Delilah," I said. "I had a feeling you'd show up. Everyone, I give you the mastermind—Delilah Vaillancourt."

Delilah removed a blonde wig and tossed it aside, exposing her braided hair. She was holding a Smith & Wesson .38 snub nose. At this range, she could be blind and still put a hole through me. She took the guns from my holsters, tossed the fake Schofield, kept the real Peacemaker, and stepped back.

Vivian roared, "Delilah, he was your uncle!"

"Quiet, Auntie, or my gun might go off."

The audience was mesmerized, unsure whether this was real or dinner theater.

"This is fascinating," Delilah said, motioning with the gun. "Keep going."

"I was about to talk about your connection to McCourt," I said. "Without even realizing it, Kat Styles gave me some crucial information about your identity." I winked at Kat. "She told me McCourt had been fired from a college in New York City for having an affair. Meanwhile, McCourt told me that he got his Ph.D. from

NYU. But that was a lie, a lie to cover up where he really attended graduate school—Columbia. McCourt was kicked out of Columbia for having an affair with one of his students. That student was you, Delilah."

"Right so far," she said. "Go on."

"When McCourt was kicked out," I said, "you asked Sidney to give him a job. But soon after he started working here, McCourt somehow discovered the terms of Sidney's will, which stipulated you would inherit a trust fund of only twenty million. When he told you, you lost it. Some woman you'd never heard of was getting a hundred million. So, you decided to murder your uncle and frame Heather for it."

"Yeah? How?"

"Well, first you went to John Roman, a tough-talking mercenary type you'd met at Club Purgatory. You paid him in money from the smuggled gold, and I imagine you paid him in other ways, too."

"Shut your mouth," Delilah said.

The actresses giggled.

"Roman and McCourt murdered Sidney. But even before that, you were going into Roman's house when he was out, making calls to Yellowstone, Ricochet, and Gardiner—where Heather's boyfriend lives."

"And why would I do that?" she said.

"To begin framing Heather," I said. "If she was found guilty of killing Sidney, you could get everything. But your plan hit a snag. You got Louis to recommend Roman as the private detective on the case, but Vivian ended up hiring Svetlana and me instead. You weren't able to control the investigation like you'd hoped."

Briggs started to draw his gun. I shook him off and turned back to Delilah.

"At that point, you started eavesdropping on Louis, and probably sleeping with him, too, to get other information, like Vivian's safe combination. Louis also told you that his former boss, Randal Shaw, wanted to hire me and Svetlana, so you told Roman about it."

"And why did I tell Roman?" Delilah said.

"So he could hire a sniper to kill Shaw, before Shaw could tell us about the gold. Roman used his seaplane to transport the sniper to and from Martha's Vineyard, and the two of you used the seaplane again to fake Louis's disappearance."

"Wait!" Delilah said, her eyes wide. "This is good, make sure they hear it." She waved the gun at the audience.

"After Louis disappeared," I said, "to avoid suspicion you personally showed me his bungalow. Several things were out of order, but one clue gnawed at me—those deep wheelbarrow tracks. I kept wondering, 'What did Louis take down to the boat that was so heavy?'"

Delilah's face beamed with rapture. She jabbed the gun at me.

"Don't stop, go on!"

"Louis didn't take *anything* down to the boat," I said. "You killed Louis and used the wheelbarrow to take *him* down to the boat, wearing his shoes to do it. Then, with Louis's body on board, and the cash and gun from Vivian's safe, you sailed out to sea, where you met Roman with his seaplane. He exploded the ship's hull, the boat sank, and the two of you flew back together."

"My poor Louis," Vivian said.

Delilah swung out a hip, put a fist on it. "You've got to admit, it was an awesome plan."

"Yeah, they should give you the Nobel Prize," I said. "Too bad you scratched yourself on that seat lever in the plane. You left a piece of your Daisy Dukes behind."

I held up the baggie with the thread again. Delilah smiled wistfully.

"Yeah, bummer," she said.

Vivian said, "But Roman—what happened to him?"

"Delilah killed him, too," I said. "The day after they got rid of Louis, she went to Roman's presumably for a party and shot him with your gun. But without Roman around, she still needed muscle, so she anonymously hired a couple of thugs to get me off the case. It didn't work."

I kept an eye on Delilah and the gun. This situation could go south in a hurry.

"Finally," I said, "when Svetlana and I were getting close, Delilah made a last-ditch effort to frame Heather." I turned to her. "You flew out here on a private jet, right?"

"Jackson Hole, actually. So what?"

"So," I said, "that's how you got the gun out here. No bag inspections."

"Right," Delilah said.

"But your *first* time to Jackson Hole, you hired another P.I. yourself—Jim Slade. You hired him to monitor my activities and report back to you."

"Very good."

"This flying around of yours raises another point—opportunity," I said. "When I was piecing this together a couple of days ago, I realized that while several suspects had motive and means, no one had the unfettered opportunity that you had. Several times, Svetlana and Vivian reported that you weren't around. That's because you were working behind the scenes, either in New York or out here, setting up the next part of your frame. Which leads me back to the gun."

I pointed at Delilah. "To implicate Heather and Patrick, you planted the gun in his trailer, along with a set of nurse's scrubs. Then, wearing a second set of scrubs, you killed Boone with a massive dose of horse tranquilizer. A drug you stole from Vivian's vet when he put down her horse. My bet is, you used the tranquilizer on Louis first, although I can't prove it."

"That was hot," she said.

I sighed. "The sad thing is, you were even better at playing dumb. Like that bit when you picked us up the first day—pretending you didn't know who Daisy Buchanan was."

"And *you* fell for it," she said.

"Yes, sweetie, I fell for it. And now it's over."

She looked at me as if I'd said the world was flat.

"That's right, you're going to jail," I said. "Now, give me the gun."

Someone coughed. I'd forgotten all about the audience. Looking down the barrel of a .38 has a way of making everything else irrelevant.

"Nope," Delilah said. "Afraid I've made other plans." She snapped her fingers at McCourt. "Come along, honey."

He was slumped over in his chair, contemplating the pebbles at his feet.

"Let's go," she said.

McCourt rose and went to her side. She gave him my Peacemaker.

"You're pretty smart, Dakota Stevens," she said. "It's been fun sparring with you."

I was taken aback by her nonchalance. When this went to trial, I could see her getting an insanity plea; the girl was certifiable. She approached Briggs's table and held the gun on the back of Heather's head.

"Your gun, sheriff."

Gritting his teeth, he handed it to McCourt, who slipped it in his coat pocket.

"And your cell phone," Delilah said.

Briggs tossed it on the ground.

"Cute." Delilah lowered the .38 and shot the phone. Amazingly, she hit it on the first try. She smiled at me.

"I've been practicing," she said.

"We're all very proud."

She glanced at McCourt. "Nobody else has a phone, right?"

"They shouldn't."

McCourt handcuffed Briggs to the metal chair and took the keys.

"And the gold, dear," Delilah said.

McCourt approached Svetlana. As I moved to cut him off, Delilah fired a round at my feet. I stopped.

"The gold, Ms. Krüsh," McCourt said.

Svetlana's defiance worried me. She glared up at him so intensely, he had to look away. Those eyes of hers were intimidating enough when she was in a good mood.

"You get it," she said.

He dragged the carpetbag out and heaved it off the ground. Delilah jammed her gun into Heather's temple, grabbed her by the arm and yanked her out of the chair.

"Let's go, *cuz!*"

They wove through the crowd to the idling train. Delilah told the engineer to start it, the three of them boarded the passenger car, and a moment later the train crept forward, gathered steam and disappeared around the bend. They were gone.

"Does anyone have a cell phone?" I asked.

Nobody said a word. I knew it was crazy, but I had no choice: I had to follow them. Heather was in serious danger. Delilah herself had killed Louis, Roman and Boone, and she showed every sign of killing again.

When I looked up next, there was a burst of activity. The actors were out of their seats now, some shouting, some crying, some running around. I pushed through the crowd to Briggs's table. Kat was stooped over, picking his handcuffs with a hairpin.

"Kat, how do you…? Never mind, I don't want to know."

She grinned and removed the cuffs. Briggs sprang out of his chair rubbing his wrists.

"Briggs," I said, "you go back to Ricochet and call the cops. I'm going after them."

"Stevens, listen—"

"Look, Briggs, Delilah's out of her gourd. You saw it. She's going to kill Heather. Now, do you have a gun or not?"

"Backup weapon's in the truck. Didn't think I'd need it for a picnic."

"I'll think of something," I said.

I climbed aboard my horse and was about to ride away when Svetlana called out.

"Dakota!"

She and Keller ran over to me.

"Make it fast," I said. "I've got a train to catch."

"That's just it," Keller said. "You won't catch them following the rails. See that path over there? Take it until it forks, then go right. That'll cut you through the woods. If you haul ass, you just might beat it."

Svetlana laid a hand on my ankle. "Be careful, Dakota."

I nodded solemnly to her, snapped the reins, and was off.

61

CHASING DOWN A TRAIN

The path was little more than a strip of dirt through dense weeds along the railroad bed. At the fork, I jerked the reins right and plunged into the woods. I rode with my head tucked into the horse's mane, keeping low as the horse raced across the spongy forest floor. Its hoof beats were eerily quiet. Gradually the path disappeared and I followed the outlines of it between the trees. The woods were cool and shadowy, and then I began to see light ahead. We had reached the tree line.

I emerged from the trees onto a broad field. In the distance, maybe a quarter-mile away, I spotted the high walls of the gulch and black smoke billowing into the air.

I hadn't beaten the train.

It exited the gulch and began crossing the open ground. I steered the horse toward a point farther up the tracks, and cut diagonally across the field until the train was a hundred yards away.

It seemed fitting that the case should end this way—with me chasing down a train. I lowered my head and veered toward the tracks.

As I slid alongside the flatbed car, I leaned toward the rail. But before I could grab the rail, the horse lurched away from the train. Hanging sideways off the saddle, I cursed every western I'd seen for making this look so easy. I righted myself, cracked the reins, and swerved in for a second try.

"Come on!"

Even though the train couldn't have been moving faster than 25–30 mph, the clacking of the wheels was deafening. With the horse churning beneath me, I let go of the reins with my left hand and leaned out of the saddle again. My fingers wrapped around the steel. In one motion, I pushed myself off the horse and hooked my arm around the rail. My boots whacked against the railroad ties. The train wheels licked their chops, daring me to let go. I began to slip.

Then a memory flickered in my head. I was back at the FBI Academy, on the chin-up bar in the sweltering Quantico woods, willing myself over the bar one more time. Still hanging off the platform car, I willed myself over the rail and landed face-down on the deck. The horse peeled away.

I lay there for a moment with the wind chilling the sweat on my neck. As I got to my feet, I realized how foolish this was—walking into a hostage situation un-armed, against two mentally unstable people with guns.

But what choice did I have? If I didn't, Heather would surely die.

I crawled to the end of the flatbed car and stopped at the door to the passenger car. I peeked inside.

McCourt was alone on one side of the car, staring out the window. Delilah had Heather cornered across the aisle.

I sat down and tried to think. As if mirroring my state of mind, the countryside drifted by in a green-brown blur. Now what? With nothing for a weapon, the best I could do was stall. They were certain to be wound tight in there, so I had to assume I'd startle them. I crouched to the side of the door, knocked on the window and jerked my hand away. There was a gunshot and the glass exploded. I hate being right.

"Stop shooting, I'm not armed," I said.

"Stevens?" Delilah shouted. "How the hell did you get here?"

"A jet pack. Does it matter? Look, I've got a proposal."

"Hold your hands up in the window first," she said.

I did.

"All right, come in. Easy."

Keeping my eyes on her, I opened the door, stepped in and closed it behind me. It was instantly quieter, and about twenty degrees hotter. I stood at the end of the car with my hands raised, sizing up the situation. McCourt was staring out the window, sweating, the Peacemaker dangling from his hand. But I couldn't grab the gun because Delilah had Heather shoved against the window with her gun jammed against Heather's temple. She stroked Heather's head with her free hand.

"I was admiring my cousin's hair," Delilah said. "It's *so* soft."

Heather's pupils were the size of manhole covers. Tunnel vision. The adrenaline did that. She didn't notice me at all, and her whole body trembled. Across the aisle, McCourt mumbled at the glass with his chin in his hand.

I kept my arms raised. It was time to put my acting skills to the test.

"Delilah, I've been talking with your aunt. She wants to help you. She's going to get you the best lawyer. And she's going to give you half of Heather's inheritance."

"You're lying." She spat out the words like they were poison.

"You're a smart girl," I said. "Think about it. Would I risk coming here to lie? Unarmed?"

"Maybe you didn't have a choice," she said. "I took all the guns."

"It can't be true," Heather said.

I glared at Heather. If I didn't make this look good, in a minute we'd both be dead.

"How the hell would you know?" I said. "You just met Vivian. Delilah's been taking care of that woman's sorry ass for years. And then you come along, lah-dee-dah, and collect a hundred million bucks."

"Fucking-A." Delilah jabbed her with the gun barrel. Heather cowered.

"Delilah, wait a second," I said gently. "Vivian said if you kill her, the deal's off. One more thing. I want a taste. You know, a couple of million for setting it up."

She moved the gun off Heather and leveled it at me, sighting down the barrel with one eye shut.

"I should put a bullet in you for all the shit you caused."

"Dakota," McCourt said, "I strongly advise against getting involved with her. She'll destroy you."

"You fucking eunuch, shut up," Delilah said. "You had two years to get that gold out."

"We had something," McCourt said. "Love maybe, I don't know. I was alone. She was so bright, so beautiful. And I wouldn't have done a thing about it either. But she came on to *me*."

McCourt's arm holding the Peacemaker went rigid, like a robot switching on. He pivoted in his seat to face her.

"But she couldn't keep her mouth shut," he said. "She had to tell her friends, who told their friends, and before you know it, the Dean is calling me in. No warning, nothing. I'm out. Years of work down the drain. And then she gets me on this gold escapade, and I go along with it because I love her and I think she loves me."

My eyes darted between their two guns, watching for the slightest twitch that would mean disaster. McCourt rested the Peacemaker on his knee.

"But it was never about love for you, was it, Delilah?" he said. "Always the money. And you never let me forget it. I'd smuggle out fifty thousand, a hundred thousand, but it was never enough. And now I find out you weren't even faithful to me. Roman, Louis, probably the man at the raw gold exchange—who else? How many?"

Delilah shrugged. "Hard to say. Five, six maybe. What'd you expect? You were never around."

"I was never around because I was trying to find the gold!" McCourt shouted. "For you!"

"So, I'm selfish," she said. "Sue me."

McCourt snapped back the hammer on the gun and thrust it across the aisle at her.

"You...you ruined my life!"

"Put the gun down, William," she said softly, motherly almost. "We'll have plenty of money soon, enough to get you a new life."

Tears welled up in McCourt's eyes. "You crazy bitch. Don't you get it? There's no deal. They're going to arrest us the second we get to the depot."

Delilah blinked. The truth of what McCourt said was sinking in.

"Don't listen to him," I said. "He's angry and not thinking straight. Your aunt's extremely wealthy and powerful, and if she says she can do this—"

"I'll tell you what, honey," McCourt said, "I'm not going down alone."

She let out a breath. "I should have done this a long time ago."

In the half-second it took Delilah to raise her gun, McCourt fired. The big Peacemaker slug ripped through her stomach. Delilah's arm froze, and the gun toppled to the floor. Heather screamed. Sprayed with blood, she slid off the seat and cowered against the wall. I spun around to face McCourt, but the Peacemaker had already fallen out of his hand. I nailed him with a solid uppercut and he slumped over. Quickly I secured all of the guns, checked to see that Heather was okay, and hurried over to Delilah.

Her white blouse was already dark with blood. I ripped it open and pressed my handkerchief against the bullet hole to stanch the bleeding. In moments the handkerchief was soaked and my fingers warm with the life draining out of her. I propped up her feet and cradled her head in the crook of my arm. Her face went pale.

"Dakota, tell me I'm smart."

I hated even thinking it because I knew it was an insult to all the people she had killed. Still, a feeling of macabre admiration rose up in me, and I knew it would be the last thing this troubled girl would ever hear.

"Incredibly smart, Delilah. One of the smartest I've faced."

The natural opiates in her body must have kicked in. Her face relaxed, and the hard lines from her intense scheming melted away, leaving nothing but ecstatic bliss.

"Really?" she said.

"Really."

She gazed up at me and swallowed. "Then why didn't they love me?"

With that, her eyes flickered out and her body went limp in my arms. I closed her blouse, crawled to the side of the car and collapsed against the wall. Heather crawled over and clung to me, sobbing.

I looked at Delilah. As the train car swayed, her head rocked minutely side to side. Dead before she was 21, and no one would grieve for her. But even if I had wanted to shed a tear, I couldn't. Catching her had taken everything in me. I had nothing left to give.

62

FENDI, FERRAGAMO, VERSACE AND SAKS

W̲e were in the Trump Tower office of Vivian's lawyer, settling the final details of the case. Sitting across the conference table were Vivian, her lawyer and her newfound niece, Heather Van Every. The lawyer spoke to Svetlana and me as though his clients weren't in the room.

"Vivian and Heather were impressed with your results. They trust you will be happy with your fee."

He held out a check. I pointed at Svetlana and watched her eyes as she took it. They dilated imperceptibly before she tucked it into her handbag.

"Well?" Vivian said.

Svetlana nodded. "It is extremely generous. Thank you, ladies."

The lawyer gathered his papers and left. Vivian and Heather came around the table.

"Excellent work, Mr. Stevens," Vivian said. "And you, Miss Krüsh. You're quite a team, you two."

Heather shook my hand. "I can't thank you enough."

"You're an incredibly rich woman now," I said. "How much gold was there anyway?"

"So far, about seven tons."

"Well," I said, "if things with Patrick don't work out, you know where to find me."

"And," Vivian said, "the gold found on the disputed land, she gave to the reservation."

"It was good of you to help them," Svetlana said to Heather. "By the way, how is your mother?"

"She's here at Sloan-Kettering, but the doctors don't have high hopes."

"I'm really sorry," I said.

"Dakota," Vivian said, "you were with Delilah at the end. Did she say anything?"

I considered telling her the truth. However, Delilah was gone and the truth would only hurt now.

"She said she was sorry," I said.

Vivian's face crinkled up. I patted her on the shoulder and met Svetlana at the elevator. We rode down together in silence.

Out on Fifth Avenue, the afternoon heat hit us like a crosstown bus. We went to the corner of 56th Street and just stood there, watching the traffic whiz by, wondering what we were supposed to do next. Go back to the office? Go to the movies? Go home? Bright sun glinted on car windows. A river of pedestrians parted around us. Standing close to me, gazing into space, Svetlana seemed as lost as I was—an unusual state for her. If her thoughts were anything like mine, she missed Ricochet, missed the quiet and the antique way of life, missed the countryside and the sense of clarity. Although we'd been back for nearly a week, neither of us had fully re-acclimated to the relentless pace of Manhattan.

But there was one subject that always perked her up, a subject close to her heart: the money.

"So, Muse," I said, "how'd we do?"

Svetlana came back to reality with a smile on her face. She clutched her Gucci bag in front of her and swung it like a pendulum.

"I should not. It will go to your head."

"Maybe you're right. Yeah, don't tell me." I pointed west on 56th. "Hey, you know what's down there."

"Benihana," she groaned. "But Fendi, Ferragamo, Versace and Saks are all that way." She gestured down Fifth.

"Tell you what, kid." I held out my arm. "Buy me lunch and then I'll buy you a sexy pair of shoes."

"Make it a closet of shoes," she said.

And with that, she looped her arm through mine and together we turned heads crossing Fifth Avenue.

ABOUT THE AUTHOR

Chris Orcutt has written professionally for over 20 years as a journalist, fiction writer, playwright, scriptwriter, technical writer and speechwriter. As an adjunct lecturer in writing for the City University of New York, he received the Distinguished Teaching Award.

Orcutt is the creator of the critically acclaimed Dakota Stevens Mystery Series, including *A Real Piece of Work* (#1) and *The Rich Are Different* (#2). He is the author of *The Man, The Myth, The Legend*—a short story collection voted by IndieReader as one of the Best Indie Books of 2013.

Orcutt's short fiction has been published in *Potomac Review* and other literary journals. It has also won a few modest awards, most notably 55 Fiction's World's Shortest Stories. As a newspaper reporter he received a New York Press Association award.

If you would like to contact Chris, you can email him at corcutt007@yahoo.com or tweet him: @chrisorcutt.

For more information about Orcutt and his writing, or to follow his blog, visit his website: www.orcutt.net.

EXCERPT FROM *A REAL PIECE OF WORK*

Book 1 in Chris Orcutt's Dakota Stevens Mystery Series is also available. *A Real Piece of Work*, the 1st novel in the series, delves into a world of art forgery, secret identities and murder. Following is the opening of *A Real Piece of Work*.

B ack in my FBI days, during soporific stakeouts when I dreamed about the life I might lead as a private detective, I never imagined the job would one day require me to scuba-dive across a half-mile of ocean brimming with sharks.

Basically, anything capable of eating me was absent from my business plan.

Right now, despite the Caribbean sun on my face and the piquant salt air in my nose, I wished I were back in snowy Manhattan, safe behind my desk, listening like Sam Spade to some elegant dame tell me her troubles. Instead I had a 20-year-old scuba bum and my bikini-clad associate, Svetlana Krüsh, all but shoving me into the water. They stood silently beside me as wave after wave spanked the hull. Under my wetsuit, the heat began to rise.

"You're positive they're both on there," I said, nodding at the 80-foot motor yacht in the distance.

"According to the chambermaid," Svetlana said, "they left together this morning."

"And we're sure they're, ah, busy?"

"I am told they never leave the room."

She adjusted her bikini strap. After three days down here, Svetlana had only a whisper of a tan, but the way the leopard print hugged her aristocratic curves, you didn't care. Kyle, our alleged guide, leered at her. I grabbed him by the mouth and pinched his cheeks together.

"How about it, *dude*?"

"Wha?"

"Our friend on the yacht."

"Already told you—guy runs their slip says they put out every morning, come back around one."

"What time we got?"

With a flourish, Svetlana held out her watch. High noon.

"How long to get over there?" I asked.

"Half an hour, tops." Kyle scratched in his ear. "Quit stalling, man. I've gotta meet somebody at Sloppy Joe's soon."

I looked over our stern. Key West was a purple mist on the horizon. I turned back to the yacht.

"Let me see, one more time."

Svetlana passed the binoculars. While the captain and his mate read newspapers on the bridge, three bodyguards sunned themselves on the bow. Conover and his mistress had to be inside, doing what mistresses and CEOs of financial services companies did.

"*Moneta?*" Kyle said. "What the hell kind of name for a boat is that?"

"Goddess of money," I said. "Greek, I think."

"Roman," Svetlana said.

"There you go—Roman. We know what he worships anyway."

To the south dark clouds were creeping in, and the mounting wind flapped Svetlana's hair across my cheek. Between their boat and ours was a gulf of iridescent blue-green water that looked like it would take a week to cross. I wanted to call it off, but if I chickened-out now, in two weeks my business would shrivel up. Besides, Mrs. Conover was counting on us. I handed the binoculars back.

"Ready, Mr. Stevens?" Kyle said.

"Stop with the 'Mister' already. It's Dakota." I strapped on the flippers. "Why am I doing this again?"

Why? Because Mrs. Conover had made it sound so simple—snap a few photos, collect a big check. "I'll cover any expenses," she said. "Consider it a vacation…take a week, a month—I don't care. Just catch the bastard."

Svetlana nudged me. "Because you are sucker for jilted women. Especially when they are rich." She handed me a mask. "And don't forget, a blizzard is starting in New York, so we must catch six o'clock out of Miami."

I spit in the mask, rubbed it around and put it on.

"Sharks?" I said to Kyle.

"Sure. Blacktips, a few bulls maybe. No big deal."

I squatted down and slipped into the vest with the scuba tank. Kyle showed me the buttons for the buoyancy compensator.

"So, Miss Krüsh," I said, "while I'm risking life and *limb*, what will you be doing?"

She donned a pair of Dolce & Gabbana sunglasses and tied a mocha sarong around her waist so it hung fetchingly off one hip.

"Wave when you finish, and I swoop in like cavalry." She plopped down behind the wheel, crossed her runway legs and rubbed sunblock on her shoulders. Kyle jammed the regulator in my mouth.

"Remember what Nietzsche said, man—the shit that doesn't kill you makes you stronger. Trust me, you're gonna love it." He tipped backwards into the deep.

I patted the vest's waterproof pouch to check for the camera and plunged in...

Made in the USA
Charleston, SC
28 May 2014